Grizzly Cove: Crossroads

Storm Bear

BIANCA D'ARC

Copyright © 2019 Bianca D'Arc
Published by Hawk Publishing, LLC

Sabrina is a weather witch losing control of her one and only power. She's never been much of a threat, magically speaking, but just recently, things have changed and almost everyone in the remote town where she lives, has turned against her. The local werewolf Alpha even called the Lords on her.

When Ace goes walkabout, he decides to call in on an old friend who works for the Lords. But Rocco gives him the bum's rush, and the Lords task him with a mission he can't turn down. He's to go to Canada and help a weather witch who is causing trouble for one of the wolf Packs up in the mountains.

Ace finds Sabrina being stalked by more dangerous predators than the wolves. Evil is after her. They want to steal her power and use it for their own ends. But that can't happen. Not while Ace is on the job. And, not while Sabrina is so intriguing to not just Ace's human side, but his inner bear, as well.

They make a run for the border but keep encountering trouble. The Lords asked Ace to bring her back to them, but the way is blocked at all turns and they have to re-think. Grizzly Cove seems like the best solution…if they can just get there.

Showdowns on the road, magic flying in all directions, and a young witch who doesn't know what's happening to her suddenly blossoming powers. Ace and Sabrina will face it all, while their attraction grows into something a whole lot steamier. Will they make it to the relative safety of Grizzly Cove?

DEDICATION

I'd like to thank all those fans who have followed my *Tales of the Were* from werewolves, to big cats, to bears and back again. It's been a wild ride and it's nowhere near done! We still have a few bad guys to vanquish before I'll call a halt to this series, which has sprouted so many tentacles. I'm enjoying the world too much to wrap it up without making sure I've tied up all the loose ends and corralled all the plot bunnies. Never fear, there will be more *Tales of the Were* for at least another year or two.

Special thanks to Peggy McChesney, my dear friend and proofreader extraordinaire. Best of luck in your new adventures!

As with all my books, I dedicate this one to my family, who were always there for me when I needed them.

PROLOGUE

"No! Get back here!" Sabrina ran down the slight hill she'd been standing on to cast her spell. How had it all gone so wrong so fast?

She'd intended to just nudge the heavy rain that was headed in the direction of the town's weekend carnival away toward the other side of the valley. Instead, she'd somehow spawned a whirlwind, and it was heading right for the Ferris wheel!

Sabrina ran after it, waving her arms and trying to cast a counter spell. She almost didn't care who saw her. It was more important to stop the whirlwind, right now, than to protect her dubious anonymity. Besides, most of the residents of the tiny town tucked into the Canadian Rockies were shifters, anyway. No real reason to hide from them. They could probably sniff out her magic, regardless.

Thankfully, she'd been cautious this morning, only casting something small, because lately, her bigger magics had gone terribly awry. Thank the Goddess Sabrina had decided to start out small this morning, otherwise she could have been looking at a full-blown tornado, rather than just a small-scale dust devil. Still, the thing could do some damage if it traveled through the wrong place.

She cast like a crazy woman—probably looked it, too—as

she followed the whirlwind down into the grassy meadow just outside of town, where the carnival had set up shop. Only a few early risers saw her, shaking their heads or scratching them as they watched her headlong flight after the small whirlwind she'd created. Nobody stopped to offer advice or help, but that was okay. They were shifters, not mages.

It probably would have taken a real master-level mage to suppress her whirlwind, now that it had got going. Hells bells! She was a weather witch. She should be able to control any sort of weather out there—especially something that she had whipped up herself.

But it wasn't working that way lately. Sabrina didn't know what was wrong. She didn't know what to do. She just kept fumbling around, trying to fix whatever had happened to her innate magic. It had never been this difficult before.

She had grown up without any real knowledge of magic, so she'd never had any truly formal training. In college, her weather sense had awakened and she'd had to figure things out for herself, but it hadn't been strong, and it had only been the one gift. She wasn't a mage by any stretch of the imagination.

She'd muddled along, figuring out how her one tiny gift worked and she'd become good at steering weather. Unfortunately, it felt like suddenly, everything was different. Her abilities were spiraling out of control, just like that whirlwind she was chasing. Nothing made sense to her, anymore.

She needed help, but she had no idea where to get it. Weather witches weren't recognized as mages by almost all of the reputable mage schools. She couldn't just call up one of the ancient families that trained wizards and witches and ask for an appointment. Not with just a measly weather power to her name. They'd laugh at her and hang up. They weren't interested in one-trick ponies. They only dealt with those who had real power. The full package.

Weather witches didn't really even count as magical folk to real mages. They were tolerated because they were useful, but if one malfunctioned—like Sabrina was doing lately—there was no recourse. They'd probably tell her to just stop using what little magic she had. It would be like cutting off a limb, Sabrina knew. She'd tried it when things had first started going awry, but she just couldn't do it. The magical build up demanded release, and things were much worse.

Better, she had decided, to let off the steam, so to speak, a little at a time. Use her talent in small increments to make the town a better place. Bring rain to the crops. Keep things like downpours away from town celebrations. That should be simple enough, right?

Apparently not.

One of the early morning observers shook his head as Sabrina passed by, chasing her whirlwind.

"Well, that does it," he said to himself. Still shaking his head, he pulled a cell phone from his pocket. He punched in a number and waited for someone to pick up on the other end. "Rafe? Yeah, hi. It's Tobias. Can you spare Rocky or someone like him to come up here? Our weather witch is broken and needs fixed."

"Isn't that more a job for a mage?" the man on the other end of the line asked.

"Nah. A bear ought to be able to handle it. Someone with more magic sense than me and my wolves, at any rate. She's only got the one talent, and it's not very big. From what I hear, mages want nothing to do with her kind," Tobias explained. "She's nice enough, and I'd like to help her. She's done a few good turns for our town, and my Pack, in the past. If you could send someone who could straighten her out, I'd be much obliged."

"Well, I doubt if Rocky can do it, but I'll ask him if he's got a friend that we can send up your way," the man promised. "What exactly is the problem?"

"After we hang up, I'm going to send you a video file. It'll be self-explanatory," Tobias assured the other man.

They hung up not long after, and Tobias used his

smartphone to capture some images of poor little Sabrina chasing her whirlwind, cussing at it like it was a misbehaving pet. Tobias's head was pretty much constantly shaking as he sent the file to Rafe.

Sabrina was messed up. Tobias only hoped the Lords would be able to send someone to help her.

*

Near Sturgis, South Dakota, the three bear brothers said their farewells. Each was headed in a different direction, looking for adventure in parts unknown. It was time. Time to test their mettle and do a little solo roaming.

Ace loved his brothers, but they'd had a bit too much together time lately. Bear shifters liked to be on their own a lot more than other types of shifters. Ace knew it would be good for both him and his two younger brothers to get out there and do some things without constant sibling supervision. So, they'd decided to go their separate ways once they finished helping a friend out in Sturgis.

Ace was going to take I-90 and head up into Montana. He had some contacts up there that he intended to look up, then he'd figure out where to go from there. He'd finished with commitments and schedules and just wanted to see where the wind took him for a little while.

He had been feeling increasingly restless over the past year or so. He'd been feeling an urge to claim a territory of his own and settle down, but there was no female bear shifter on the horizon. Heck, there hadn't been any sort of serious female in his life for a while now.

He hoped, by giving in to the urge to roam, he'd allow fate to take a hand in his life. Maybe he'd find his true mate. Maybe not. But, either way, he was looking forward to an adventure.

Ace revved his Harley and headed west. The wind buffeted him, welcoming him as he got up to highway speed. Ah. There was nothing like it. The open road, his hog under him and no timetable in sight.

It was time to answer the call of the wild…

CHAPTER 1

Ace drove his Harley up into Montana and decided to pay a visit to an old friend. Rocco Garibaldi was a well-known associate of the current Lords of all *were*folk in North America. He was also a bear shifter who had been working for the Lords for many, many years, and he was a personable fellow who made friends easily as he liaised between the various bear Clans and the Lords.

Ace looked him up, and though he was friendly enough, Rocky passed Ace on to the Lords before he really knew what was happening. Rocky introduced them and then left Ace on the Lords' doorstep, relying on their hospitality.

It was an odd situation, but Rafe and Tim, the twin Lords, turned out to be nice guys who welcomed Ace readily. In fact, they invited him to dinner. Rafe and their mate, Allie, were inside the house while Tim and Ace sat on the veranda, out of the way of dinner preparations, talking.

"What do you know about weather witches?" Tim asked Ace.

"Aren't they considered a minor power among magic users?" Ace replied.

Tim nodded. "Most of them only have that one talent, and it's usually not enough to get the real mages interested in them. They're left to their own devices, for the most part.

Occasionally, one will team up with a younger person to teach the craft, but that's about as formal an education in magic as any of them get. Mostly, they're self-taught. It's an earth-based magic somewhat akin to our own."

Ace hadn't realized that, but it made sense. "So, why the interest in weather workers?"

"We got a call from a small town in the Canadian Rockies that's having a little problem with their local weather witch. The town hosts a werewolf Pack and a few other assorted shifters. A lynx family and some others, but nobody with enough magic of their own to try to help their weather witch," Tim explained. "They asked us to send them a bear, if we could get anyone to go up there."

"You think a bear shifter will be able to help the witch?" Ace wasn't so sure. While it was true that most bear shifters had way more innate magic than other shifter species, just being a bear shifter didn't guarantee an aptitude for human magic.

Tim shrugged. "At the very least, you could sniff out exactly what's going on up there and report back. The most the local wolf Alpha would tell me was that she was *messed up*." Tim pulled out his smartphone and began tapping the screen. "He sent a short video, and it's actually kind of funny."

Tim brought up the video and turned the phone toward Ace. What he saw almost made him laugh out loud. A woman was running after something, then the angle widened to show a small dust devil whirling in front of her as she ran after it like a runaway dog. She was shouting at it to "get back here" and to "stop" just like he'd heard people yell at their pets who wouldn't cooperate. He couldn't help the smile on his face.

When he looked up as the video ended, he met Tim's gaze. He was grinning too. Both men shook their heads.

"She's definitely got spirit," Tim observed, turning his phone back to look at the image frozen on the screen.

"I'll go," Ace heard himself saying. He hadn't even realized he was going to agree to the mission, but there was something about the woman on the little screen that had captured his attention—and that of his inner bear.

Tim's grin grew wider. "I thought you might," he said with a hint of satisfaction.

"Do me a favor," Ace said, once again speaking before he knew what he was going to say. "Send me that video file."

Tim shook his head and chuckled, tapping the screen of his phone a few times. "Sent," he said a moment later. "Just go up and see what's what, then report back if it's anything you can't handle yourself. Frankly, I think she just needs someone to help her figure out her powers. According to the Alpha up there, she's gotten stronger in recent months, and that's probably throwing her off. A few days of observation and maybe a few pointers from you, and she should be good as new."

Personally, Ace didn't think it was going to be that easy, but he held his tongue, finally stopping himself from speaking every word that came to mind. What was it about these Lords of all were that made him blurt out his thoughts without realizing what he was about to say? Or, maybe, it was seeing the woman on the screen that had momentarily robbed him of caution. He wasn't sure, but he did know there was something about her. Something compelling that made his inner bear sit up and demand that he ride to her rescue.

"Looks like I'm working for you, for the time being," Ace said on a rueful sigh.

"There are worse things, I'm sure," Tim joked. "Don't think of this as work. Think of it as an adventure."

"That's what our recruiter said when my brothers and I joined the military," Ace replied. "If you hear news reports about a bear being swept up in a tornado, you'll know what happened." Both of them chuckled as they watched the sun set through the tall pines. "Sure is pretty up here, Tim. Thanks for making me welcome."

"Any friend of Rocky's," Tim replied. "Besides, you bear shifters have been stirring things up in the world lately. We welcome a chance to make friends and allies among your species."

"You mean the guys who founded Grizzly Cove?" Ace asked. As far as he knew, those dudes were the ones shaking things up. It wasn't normal for so many bear shifters to gather in one town, but somehow, they were making it work.

"You know any of them?" Tim asked, sounding intensely curious.

Ace shrugged. "Yeah, I've crossed paths with a few of the founders, and I have a close friend living there now with his new mate. I thought maybe, if my travels took me in that direction, I might check the place out. My buddy invited me and my brothers to visit."

"Well, when you're done in Canada, maybe you can swing by Grizzly Cove and help them out. From what we hear, they've got a tiger by the tail over there, but they claim to have things under control." Tim shrugged. "I know they've already sought specialist help, but we're all waiting for the guys they need to be free to go up there and try their luck."

"Against the leviathan, you mean?" Ace asked. His friend, Ezra Tate, had told him and his brothers about the problems Grizzly Cove was having with evil in the ocean.

Tim's gaze narrowed. "I know the guys they're waiting for—the sons of Admiral Morrow. They're Navy SEALs with elemental power over water. But I also know the Morrow boys are deep undercover in far off lands, right now. I just hope your friends in the cove can hang tight until the Morrow brothers are free to help."

"I have every confidence in that group. They were hell on wheels in the service, and they've stuck together ever since. They're more like a family of bears than a group of loners, and they work really well together," Ace told Tim. "I mean, look what they've accomplished since retiring from the military. Not every shifter group could manage to create an entire town from scratch in just a few short years. And they're finding mates and settling down. That was their plan, and they're actually executing it, which is kind of remarkable."

"I know their military reputation," Tim said. "If any group

of shifters can hold it together, it's them, but none of us have ever dealt with something like the leviathan before."

"They've done remarkably well in holding the thing at bay," Ace allowed. "I heard they'd managed to protect the entire coastline."

"One of the new mates you mentioned is a powerful witch. And they got some other help from a new kind of shifter. Or, perhaps I should say a really old kind of shifter." Tim's smile was wry.

"What kind? Or should I not ask?" Ace probed. Tim and his brother were the Lords of this generation. They had any number of secrets Ace didn't need to know. He'd follow Tim's lead as to whether or not to reveal what he knew.

"You're going to hear about it sooner or later." Tim sighed. "Apparently, there's a dragon out there in the world."

"A dragon? No way," Ace replied, shocked.

"Way," Tim replied. "He's Romanian, apparently. We haven't met him, yet, but it's something we'd like to do as soon as can be arranged. We hear he's found family among the bears in Grizzly Cove, so he might settle there."

"Bears related to dragons?" Ace mused. "And Romanian?" He thought for a moment. "I know there's a big-assed Russian bear there named Peter. Is he the relation?"

Tim nodded. "That's what we've heard."

Ace was impressed. "Pete's not any more magical than the rest of us, but he's one big mofo. I guess I could see the relationship, but it would've had to be far back in the family line for him to be so much a bear and not have anything *Other* about him. I've met him a few times, and he's always felt one hundred percent bear to me."

"Yeah, they think maybe his great-grandfather—or maybe even further back than that—might've been a dragon shifter."

"Man." Ace shook his head. "I thought they were just a myth. Didn't actually realize dragon shifters were a real thing."

"We have records from millennia ago that show they were around at one point, but there were never that many of them, and we believe they were specifically targeted in the past centuries by the *Venifucus* and hunted to extinction. They were serious opponents to Elspeth and played a pivotal role in her banishment."

"So, if the *Venifucus* are planning ahead to bring back their leader, Elspeth, from the farthest realm to which she was banished, they would naturally try to get rid of her greatest enemies beforehand," Ace said, thinking it through. "Makes a horrible kind of sense."

"Yeah," Tim agreed. "But they seem to have missed one, at least. We're very eager to talk to him, but he isn't in Grizzly Cove at the moment. He was called away by something, Peter said, but he promised he'd be back as soon as he followed whatever trail he was on to its end."

"What's he searching for?" Ace couldn't help but ask.

"Others like himself," Tim answered with a bit of pity in his tone. "The poor bastard. He was raised in a Romanian orphanage at a time when such places were like horror chambers. He didn't know what he really was until he started shifting."

"Damn." Ace thought about the rude awakening that guy must've had when he turned into a freaking *dragon* for the first time.

Their conversation was interrupted when Rafe came out of the house, joining them on the veranda. He had brought fresh bottles of beer with him and handed them around to his twin and their guest. Ace took the frosty bottle, thanking the Lords with a nod.

"So, you're all set," Rafe announced. "I called the Alpha up there, and they'll be expecting you."

"But how did you know I'd agreed? You got this place bugged?" Ace half-teased.

"Dude." Rafe shot him a look, shaking his head. "We're the *Lords*."

Tim guffawed. "Don't let him fool you, Ace. My twin is a shameless eavesdropper."

Ace didn't know what he'd expected when first meeting

the all-powerful Lords of North America, but these two had set him at ease. They were just regular guys—if you didn't mind hanging out with clones. Essentially, that's what identical twins were, right? Ace had mastered enough knowledge of genetics in college to remember that much, at least.

But where Tim was more serious, Rafe was much more the jokester. Still, they made a good team, and their people clearly loved and respected them. Rocky spoke highly of them both, and he'd been with them for decades.

Rocco Garibaldi was sort of a hero to most bear shifters. He was the go-to guy for the North American Lords, which gave him a special status even among his own kind. He'd been hiding out up here in Montana ever since his mating, and even now, he'd basically just provided the introduction to Tim and Rafe, then left. Something was up there, but it wasn't Ace's place to pry. Still, he wondered if everything was okay with Rocky.

"Something troubling you?" Tim asked quietly. Ace must've let some of what he was thinking show on his face, though he hadn't meant to. Or, maybe, the Lords were just that sensitive to other shifters.

Ace didn't want to stick his muzzle in, but he really was concerned. "Is everything okay with Rocky? He seemed a bit...uh...preoccupied, and he hasn't really been in touch with anyone outside of your immediate circle in a long time. Bears all around the country look up to him, and since he's gone silent, there has been some concern expressed. In fact, once my brothers knew I was heading in this direction, they asked me specifically to check in on him, but he's not the same approachable bear I once knew."

"He's got a family to protect, now," Rafe said before Tim shot his twin a quelling look.

"Look, Ace," Tim said in a more serious tone. "There are reasons for his change in behavior, and I can promise you, they're nothing bad. He does have a mate and children to consider, now," Tim elaborated but didn't go into detail.

"More than that, I can't say, but know that we're looking out for him and his family, and he's doing the same."

Ace wasn't entirely placated, but he'd basically been told to mind his own business in a very polite way. One did not argue with the Lords. They hadn't gotten their position through popular election. No, they'd been marked from birth by the Mother of All. Their position of power was a quasi-religious thing that all shifters respected.

The shifter birth rate was naturally low. Twins were extremely rare. Identical twins were limited to one set per generation, per region of the world. A very small number of sets of identical twins that were marked out, by their very existence, as special. Chosen of the Goddess to lead the next generation of shifters in their region of the world.

The species varied. Tim and Rafe were werewolves, but the Goddess only knew what form the next set of twins would take. The Goddess…and the parents who were raising the twins. A suspicious thought began to form in Ace's mind about Rocky's withdrawal from the public eye, but he didn't ask. For everyone's safety, it was better to just let some secrets lie until they were ready to be revealed.

"I can respect that," Ace told Tim quietly. "Just… Tell him he's got a lot of people out there who would be glad to help him, if he ever needs it. He's well liked among bears, and though we're not as big on togetherness as you wolves, we do care deeply for one another."

Tim nodded. "He knows, but I'll mention your concern. I'm sure he'll be touched by it."

The moment stretched until Rafe moved closer. "After you deal with the woman up north, why not come through here again on your way back into the States?" he suggested. "We can always use more friends among widespread communities, like bear shifters, and you seem fun. We can have a barbeque and make fun of cats."

"Is that a werewolf's idea of a good time?" Ace just shook his head, even as he had to chuckle at Rafe's bizarre sense of humor. "Some of the big cat shifters I know would claw your face off just for looking at them funny."

"Yeah, I know a few like that, too. Can't take a joke for the life of 'em," Rafe complained with a mocking scowl. "But they do say bears know how to throw a party. Sadly, we've never been invited to a bear party." Rafe gave a mock forlorn look, and Tim just shook his head.

"Dinner's ready." A feminine voice came from the open door into the house.

It was Allie, the priestess and mate to the Lords. It was an unusual arrangement, but none of the normal rules applied when it came to the Lords in each generation. They were Goddess-touched, and their mate was always a priestess of the Lady. Ace didn't pretend to understand it, but like most things related to the Goddess, he accepted with no judgment. She worked in mysterious ways, and it was always better, he thought, to not mess with a deity who had such power in this realm. Better to live life unnoticed and happy than have some grand destiny and a ton of struggle and strife.

He wasn't sure he'd get away with it, but while it lasted, the peaceful life was nice. Of course, now that he'd met the Lords and was even agreeing to do a job for them, he wasn't sure he was keeping a low enough profile, anymore. Then again, *nothing ventured, nothing gained* was another motto he had learned to value in recent years.

It was that last philosophy that had led to him and his brothers taking off for parts unknown—separately. Their lives were full but had become way too predictable of late. Bears needed a bit of excitement from time to time or they got fat and lazy. The brothers' occasional solo explorations of the country were supposed to help them each inject a bit of excitement into their lives. So far, Ace had to believe it was working. At least, for him.

Only a few days apart, and already he had met the leaders of their kind on this continent and been given a mission in a new part of the world for him. He'd never been up into the part of Canada where they were sending him. It ought to be nice, if nothing else, to see the mountains up that way.

Ace followed Tim and Rafe into the house and then enjoyed a hearty meal with the priestess, Allie, and the twin Lords. They were nice people, and Ace thought maybe he was well on the way to making them friends. If a plain old garden-variety bear shifter could be friends with such powerful beings. He wasn't Rocco, after all. He was just the eldest of three brothers who all made their livings as mechanics nowadays.

Still, the trio made him feel very welcome, so the possibility of friendship—or at least a cordial acquaintance— was very real. Ace felt good about his adventure already. Meeting new people and expanding one's horizons was a big part of why the brothers had decided to go their separate ways for a while.

The next morning, when Ace was ready to take off for Canada, the Lords saw him off with words of advice, supplies for the trip, and their best wishes. The ride was refreshing, the temperatures dropping as he went farther north. His inner bear appreciated the colder air. He loved spring and autumn best, and that's what it felt like as they crossed the border into Canada—a crisp day that appealed to both sides of his nature.

He slept in the wild that night, shifting into his bear form after hiding his bike in a thicket at the side of a mountain road. There was nobody around for miles, and he was able to bed down in his fur, near his bike and belongings. Yeah, this was the life.

He did that for the next two days, making his way slowly up into the mountains on twisty roads that challenged his riding skills. It was incredibly invigorating. Then, on the third day, the weather went crazy.

CHAPTER 2

Sabrina didn't know what was going wrong, but something was definitely wacky with the storm she was trying to control. First, the winds picked up, instead of dying down the way she'd intended. A chill had come blasting through, freezing some of the rain so that the raindrops became ice pellets that really hurt when they hit bare skin. Then, the snow started to fall. Just on one side of Main Street.

Sabrina rushed outside to try to stop what she'd unwittingly set in motion, but the frozen rain hit her in the face, nearly blinding her. She kept walking, and three steps later, she was on the curb in pure rain. She blinked a few times. It was snowing in the middle of the street, and hail was hitting on the opposite sidewalk. Yeah, no way this was natural.

It was her latest screw up. Damn. She'd meant to coax the clouds away from town. Instead, she'd whipped up a hell of a winter storm. Only, it wasn't winter. And this storm was in no way normal.

She heard the rumble of an engine before she caught sight of a motorcycle coming cautiously down Main Street. Whoever that was, he should know better than to ride a motorcycle in a storm like this. Only...the storm had come up so suddenly—thanks to her—that he probably hadn't had a chance to find shelter.

Nice. Her guilt escalated. She'd caused this poor biker possible hypothermia and dangerous driving conditions.

Scratch that. Not just dangerous conditions, but an actual accident. Even as she watched, he skidded on a patch of black ice, and his wheels went out from under him. It felt like it all happened in slow motion as he slid, the heavy bike on its side, the big man trapped with one leg beneath it. They were moving fast, thanks to the road paved with ice. At least he wouldn't get friction burns. At least, she didn't think he would.

She put out her hands, hoping to slow him, and from out of nowhere, a chilly wind came to her aid. He was on a trajectory heading directly for her, but the wind helped stop the slide, and he came to a halt just a few feet from where she stood on the curb, her hands outstretched.

The moment he stopped, she went to him.

"Are you all right?" she asked, kneeling to get a better look at the man. He was wearing leather, which hopefully had protected him from the slide.

"I'm—" He looked up, and their eyes met...and held. Time stood still. Even the winds died down.

He reached out one hand to her, and she took his big hand in hers, and a jolt of magic shot through her, feeling...delicious. Why that word sprang to mind, she didn't know, but if this man's magic had a flavor, it was something she found almost irresistible. Like her late father's famous Irish coffee. Rich and powerful, with a kick of something forbidden.

The magic felt somehow familiar, as well. He was a shifter, of that she had no doubt, but he was much more magical than the wolves in this town. He was something else altogether.

His magic calmed hers, and before she knew what was happening, the storm died, and the clouds began to disperse. Snow and rain stopped altogether, and even the ice began to melt as the cold winds ceased to freeze everything in sight.

When the first rays of the sun hit their hands, she became aware of where they were and that she was still holding a stranger's hand. "Um…" She retrieved her hand and stood, reaching for the handlebars of the bike. She wasn't sure she could lift it, but she wanted to help the man. She *had* to help the man.

He was going to be important to her future. She didn't know how or why, but he was. For good or ill, she didn't know either, but she had to help him. She'd caused his accident. The least she could do was attend his recovery from it.

She tugged up on the handlebars while he pushed from below. Honestly, he did most of the work, but she guided the big bike off him and rolled it into a parked position. She knew how to lower the kickstand because the Harley was a lot like her father's old Indian. At least in some respects.

He remained on the ground, watching her, and she began to feel self-conscious. "You know bikes?" he asked, his voice a rumble that she hadn't quite expected.

Still, he was a big man. Big voice for a big man. It fit.

"My father had an Indian," she told him. "He taught me to ride when I was a teenager. I still keep my license current, though I don't have either a car or a bike, right now." Why was she telling him her life story? What was it about this guy that invited her to share information? "Are you okay? Did you hurt your leg when you skid?"

Before answering, he straightened both of his legs out in front of him and seemed to do a quick inspection of his leathers. The chaps he wore had protected his jeans and were only a little scuffed. The ice had limited the friction, as she'd hoped.

Of course, he wouldn't have skidded in the first place if she hadn't lost control and allowed ice to form. This was all her fault, and she felt terrible about it, but at least he didn't seem too damaged.

"I seem to be intact," he told her. "No harm done."

"You better stand up before you make a statement like

that," she told him, offering a hand.

He hesitated only a moment before taking her hand, and a little sizzle of magical energy worked its way up from her fingertips to sizzle and snap its way through her whole body. Yowza. The man packed a punch, magically speaking.

She leaned back as he stood, allowing her to help a bit. He favored the leg that had been trapped under the bike for a moment, then tentatively put weight on it. He then walked a few steps, hopping up the curb and onto the sidewalk, shaking his legs out and walking off whatever pain he might be experiencing. She cringed, watching him, hoping he was going to be all right.

Ace felt the impact of the woman all the way down to his toes. She was the weather witch he'd come to see. Her magic felt like wind and rain, ice and snow, but mostly like air currents buffeting him gently in her presence. That moment when she'd first touched his hand had marked him, and he knew, beyond the shadow of a doubt, that his life would never be the same, again.

Whether that was going to be a good thing or turn out to be a bad one, he wasn't sure, but he did know something momentous had happened. He knew damned well that her loss of control had caused the freak storm and the ice he hadn't been able to see on the black pavement. Her guilt couldn't have been clearer. Nor could the way she agonized over what she had caused.

Poor baby. He was fine. Or, he would be, given a chance to heal. No harm done. He didn't want her to feel bad. He never wanted her to feel bad.

And, *what the actual fuck* was he thinking? Those kind of thoughts weren't something he was used to having. Had he cracked his head during the slide? No. He thought he probably would've remembered that. Still, he ran his hands through his hair, looking for bumps as he walked off the leg pain.

Finding no evidence of head trauma, he turned around to

find the witch watching him warily. She looked so afraid that he might be hurt, he had to—just *had* to—put her at ease. It was like a compulsion.

"I'm fine. Seriously. Just a little sore."

"I'm so sorry," she whispered. "I didn't mean—"

"This is the absolute last straw." A new voice came from behind Ace's back, and he spun to confront the threat. "I've warned you before, Sabrina. We can't have stuff like this happening in our town. You need to get your shit together, or you need to go." The man looked at Ace, giving him an appraising glance. "You okay, mister?"

"I'm fine, Alpha." Ace figured it was better to be clear on who he was and what he knew from the get go. This was the Alpha wolf of this town. Ace would stake his bike on it. Or, whatever was left of his bike after that skid.

The other man looked more closely. "You the bear?" he asked in a quiet voice. Ace nodded. "Well, I hope you can do something with her. She's causing havoc all over the place, as you can see."

"The Lords sent me up here to assess the situation. I'll report back to them, and we'll take it from there. Right now, I just want to get the lay of the land around here. I've never been up this far in the Rockies before," Ace admitted.

"You called the Lords on me?" Sabrina's voice held both betrayal and anger.

Her face was pale when Ace turned to look at her, putting himself sideways between her and the wolf Alpha. He wouldn't turn his back on a predator, even if the wolf wasn't much of a threat to a full-grown grizzly shifter. It was also a sign of disrespect, which could set the wolf Alpha off, if he was the sensitive type.

"I told you I was out of patience, Sabrina," the other man reminded her in a scolding tone. "Something has to be done to get your magic under control. If this guy can help, so much the better, but if he can't, then you're going to have to find another place to live. You're drawing too much attention to our little town. We're trying to live a peaceful life here, and you're making that difficult."

"Well, I'm sorry for breathing in your nice, peaceful town! Excuse me." Sabrina gathered up her dignity and stormed off down the street.

Ace wanted to follow right after her, but the wolf Alpha caught his arm. "Better let her go. She gets in snits like this, now and again," the man said disdainfully.

Yeah, Ace thought, I'd be *in a snit* if some asshole treated me like crap in public, too. Of course, when a bear got testy, people bled. Still, Ace knew enough about women to realize she needed some time and space to cool down. Hopefully, she'd allow him to start over after Alpha Jackass—Ace's new designation for the not-too-bright werewolf—was out of sight.

"How long has she been in town?" Ace asked, both because he found himself intrigued by the woman, and because it was pertinent information for the job he'd been sent here to do.

"About two years," the Alpha told him. "She's been out of control only for about the last two months, bringing all kinds of wacky weather down on us."

Two months? That wasn't much leeway the Alpha was giving her. A more sympathetic fellow probably would have given someone he'd known for two years a bit more time before reporting her to the Lords and demanding help in sorting her out. This guy wasn't much of an Alpha, Ace decided. He was rude and not very considerate of the feelings of his people.

Ace would do more observation of the town and its residents. If this Alpha was a bad one, the Lords would need to know. If he was just indifferent, perhaps the Lords could send *him* help. Maybe someone who could teach this jerk how to be better to his people. Ace wasn't exactly sure how wolves handled this sort of thing, but hopefully, something could be done, if necessary.

"Name's Tobias," the wolf said, holding out his hand to Ace.

Ace looked after the woman. She'd already disappeared from sight, but he could track her, both by her magic and the delectable scent of her skin. She wouldn't get away from him so easily, but first, he had to deal with this guy.

"I'm Ace," he replied, returning the man's handshake.

"You a friend of Rocky's?" Tobias asked point blank. The man was blunt, that was for sure.

"Yeah. I've known Rocky a long time," Ace admitted.

"I asked them to send him, but I guess he's busy," Tobias went on. Was the man *trying* to be insulting? Ace did his best not to take offense. He'd only just driven into town. He'd give it a day or two to decide if this guy needed to die or not.

"Yep. Real busy. So, you got me. And, if you don't mind—" Ace turned away, intending to head in the direction Sabrina had disappeared, but the Alpha grabbed his arm, again. Ace swore. If the wolf did that one more time, he was going to lose a limb.

"I need an update first. Tim said you'd have some data for me," Tobias reminded Ace of the small package Tim had given him to give the Alpha.

"It's in my saddlebags," Ace told the other man with a long-suffering sigh.

He was going to be stuck with this guy for at least a little while longer. Ace didn't know what was contained in small package, but he was obligated to deliver it. Leaving it unattended while he pursued a woman probably wasn't the best move he could make at this point.

Ace bent down to retrieve the package and caught sight of the deep scratches on the side of his bike. Damn. They weren't as bad as they could have been, due to the smooth sheet of ice, but there was still quite the mark left on his beloved Harley. He'd have to fix that at some point.

"Here you go," Ace said, wiping the grimace from his face as he straightened and faced Tobias. He handed over the package gladly. Anything to discharge his duties and be able to go after Sabrina.

"Your bike will be safe there. Join me for a beer." It

wasn't really a request, Ace could tell from the tone of the Alpha wolf's voice. This was a man who was used to getting his way and being obeyed.

"If you don't mind, I'd rather check on your weather witch," Ace told him.

But Tobias shook his head. "You won't get any sense out of her 'til she calms down. She's weird. Let her be and come on over to the pub. I'll buy the beer, and there's good food if you're hungry."

That was kind of a stupid question to pose to a bear. They were always hungry. And, right now, Ace's stomach was reminding him that he'd skipped breakfast in order to make better time. While he objected to the Alpha's characterization of Sabrina as *weird*, the wolf knew her a lot better than Ace did. If he said she needed time alone, then perhaps he was right.

Also, Ace was still trying to decide if he would leave this asshole intact when he left this town. Perhaps he was just bad at first impressions. He'd give the Alpha a chance to redeem himself, and a beer and a burger sounded like just the ticket.

Ace wouldn't admit it to himself, but there might just be a little fear involved in his decision, as well. It wasn't every day a man met a woman who could change his destiny. He didn't really know how he knew that, but the knowledge was there. His bear half felt it deeply.

Better to eat first, and then confront fate on a full stomach, both bear and man side agreed.

Sabrina was humiliated. She was as embarrassed as she'd ever been and went to hide in the back of her friend's coffee shop. Marilee was just about the only friend she had left in this town, and the moment Mar saw Sabrina's face, she led her right into the back corner. She broke out the cinnamon buns and a pot of chamomile tea and sat with her as they noshed and didn't speak for a while.

"Now, honey, are you okay?" Mar asked in a soft voice. She was a good wolf. A wolf who cared for others. Maternal, they called it, even though Mar wasn't mated and didn't have any pups yet.

"I'm…" Sabrina didn't want to say it out loud. "Oh, Mar, I caused that storm just a little bit ago, and Tobias called the Lords on me. They sent some guy, and he skidded out and scratched his Harley and hurt his leg and landed right in front of me. And he touched my hand, and the magic went all docile and quiet." Her words trailed off, and she realized what she was saying. She'd been too upset before to realize what had happened.

"That's a good thing, surely," Marilee prompted. "Maybe this man really can help you."

"He's a shifter, just not like you. He's…something else," Sabrina told her friend.

"Not a wolf?" Mar looked thoughtful. "Well, there are other species that have way more magic than we do. Bears. Some kinds of special cats. The occasional aberration in other populations. You say the Lords sent him?" Sabrina nodded, feeling glum. "There's a bear who works for them, and Tobias knows him. Maybe he's a bear. Is he a big man?"

"A giant," Sabrina agreed, nodding morosely. "Tall. Big all over, really, but not fat. Muscular, at least from what I could see under the leather he was wearing. He had chaps on over his jeans, but he had a nice butt." Sabrina blushed, even as she giggled a little. Had she really noticed the guy's butt even as the Alpha was complaining about her?

"You noticed his butt?" Mar was always on her wavelength, which was why they'd become such good friends. She was smiling in a conspiratorial way.

Sabrina nodded. "It was hard not to notice. The man is hot. In a giant-sized way."

"Don't look now, but I think your hot behemoth is heading this way." Mar nodded toward the big windows at the front of her shop. "Do you think he tracked you down?"

CHAPTER 3

Ace followed the luscious scent of Sabrina into a small café. He found her sitting in the farthest corner, a half-eaten cinnamon bun in front of her. His half-assed plan to eat with the Alpha then track her down had been blown to smithereens. The moment Tobias had mentioned other newcomers to their small town who seemed inordinately interested in the local weather, Ace had left the pub without even placing an order.

Just hearing that someone might be a little too interested in Sabrina's area of influence set his teeth on edge. Strangers in a shifter town were always worth noting. This sleepy little mountain village didn't get a lot of visitors in the normal course of business. Ace had been invited here, and he was a shifter. Wolves liked togetherness, and their Packs—if large enough—often formed towns around themselves and their holdings, over time. They protected their lands and territories with ferocious intent.

Strangers didn't just walk into such places every day. And, once in a wolf town, non-magical folk seldom stayed long. Sooner or later, the suspicion of outsiders got them moving on to someplace wholly human, where they were made much more welcome. That someone was asking about Sabrina's weather was somewhat expected. Non-magical humans spent a great deal of time studying the weather. But that these newcomers hadn't taken the hint and left town already made Ace feel wary.

That, and the fact that the werewolf Alpha didn't know where the strangers—supposedly hikers—were staying, sent alarm signals tingling down Ace's spine. How could a freaking werewolf Pack not know where human intruders were camping in their own territory? How were they masking their presence? At least one wolf should have run across them. The werewolves patrolled their territory all the time. *Somebody* should know where the camp was, but Tobias had told Ace that the humans were seen in town last week, and then, when everybody thought they had gone, one of the men showed up at the pub, asking more questions.

He'd been asked things in return, of course. Things like where he'd come from and where he was staying, but he'd been cagey. Downright rude in one instance, which had earned him a cold shoulder from the bartender, who had a touchy temper. Ace wished the bartender had been able to contain his temper and find out more about the strangers, but that was water under the bridge. All Ace could do now, was keep an eye out for trouble.

In fact, he'd keep one eye on Sabrina and one on everyone else. If strangers had come to town looking to make trouble for her, they were going to get a rude awakening. Ace was on the case, now. Nobody would get to Sabrina unless they went through him first.

He walked cautiously closer to her table in the corner, making eye contact before she could look away, pretending not to see him. He wouldn't allow that. They would meet face to face, eye to eye. They would be equals, regardless of the fact that he was a grizzly and she wasn't even a shifter at all.

"I'm sorry about before," he told her as he stopped in front of her table. "That guy seems to say out loud whatever fool thought crosses his tiny mind."

Sabrina gasped. "You shouldn't talk about him that way," she told him, surreptitiously glancing around to see if anybody else was listening.

"I've only just met him," Ace replied slowly. "He'll have to do a lot to change that first impression." Ace sighed and consciously relaxed his stance. "Look, can we start over? I just rode up from Montana, and this is my first time this far north in the Rockies. I came here at the request of the North American Lords to see if I could give you a hand regaining control over your gift. I'm not the bad guy here. I'm truly just here to help."

He seemed so sincere. Sabrina wasn't sure what to think. The fact that Tobias had ratted her out to the Lords—a hierarchy she didn't even belong to, thank you very much— still hurt. A lot. How dare he? She'd always done her best to help the people in this town. She'd expected a little more gratitude, and maybe a bit of lenience and understanding when her powers started going wonky.

Instead, he'd tattled on her to the Lords. And this guy was the result.

Of course, her sudden ice storm had almost killed him. She felt a bit guilty about that still, even though he'd come through it mostly unscathed.

"I'm sorry, too," she told him. "About the ice. I truly didn't mean for that to happen. Are you sure you're okay?"

"Fine," he assured her graciously.

"And your bike?" She hadn't gotten a very good look at the Harley, but she was pretty sure it had to be scratched up. "I can't offer to pay for repairs because...well...I'm broke, but maybe I could help, somehow? I'm pretty good with paint and buffing if it's just scratches on the finish."

"That won't be necessary. I'm actually a mechanic. If there's anything wrong, which I doubt, I can fix it myself, and the cosmetics can wait 'til my brother can do it. He's a genius with finishes." He seemed surprised he'd said so much, then shrugged. "Thanks for offering, though."

Well. He was being nice, again. Maybe he really *was* nice. Unlike some wolves, named Tobias, she knew.

"Would you like a cinnamon bun?" she offered, deciding to take the hint as he seemed to glance more and more at the plate of pastries.

"Thought you'd never ask," he said, sitting down opposite her and grabbing a bun off the plate. His first bite took care of more than half the giant cinnamon roll. Sabrina watched, impressed, as he chewed, a big smile breaking over his face.

"These are delicious," he said after he'd swallowed. So, at least he had manners. Somebody had trained him well.

Shit. He was probably married.

Here she was, having lustful thoughts about a married shifter. She knew they mated for life. There was no fooling around and no finding someone else once they'd found their true mate. She'd always thought that was kind of beautiful. And she definitely wasn't the kind of woman who would even think about stealing another woman's man.

"Marilee does all the baking. She's really good," Sabrina told him, trying to disguise her turbulent thoughts.

"What's wrong?" he asked, putting down the cinnamon roll and looking at her.

"Nothing's wrong," she replied, speaking too fast for it to be the truth.

"You smell upset."

She did a double take. "Smell? You can *smell* the way I feel?" She felt violated.

He tapped his nose. "Bears are very sensitive to scent. So are wolves. Don't tell them I said this, but they might even be better at sniffing out people's moods than I am."

"They can smell things like that?" Now, she was *really* upset. Had all her so-called friends in this town been reading her so easily? Was that why she'd had such a hard time fitting in?

He looked surprised. "They didn't tell you?"

"No," she snapped. "Nobody saw fit to educate the poor human witch with only one gift." She felt brittle all of a sudden. Marilee was watching her with a concerned expression. She could probably hear what they were talking about. "Everybody in this town has better abilities than I do. I tried to help them, but they ratted me out to your Lords." She stood, so upset she didn't really care if he *could* smell it. "I can tell I'm not wanted here."

She lifted the empty plate and brought it back to the counter where Marilee was watching with wide, stunned eyes. Sabrina put the plate on the counter between them.

"You've been a good friend to me, Mar. You're probably the only one in this entire town who gave me a chance." She hated that she sniffled in the middle of her little speech. "You can tell Tobias I'm leaving."

"Where will you go?"

Marilee looked really upset, but it wasn't her life that was falling apart. Sabrina would regret losing her friendship, but it couldn't be helped. This town didn't want her, and she wasn't any good to anyone until she got her head back on straight and her power under control.

"I don't know," Sabrina admitted with another betraying sniffle. "But, when I get there, if I write to you, will you send my things to me? I can't take everything with me, right now."

Marilee reached out to put her hand over the top of Sabrina's. "Of course I will. But, Brina, you shouldn't leave like this."

"She's right, you know." The man's voice came to her from just behind her shoulder. He'd moved silently—like the rest of the shifters in this town—and snuck up on her. People had been doing that ever since she came here, but she still wasn't entirely used to it.

"I thought you'd be happy if I took the problem out of town with me," she countered without facing him. "You were sent here to fix the situation, right? I'm leaving. So, problem solved."

"It's not quite that simple," he told her. "Whether you stay here or go someplace else, you still need to get your magic in balance. I'm willing to do what I can to help you with that, no matter where you go."

That made her turn to look up into his warm brown eyes.

"Why?" she asked. "Why do you care what happens with me and my ridiculous little talent?"

He stepped closer. "It's not ridiculous, and judging by the ice sheet I hit on my way into town, it's not little either." He looked around, and his voice dropped into a more confidential tone. "There are things happening in the wider world that you don't know about. Dangers to magic folk. If your wild magic attracts the wrong sort of attention, you could be in real danger."

"What?" Marilee and Sabrina voiced their shock in unison.

"There are strangers in the woods," the man went on. "Did Tobias send out a warning to his Pack?" Here the man looked straight at Marilee, though they hadn't been introduced. He seemed to know she was a werewolf. His nose probably told him, since shifters could apparently scent things like that.

Marilee nodded, her eyes wide. "I heard to keep an eye out for strangers and try to learn what I could if any of them came in here."

"How could any human camp out in werewolf territory and not be seen except when they want to be seen?" he asked, a steely look in his light chocolate eyes.

Marilee gasped, and even Sabrina knew what he was getting at. "You think these strangers are somehow masking their presence?" she asked. "With magic?"

"Possibly," he said, refocusing his attention on Sabrina. "Whatever they're doing, it doesn't seem friendly. If they were on the level, they would have approached Tobias when they arrived in his territory. All magic folk know enough to observe the polite conventions. If they're non-magical humans, then how can they be so good at hiding their presence? Even some Special Forces soldiers I've known don't have those sorts of skills, though they can hide in ways most people can't even imagine. Ditto for hunters. No human is that good that they can fool an entire wolf Pack of trained hunters patrolling their own territory. It boggles the mind."

"He's right," Marilee whispered. "If they're hiding their presence in our territory, they're definitely up to no good."

"And you're suggesting they've come here after me?" Sabrina squeaked.

"It's very possible they were attracted by your wild magic. I know, for a fact, that the *Venifucus* has been very active in trying to convert or capture mages and Others who were just coming into their powers," he pronounced in a dark tone that almost made her shiver.

"The who?" Sabrina asked, confused.

"Oh, Brina, I've heard of those guys. You don't want to get mixed up in anything they're involved in, believe me," Marilee said, her expression tight with worry. "They're, like, pure evil."

"The *Venifucus* is an ancient organization of mages and Others who are dedicated to returning the Destroyer—their leader—a fey sorceress named Elspeth, to the mortal realm. Some think she's already made it back, and a big war is coming," he told them.

"You know how crazy that sounds, right?" Sabrina asked. "It's like something out of a fairytale."

"I wish it was a fairytale," he agreed. "But it's not. The *Venifucus* have stepped up their game in recent years, and they're actively going after young mages who aren't fully in control of their gifts, and Others who have power they can corrupt. Your wild magic would be attractive to them." He paused a moment, then his gaze softened. "I can help you control it, if you'll let me."

That took the wind out of her sails. She had to think, but she needed more information, first.

"But, if the bad guys are already here and the Pack can't seem to pin them down, then I'd be safer if I left, right?" she reasoned aloud.

"Possibly, but you're vulnerable as long as your magic is out of control. The minute you use it, they'll be able to zero in on your location, again," he warned. "But, if we travel together and we head for a safe place, you have my oath that

I will do my best to protect you."

"A safe place. Like where?" she wanted to know. No place sounded safe to her after what he'd just told them.

"I believe the Lords would help you. Their mate is a priestess, gifted with magic. If, for some reason, I can't help you gain control, I know she can," he promised.

"Where are they? Is it far?" Sabrina asked the next logical question.

"Montana. More than that, I can't say, but I can take you there," he told her.

Sabrina looked at Marilee. She trusted her friend more than any other wolf in this town. "What do you think, Mar?"

"I think, first, we should verify that he is who he claims to be," Marilee said boldly. "No offense intended," she said, glancing somewhat nervously at the man. "Then, if he checks out, I think it's probably safer for you to get help. Much as I hate for you to go, it might be the only way to keep you safe. You can trust the Lords without question. If this man was sent by them, then I suppose you can trust him, as well."

"But I'm not a shifter. Why should they care what happens to me?" Sabrina asked the thing that was really bothering her.

"Every soul the *Venifucus* corrupts will make the coming battle that much more difficult," he told her. "All beings who serve the Light will have to band together as they once did, to fight evil. If you're committed to the right side, the Lords— and I—will help you. Simple as that."

"What happened the last time good and evil fought?" Sabrina asked, almost dreading the answer.

"Have you heard of the Dark Ages?" One of his eyebrows rose, and the hint of a smile teased over his lips.

"Seriously?" Sabrina gulped. He nodded, and her heart sank. Damn.

Ace hated breaking such bad news to this pretty woman, but it had to be done. She had to know exactly what kind of danger she was in. It was clear she had never really considered her weather-working skills anything anyone else would be interested in exploiting, but he had to make her aware of the truth.

From the little he'd seen of her power, it wasn't insignificant. In fact, it was a lot more potent than he'd expected. Whatever was happening within her to create such chaos outside, it wasn't something small. She seemed to be...evolving. Her power growing in fits and starts, like a youngster's. That's the kind of loss of control he'd seen when he drove into town. It looked very much like someone who'd grown used to one intensity of power suddenly being ramped up to a whole new level.

"Look, leaving town is probably a good idea," Ace told her quietly. "I've met the Alpha, and he doesn't impress me as the type who would go out of his way for anybody who wasn't Pack."

Sabrina nodded slowly, and Marilee looked pained. "He's right," the wolf woman said after an uncomfortable moment. "He's fiercely protective of us, but anyone who's not Pack doesn't really scan on his radar, I'm sorry to say." Marilee turned her attention to Ace. "You're a bear, right?"

He was somewhat taken aback by her direct question, but he liked her straight-forward approach. Ace nodded confirmation.

"Brina, bear shifters are among the most magical of all," Marilee said, reaching for Sabrina's hand. "The Lords sent you a bear for a reason. He can protect you—both physically and magically. If you go with him, he'll get you to safety, or die trying."

Sabrina looked alarmed. "I don't want anybody to die," she said in a shaky voice.

Ace wanted to reassure her. "I don't want that, either," he said in as light a tone as he could manage under the circumstances. "But I did give my word to the Lords, which means I'm committed to your safety. Your friend is right. Once one of us is given a task by the Lords, it becomes a sacred trust. You are safer with me than anywhere else, right now…unless you have allies we don't know anything about?"

Sabrina shook her head, looking a little lost. She looked away, and he wanted nothing more than to reach out and give her a hug. She seemed so alone just at that moment. But then, she looked up at him, her big blue eyes wide.

"And you…turn into a bear?" She seemed hesitant about asking.

Ace nodded solemnly. "A grizzly," he clarified. "I assure you, my furry form is as in control as my human shape. Just like the wolves. We remember who we are when we shift. I will never hurt you."

He gave her that information just in case she was worried he'd attack her when he was in bear form. Humans didn't know much about shifters, even those humans who had magical gifts. Shifters usually liked to keep it that way. They liked having their secrets. But, if she was going to be traveling with him, she needed to trust him.

Sabrina looked at her friend, as if for confirmation. Marilee nodded, and Sabrina seemed to relax a fraction. It was good to see the true friendship between these two women. Ace regretted that the rest of the Pack hadn't been so welcoming to this poor little weather witch. The Alpha could have protected her and helped her, but instead, he'd just called for help—which at least was *something*—and brushed his hands, glad to let someone else handle the so-called problem.

Sabrina wasn't a *problem* to be dealt with. She was a lovely woman who was having trouble with her gift. If Ace had been in charge around here, this whole situation would have been handled a lot differently. But he wasn't in charge, and he had to make the best of the situation. Taking Sabrina to the Lords sounded like a good idea, especially if she'd already drawn interest from the *Venifucus*.

He had no way to be one hundred percent certain the strangers were *Venifucus*, but it was all damned suspicious. He wouldn't know, for sure, until they attacked, and at that point, it could be too late for Sabrina. Better to remove her from the area, now, and try to sneak away from the strangers, hoping they didn't follow.

It wasn't really Ace's style to run from a threat, but he had Sabrina to consider, and he couldn't really count on these wolves for backup. If his brothers were here, the story would be quite different, but they weren't, and he had to do what was best for Sabrina.

He liked the shortened version of her name that Marilee used, but somehow, he liked her full name even better. It was more regal. It fit her better than the nickname in his mind. He wondered which name she preferred and if she'd object to his using her full name rather than the nickname. He hoped not. Of course, she didn't know him at all, yet, really. He'd fix that as they traveled together. This woman was way too intriguing to leave alone. Both his human half and his grizzly side were growing increasingly fascinated by her.

"If it helps, I've noticed that most of her problems lately are wind related," Marilee offered. Ace was touched once again by how good a friend Marilee was to Sabrina. If only the rest of her Pack were as sympathetic.

"Good to know," Ace replied, nodding his thanks to Marilee. "Now, do you want to verify who I am and who sent me? I'll do a bit of scouting nearby, and then, if you're ready, I think we should get out of here as soon as we can," he said to Sabrina.

"How do I um…verify you?" Sabrina asked hesitantly. Ace looked at Marilee.

"You call the Lords and ask them if they sent me. My name is Ace." He looked at both women as he introduced himself. "Describe me and satisfy yourselves that I am the same guy they sent. Then, tell them the code words Tango X-ray Delta Roger. They'll know that we're heading back to them, possibly with bad guys on our trail."

"You want *me* to call the Lords?" Marilee seemed hesitant.

"Do you have their hotline number?" Ace asked the woman. She nodded. "This is the kind of thing they set it up for. When someone answers, tell them you need to speak with either one of the Lords or Rocco Garibaldi. That's it. Nobody else. If they give you trouble, say I told you to call, and I'm on a sanctioned mission direct from Tim and Rafe. That'll get them hopping."

"If you're sure," Marilee said, still looking a little uncertain, but she was reaching for her phone.

Ace nodded at her. "I'll be outside to give you some privacy. Ask them what you need to. Satisfy yourselves that I am who I claim to be. I need Sabrina's trust if we're going to be traveling together, and this is a good place to start," he said honestly. They had to know he was trying to make the connection as easily and quickly as possible because the threat was real.

Ace headed out the door of the shop but didn't go far. He started by sniffing around the perimeter of the shop, looking for any scent that didn't quite belong. He went only a short distance before the pungent scent of old blood brought him up short.

Ace lifted his gaze to the direction from which the light breeze was blowing. The scent came to him from across the street. More specifically, from the man watching him on the sidewalk across the street.

Fuck. Ace thought he would have more time, but there was no doubt in his mind that the guy watching him was trouble. That scent... It made Ace's hackles rise. It was the scent of evil. Of blood magic. Something so heinous that it had been outlawed among mages since before the time of Elspeth. Only those who sought evil would follow the blood path, for their power came from the blood of the innocents they tortured and killed.

Ace suddenly understood the fate the strangers wanted to impose on Sabrina. They'd come to steal her power. To make her bleed.

Bastards.

No way would Ace let that happen.

Ace sent his senses out and realized there was another man approaching from an oblique angle. He stank, too. Both wore leather coats like they were something out of the Matrix. Stupid gear for the Rockies. These two must be city slickers, which made Ace smile. He could outsmart two city slickers any day of the week—magic or not. This might be easier than he thought.

Then, the first wave of aggressive magic hit him.

Or not.

Fuck, that hurt.

CHAPTER 4

Sabrina tried to be patient as her best friend made the phone call. Marilee got through, right away, but had to wait to be connected to one of the Lords. During the hold time, she did her best to explain to Sabrina exactly how trustworthy Ace was, if he checked out. Marilee, like every other shifter Sabrina had ever met, placed a great deal of trust in their so-called Lords.

Sabrina had never questioned it aloud, not wanting to be rude, but if she was going to place her life in this man's hands, she wanted some answers. Sabrina asked several very pointed questions of her friend and was starting to feel relieved by the answers.

Then, something happened. She felt a wave of nausea come over her about the same time she heard something that sounded like a small explosion out on the street.

"What was that?" Marilee asked, still holding tight to the phone.

"I don't know, but it didn't sound good. There's some kind of weird magic happening out there," Sabrina told her friend. "Stay back here. I'll go peek out the window and see if I can tell what's happening."

"Be careful," Marilee admonished her as Sabrina crept closer to the front of the store and the big windows that fronted the street.

Ace had gone out there. Was he in trouble? Or was this some kind of ploy to get her outside? Was Ace really on the level, or was this a trick? Sabrina approached cautiously.

At first, she didn't understand what she was seeing. There was a man in a sleazy black leather coat across the street, his hair slicked back in what he probably thought was a cool fashion statement. Sabrina didn't like the look of him. Not at all.

And then, she felt another spell of nausea, and she actually saw a wave of power cross the street in a clear shimmer, like heat off a desert highway. Only, they were in the Canadian Rockies, and it wasn't nearly hot enough to cause that sort of visual effect. And it was traveling vertically, not horizontally.

There was so much wrong with this picture, it confused her for a moment. Then, she saw Ace stagger under the impact of the nearly invisible wave of power. That was an attack!

A moment later, Ace got hit with another wave from the side that nearly swept him off his feet, but he stood strong. Sabrina had no idea how much power each one of those shimmering waves packed, but it had to be substantial. That Ace was still standing under dual impacts was impressive.

Even more impressive was the hard-muscled chest he revealed when he suddenly decided to strip off his clothing, right there in the middle of Main Street. What was he doing? Oh, yeah. He was a shifter. And shifters liked to get naked before they changed shape.

Was he intending to go furry, right then and there? As he dropped his chaps and jeans to the ground, having already kicked off his boots, she suspected he was. Goddess help her. The man was *built*.

She'd thought she'd seen some impressive physiques since coming to this werewolf-dominated Pack town, but those wolves were puny compared to Ace.

The man in the black leather coat stepped down off the curb on the other side of the street. He was moving closer.

Sabrina peered down the road at the angle from which the other attack had come and saw another man, dressed similarly in black leather, also moving closer. They let loose with a simultaneous attack, even as Ace shrugged, and a misty magic formed around him.

A blur of brown earth energy, and then, he was a bear. Right there, in the middle of town. A seven-foot grizzly bear shook out his fur. Sabrina's mouth hung open in shock as the double blast of evil magic hit the bear and sort of rolled right off his fur. Damn. Now, *that* was impressive.

She could easily see the anger on the approaching men's faces. They were pissed. Then again, so was Ace. He stood on his hind legs and let out a bellowing roar that shook the glass in the window and rolled across Sabrina's senses in a wave of power.

He was mighty when he was riled. And, looking at him standing up tall, she realized she had probably underestimated his height by a good two to three feet. The bear wasn't backing down, and the mages were heading right for him. Sabrina couldn't let him take another hit. Not for her. If these guys had come here to get at her, she would face them, and she would do her best to blow them away.

Sabrina wasn't sure where this newfound courage was coming from, but it felt right. She opened the door and walked out onto the sidewalk. Ace, in behemoth bear form, stood between her and the approaching men. They didn't seem to see her. Not at first. Not until she called on her power.

Her single, solitary, stupid little power to affect the weather. She really had no idea what she intended. She just knew she had to do something. And then, she let loose.

Her magic seemed to recognize Ace as one of the good guys, because the surge that came from the palms of her hands seemed to skip right over him but hit the two men full blast. It was a blast of wind. Hurricane force wind.

It blew them both off their feet. She watched, amazed as they sort of tumbled down the street. Sabrina cringed as they kept smacking down on the pavement. There had to be broken bones and maybe concussions involved. *Ouch.*

The bear watched them go, as she did, until they were out of sight. Her magically generated wind kept after them. She had the sense that it would not dissipate until they were a good distance away. They would be unconscious long before then, unless they had some way to protect their heads and the rest of their vulnerable human bodies.

Considering that they were both mages of demonstrated skill, she wouldn't be surprised if they could somehow generate a force field or something to protect themselves. She almost wished they could. She didn't like to think that she might be responsible for causing serious injuries, if not outright death, to one or both of them. She wasn't a killer. She would defend herself, and others, certainly, but she never wanted to be the aggressor. It wasn't a role that suited her pacifist nature.

That was part of the reason she had found it so hard to fit in among the werewolf Pack. Wolves were hunters. They saw the world in terms of predator and prey. That wasn't something Sabrina was comfortable with, and it had become readily apparent to the Pack members that her outlook on the world was very different from theirs. After that, everyone but Marilee seemed to distance themselves from her. Unfairly, she thought.

But they were Pack. They agreed with each other on most things, and it looked like they'd agreed to not accept her among them. They weren't unfriendly or threatening in any way. They just very obviously didn't want her around.

All but Marilee. The one bright spot in this otherwise difficult town.

"Brina! Are you all right?" It was Marilee, leaning out the open door of her shop, worry etched into every line on her face.

"Fine," she assured her friend as the grizzly bear turned to look at her. She read intelligence in the warm brown eyes. Ace was in there, just like he said. "I couldn't let them hurt you, again," she tried to explain her actions. "I'm sorry if I stepped on your toes, magically speaking." She shrugged, feeling vulnerable and a little silly talking to a bear. "I'll just…" She turned on her heel and headed back into the shop.

Marilee made room for her then let the door close behind them. Sabrina saw that Marilee still had the phone tucked up against her ear.

"Are you still on hold?" Sabrina asked quietly, just in case there was someone listening on the other end.

"I'm speaking with Rafe," Marilee told her. "He's one of the Lords. We've established Ace's identity and mission, and Rafe would like to talk to you. I already described what just happened." Marilee's respectful tone and the wide-eyed gestures she was making silently urged Sabrina to be on her best behavior when speaking to one of the leaders of all shifters in North America.

As if she'd be rude to such a person. Sabrina held out her hand for the phone.

"Hi," she said. "This is Sabrina."

"Hello. I'm Rafe. I'm sorry if Ace's mission took you by surprise. Your friend, Marilee, explained to me a little more about the situation up there, and I apologize on behalf of my kind for the lack of hospitality she says you've been shown. We're not exactly warm and fuzzy with outsiders as a general rule," he chuckled, his warm tone inviting her to be sympathetic to his words, "but most of our populations live alongside Others—mages, shifters of other species, and holy people, et cetera. There's usually a bit more tolerance than what you've experienced."

"It's okay," Sabrina assured the man. "Water under the bridge."

"I'm glad to hear you say that, because it looks like you're going to need Ace's help if you want to survive." His words brooked no argument. The affable tone was gone, replaced by steel. "Marilee gave me the play by play of what just happened with those two mages. If they were truly *Venifucus*, then you've got a bigger problem on your hands than just a little runaway magic. You're going to need allies."

"And if they're not from this *Venifucus*?" she asked, almost dreading the answer.

"Whatever they are, they're after you. I won't kid you. *Venifucus* is the worst-case scenario, but there are other unscrupulous rogues out there willing to kill innocents and steal their power. If that's what's going on here—and I have every reason to believe it is based on things going on in other parts of the continent—then you've got trouble. Let Ace help. He's one of the good ones, and you couldn't ask for a better man to have at your back in a fight."

The door opened, and Ace walked in, still putting his shirt back on. But for the shirt, he was dressed, again, and Sabrina realized she'd missed his shift back to human form. A part of her regretted not seeing the masculine perfection of his muscular body again. His physique was the stuff fantasies were made of... Very naughty fantasies.

"Yeah," she agreed, watching Ace approach. "I saw a little bit of that, just now. The magic just rolled off his fur. That was pretty cool," she admitted.

Ace smiled as he came closer, no doubt hearing her words. He nodded in acknowledgment, as if taking his due.

"Bears are very magical. Marilee told me wolves are your only experience of shifters, is that right?" Rafe asked gently.

Sabrina nodded slightly. "Yeah. I knew about shifters, but I've never been around any but Marilee's Pack. Just wolves."

"Then, you're in for an awakening. Bears are very different," Rafe told her. "Mostly, they're loners, but they have strong familial ties, and their loyalty, once earned, is unshakable."

Sabrina liked the sound of that. She was starting to get used to the idea that maybe she needed a bit of assistance, and maybe Ace was the right man to render it.

"Just so I'm clear, you're vouching for Ace, and Marilee is vouching for you," Sabrina recited bluntly while Marilee gasped.

Sabrina knew she was getting very close to the line of rudeness to Marilee's ruling power, but she couldn't help it. Ace was a stranger. So was this guy on the phone. The only one Sabrina really trusted here was Marilee.

Rafe chuckled. "I know it's sketchy by human standards, but that's how we do things, sometimes. If you truly believe your friend has your best interests at heart, then you'll have to decide to trust her judgment. If she says to trust me and I say to trust Ace, that would be enough for most shifters. I know it's not that much comfort to someone who was raised without that much magic, as Marilee tells me you were. I understand your discomfort. My mate was raised human until adulthood, when she finally discovered her true heritage. It was a rude awakening, but I like to believe she's okay with how everything turned out."

"Maybe I should be talking to her," Sabrina half-joked.

"If you come here, you'll most likely be working with her directly," Rafe told her. "She's got more magic than most beings, and a Goddess-blessed avocation."

Sabrina could hear the love and devotion in his voice when he spoke of his mate. That, more than anything, helped calm her suspicions. Shifters were different. They were loyal and steadfast. They saw the world in absolutes. Predator and prey. Ally and foe. Good and evil.

Sabrina didn't have to like it, but she knew her path was clear. The appearance of those two mages left her with little choice. She would have to trust Marilee and, by extension, this so-called Lord and his messenger, Ace.

"I look forward to meeting her," Sabrina told Rafe. Her path was set. "Thanks for sending Ace, and thanks for taking the time to speak with me."

Ace held out his hand for the phone, and Sabrina placed it in his palm. He said hello to Rafe and immediately began a detailed conversation about his observations of what had just happened. If there was any doubt remaining that Ace was indeed the man who had been sent by the Lords, his easy conversation with Rafe eliminated it completely. Sabrina turned away. She had things to settle with Marilee before she left, and she suspected she didn't have much time.

The mages—or their friends—would be back sooner rather than later. It would be best if Sabrina and Ace were long gone before then.

At some point, while Ace was talking to Rafe, Tobias walked into the shop. Rather than let the Alpha say something asinine to the women, Ace handed the phone to him. While the Alpha talked with the Lord, Ace went over to Sabrina.

"Are we good?" he asked in as gentle a tone as he could manage. Adrenaline was still pumping through his system after that showdown.

Sabrina nodded slowly. "I trust Marilee, and she trusts you. That'll have to be good enough."

"Then, I hate to say this, but we really need to get out of Dodge. Tobias told me there were at least three, possibly four, strangers poking around, traveling together and remaining hidden until they wanted to ask questions about the weather." Ace knew one of his eyebrows was creeping upward. That the wolves hadn't figured out these people had come for Sabrina, he couldn't fathom. "The minute I heard that, I left Tobias and came looking for you. He should've had a few of his people around you, to protect you." Anger was getting the better of him. They should probably leave before he swatted the wolf Alpha with his claws—or worse.

Marilee cringed. Sabrina looked resigned. She sighed. "Okay. Let's just go. Marilee will forward my things once I get where I'm going." The wolf woman nodded as Sabrina walked up to her. "You've been a good friend, Mar. I'll miss you."

The two women shared a hug, and Ace was touched by the tears in Marilee's eyes. She was a good woman with a big heart to take in a stray like Sabrina. Then again, everything he'd seen so far of Sabrina said she was a nice person who tried to help people. Who wouldn't like her?

The very idea that the Alpha had treated her so poorly boggled Ace's mind. The women broke apart, both sniffling, and Marilee went to the cash register. She opened the drawer hastily and took out a wad of bills, which she pressed into Sabrina's hands over her protests.

"Don't stop at your place. Buy what you need along the way. I'll go over and clear out your things once the strangers have left," Marilee promised. "Just get out of here and stay safe, okay?" Marilee had tears running down her face, now.

Sabrina gave her friend another quick hug and finally accepted the money. "I'll pay you back. I swear."

Just then, Tobias ended the call and placed the phone down on the counter with a clatter that drew everyone's attention. He sighed heavily then looked up at Sabrina, his gaze somber.

"For the record, I do regret your having to leave this way," he said, surprising them all. "But I don't want trouble here. I moved my Pack this far North to avoid trouble, and yet, it's found us, again, through you, Sabrina. You have my best wishes, but it really is time for you to go and take this menace along with you."

Ace stepped forward to confront the Alpha. "You can try to hide up here, but trouble is coming for all of us sooner or later. These are just the opening rounds, so you'd better prepare yourself and your people to deal with it."

"So the Lords said." Tobias met his stare, which was something most shifters had trouble doing. Maybe this Alpha had some backbone, after all. "You two better get going. I sent my trackers to keep an eye on where those two human bowling balls ended up, but they would've called by now if they could've captured or detained them. Likely, you only have a small window of opportunity while they're licking their wounds."

Ace didn't like the panic he could read on Sabrina's face at the Alpha's words. He would have cursed the man, but the guy was right—they really should leave as soon as possible.

"Alpha, can we count on an escort out of your territory?"

Ace asked, doing his best to hold his temper and concentrate on the task at hand.

Tobias nodded. "Already waiting. I can have one of my guys roll your bike up to the door, if you like."

There were any number of ways to interpret the Alpha's sudden cooperative actions, but Ace didn't have time to think about it. He merely nodded. Tobias went to the door and leaned out, making a gesture. A minute later, Ace's Harley rolled into sight, being pushed by a tall fellow who nodded as Ace approached.

"I'm Buster, the town mechanic. She seems sound enough. Just banged up. I think the damage is just cosmetic," the guy told Ace as he handed off the bike to him.

Ace did his own cursory check before starting her up. The engine roared to life, as it was supposed to. Everything sounded fine, but he wouldn't know for certain until he got the bike on the road. There was little time for caution. With the wolf escort, if they did run into mechanical problems, they'd at least have some help until they were clear of Pack territory. By then, Ace would know for sure if the skid had caused any larger problems with his bike.

They left without much further ado. Sabrina fit easily behind him and didn't say much. He could tell she was both sad and scared by her scent. She sobbed, just once, when she left her friend, Marilee, behind, but she got control of her emotions better than he would have expected. She was made of tough stuff, this little weather witch.

Their escort fell in around them before they even hit the edge of town. They were riding out in the opposite direction from where Sabrina had blown those two mages. Whether by luck or some sort of quick planning on her part, she'd sent the two attackers farther north, while they needed to go south to get to the border and then into Montana and the Lords' hidden compound.

They were on the western edge of Alberta, northwest of Calgary and a bit south and west of Edmonton. Ace's plan was to get them on the eastern side of the mountains and make a run for the border down into Montana. They could skirt around Calgary and maybe pick up some better transportation. At the very least, he could get Sabrina a bike of her own. Bikes were easier for making quick getaways, in his experience, and he could keep them running almost indefinitely with his mechanical skills and a little bit of gas.

They stopped a few times to stretch their legs and eat some of the snacks Marilee had packed for them, but mostly, they kept on the road. Ace wanted to make Calgary for the night. He was fine sleeping in the woods, but Sabrina needed a little more comfort. He wouldn't make her rough it if he didn't have to, and he wanted to pick up some things in a larger town that they'd need—especially a bike for her, if at all possible. Rafe had authorized that expenditure and whatever else they needed to get to Montana. Not that Ace couldn't afford to see to her needs, but it was nice to have the Lords' support in this adventure.

Clouds on the horizon drew his attention as they stopped at a motorcycle dealership on the outskirts of Calgary late in the day. Sabrina saw it, too, he was sure.

"I could try to move that away from our path," she offered.

"No," he snapped, then regretted his harsh tone. "I mean, you can't use your talent. Not at all. It'll draw the people we're trying to avoid right to you."

She seemed to consider that for a moment, then nodded. "It'll be hard. I've always used my gift, even as a kid, when I didn't realize I was doing it."

He secured his bike in a spot visible from the large windows of the store, but not too close to the doorway. He didn't like to be in the direct path of traffic in case they needed to make a stealthy getaway. It was the habit of a lifetime to be as low-key as possible when dealing with humans. And he could smell from here that everyone he could sense inside was a plain old human, with no real magic of their own.

Something told him that her ability coming so young was

significant, but the salesman inside had spotted them, so Ace didn't have time to ask more questions just then. Instead, he ushered her toward the door to the dealership, meeting the eager man inside. Ace just wanted to do this quick and then find a place for them to rest tonight.

An hour later, they rode off the lot separately, but still together. Sabrina was showing herself to be a very competent rider, and her credentials had secured the nicest of the used bikes on the lot that was sized right for her small frame. It had a powerful engine that could keep up with his, and so far, her skills were impressive. She knew what she was doing.

Ace had taken a moment to look at tourist brochures in the lobby of the bike shop and spotted an outfitter they could probably use, just a short distance away. They drove into the outfitter's parking lot, and Ace was glad to find they were still open. It was getting on toward dinnertime, and small shops like these didn't always keep city hours.

They spent about twenty minutes getting Sabrina some better outerwear. Waterproof ski jacket and layers for her legs, along with glasses and a hat that would disguise her identity as much as possible and keep her warm. Ace also picked up a two-man pup tent in camo colors, just in case they had to rough it at some point. He didn't expect they'd have to, but he believed in being prepared. He had no idea how far the bad guys' influence reached. They could have people watching the border crossings, for all he knew.

Sabrina didn't argue when he paid for the gear. At least, she didn't say anything in front of the sales clerk. No, she waited until they were outside to try to pay him back out of the cash Marilee had given her. He refused as gently as he could.

"She gave you that money for emergencies," he told her.

"This is an emergency," she countered.

He shook his head. "Not really. Not yet. If we get separated, somehow—that'll be the emergency. Until I find my way back to you. In any case, the Lords authorized me for expenses on this trip. They want you to make it to them safely, and they knew it would require a bit of outlay. And anything they don't cover, I'm happy to pay for. You're my responsibility until I get you to safety, Brina."

CHAPTER 5

Sabrina looked at him, her thoughts racing. "Marilee calls me that," she said. He seemed surprised.

"Sorry. To be honest, I actually like your full name better. Do you mind if I use it or will it remind you of getting in trouble as a child?" He laughed. "You know how some kids never hear their full name unless their mother or father is yelling at them?"

Sabrina was glad to feel genuine amusement for the first time since all hell had broken loose that day. "No. I like my full name. Lots of people have shortened it to Brina or just Bri. One daring friend even called me Sabby for a while." She basked in the happy sound of Ace's laugh when she told him that. "But I like hearing my full name. It's nice of you to make the effort to use all three syllables."

"It's a pretty name, for a pretty lady," he complimented her, which made her feel all warm and fuzzy.

She followed up with a question, just to take the focus off herself. "Is your name really Ace or is that short for something?"

He shook his head. "No, it really is Ace. Our parents were dealers in Reno, Tahoe, you name it. I have a little brother named Jack, and the middle one is named King. I'm the oldest, so I'm Ace."

"Creative," she told him, and he was struck by her unique viewpoint. Most people, on hearing the brothers' names, made some sort of crack. Mostly, they asked who the Joker was, but there were other variants people thought were clever. The three of them had heard them all from a young age. But nobody had ever said their names were *creative*, as if complimenting their parents' ingenuity.

"Do you think anybody followed us?" she asked, her mood changing as she looked at the road behind them.

"If they did, they're well back," he replied honestly. "We need to keep moving, but I think it's safe to stop for the night. They won't be able to travel at night any better than anybody else, and we've put a lot of distance between us and them today."

"I've never been on the run before," she whispered, turning away to get on her bike.

"Don't think of our ride that way," he counseled. "Try to look at it as an adventure. I mean, how many people do you know who've ridden through the Rockies on a bike with a grizzly at their side?" He smiled at her, hoping to lighten her mood.

She smiled back, shaking her head. "Well, uh, nobody," she replied. "I didn't even know any grizzlies until you rode into town this morning. And when you shifted…" Her eyes widened. "You were huge!"

Yeah, his inner bear liked hearing that. The furry bastard preened under her praise inside Ace's mind.

"As you probably noticed with the wolves, shifter forms are generally bigger than their natural counterparts," he said in as offhand a manner as he could manage while his inner bear basked.

Ace mounted his bike after securing their purchases in his saddlebags. The mostly empty cargo bags were starting to fill up. He'd made sure to get saddlebags for Sabrina's bike back at the dealership and had put all her supplies in them. If, somehow, they got separated, he wanted her to be equipped.

Less than an hour later, they pulled in to a motel parking lot. Ace went in to deal with the front desk clerk while Sabrina stayed outside where he could see her, but nobody else really could. He got a key to a room on the end of the building, in short order, and went back out to his bike.

Within moments, they'd parked under a small carport provided for guests, within sight from the room, and gone inside. It was small, but it would do for the night.

"Um…" Sabrina said hesitantly. "There's only one bed."

"And it's yours," Ace said quickly. "I'm not trying anything funny here. We're here strictly to sleep. We'll both need some rest if we're going to make tracks tomorrow." He dumped her saddlebags on the bed and put his own on the single chair in the corner. "You can have the bathroom first while I order up some dinner. Burgers okay with you?" he asked.

"Well done with cheddar cheese and fried onions, if you can," she told him, already pawing through her saddlebags. "Oh! And French fries, too, please."

Mission in sight, Ace began looking through the information binder on the small desk next to his chair that had food recommendations. He found the burger joint the clerk had mentioned when he'd asked and picked up the phone to call in their order. While he was on the phone, Sabrina disappeared into the bathroom. He heard the shower go on a moment later, and he tried his best not to think about the fact that she was in there…wet…and naked.

Down, boy.

The food arrived before she came out of the bathroom, which was fine with Ace. The less people who saw her, the better. He paid the delivery guy and gave him a tip, his stomach rumbling as the scent of the burgers hit his sensitive nose. He'd ordered a few bags of food since they hadn't really had time to stop and eat much during their day-long ride.

Ace moved the small table over next to the bedside, then set up the dinner as best he could so they could share it. She would sit on the edge of *her* bed, and he would take the chair he'd claimed earlier. He was unpacking the bags of burgers and fries when the bathroom door opened, and a swath of steam hit him, stopping him in his tracks.

The steam smelled of warm woman and some kind of soap. Delicious. *Mine*, the bear inside him insisted.

Whoa.

Sabrina came out, fully dressed, her hair wrapped in a towel. She was wearing black leggings and a black sweater she'd picked out at the outdoor store. She looked like an angelic ninja in the unrelieved black that left only her hands, feet and head bare. Wait. Scratch that. He saw she was wearing black socks, too, when she walked closer.

"That smells really good," she said, her gaze going to the wrapped burger he still held in his hand. She dropped the clothing she'd worn earlier on the other side of the bed then took her seat on the edge behind the table he'd moved.

That stirred him into motion as he realized he'd been staring in kind of a frozen stupor. Silly bear. He was a little too fascinated by the woman he'd been sent to rescue. That couldn't be good. He had to focus on the mission.

Just at that moment, the mission was food. Right. He had the food, and now, they needed to eat. His stomach rumbled, again, as he sorted out the burgers he'd ordered.

"Well done with cheddar cheese and fried onions," he read off the ticket attached to the wrapper.

"Yum," she said, accepting the wrapped burger he handed her. "Thank you."

"I wasn't sure what you wanted to drink so I got a selection of soft drinks and iced tea," he told her, unpacking the sack of drink cans onto the table. "And they put all the fries into one big container," he explained as he set the large styrofoam box on the table between them.

He shook packets of ketchup onto the table as she selected a can of soda and popped the top. Unwrapping her burger, she checked under the bun and arranged it a little more neatly before taking a dainty bite. Ace was fascinated with her fastidious manners and tried not to be too barbaric as he gobbled down his own burger. He'd ordered several for himself, but he'd share if she wanted more than one. He wasn't sure how much human females needed to eat, not having spent a lot of time around any.

She declined another burger after finishing the one, but that was okay. Food never went to waste when Ace or any of his brothers were around. Bears ate even more than other shifters, which was to say—a lot. He ate four to her one, and they both finished around the same time. They'd shared the fries, and Ace had been careful to let her have half, without being too obvious about it.

They hadn't talked while they were eating, both tired from the long day of travel and too hungry to waste time talking while there was food in front of them. But, as they slowed down, lingering over the last few French fries, Sabrina started a conversation.

"Thank you for this," she said slowly, looking down at the table. "For today. For everything." He could hear the emotion in her voice.

"No need for thanks. I couldn't leave you in danger from those creeps."

"They were awful, weren't they?" she asked quietly, still unable to meet his gaze.

"Evil," he agreed. "Their magic felt slimy against my fur," he admitted. "Blood path mages. Both of them."

"Seriously?" That made her look up. She seemed shocked. "Are you sure?"

Ace nodded. "Absolutely sure. I've felt that kind of evil before, I'm sorry to say."

"They gain power by killing other people, don't they?" she asked in a small voice.

"Torture fuels them, too. Anything that spills blood of the innocent. And, if that innocent is magical, so much the better for the blood path mage." Ace shook his head. He hated to be the one to tell her about these things, but she really needed to know what they might be up against. "Just recently, there was a case where a blood path mage was discovered to be working with a ring of humans traffickers. They were abducting women for resale to foreign buyers with the mage's help. One of the things he got in return was first choice of the women. He was separating out those with the slightest hint of magic and keeping them in his basement. He had cages down there, and they'd somehow managed to capture a shifter female along with several humans with minimal magical powers. He was draining them slowly, torturing them a little at a time until he'd used them up, then he would kill one to get what was left of her power and replace her with another abductee. It was really sick, but a colleague of mine managed to take him down."

"A bear shifter?" she asked.

Ace nodded, but he had to tell her the whole truth. "There was a werewolf woman involved, too. She's a private investigator. And a half-fey, half-human mage was with them, as well."

"It took three of them to take down one mage?" Her tone held fear and a hint of hopelessness.

He reached across the table, trying to offer comfort, but he didn't dare touch her. He didn't want to scare her, and unauthorized touching wasn't a good way to put her at ease when they had to spend the night together alone in this little room. He was very conscious of the lack of space in here, but it couldn't be helped.

"You know that not all mages are created equal. Plus, he'd had months—maybe years—of feeding off those women. He'd built up a hefty reserve of power, and he was incredibly cautious," he told her, remembering the details he'd heard through the bear grapevine.

"But there were at least two after me. Maybe more," she pointed out.

He shook his head. "Out in the open. Out of their territory. On the chase. They'll make mistakes. They're not like me. I know how to hunt. I know how to avoid the hunters and turn them into my prey if I have the chance. But your safety comes first," he promised her. "Evasion is the name of our game. We're going to dodge and weave and get out of Canada as quickly as we can. Then, we'll deliver you to the Lords, and you'll have a whole mountain of loyal shifters between you and anything that could threaten you, not to mention the power of the priestesses that live there. The Goddess Herself is said to watch over the Lords and their Lady. If you have their protection, you'll be as safe as any being can be in this world."

"I hope you're right," she muttered, taking a final sip of her drink.

"Look, we can be at the border crossing in a few hours. We'll approach it slowly and see if anybody's watching before we try for it," he told her, figuring she needed to know the plan.

He reached over to his saddlebag and took out the paper map he'd purchased earlier. Sometimes, the old-fashioned ways were better. Up here in the mountains, GPS signals weren't always available. He'd planned to give her the map to carry after they looked it over together tonight. He wanted her to know she was well equipped to take care of herself in the unlikely event they got split up.

He spread out the map as she cleared away the debris from their meal. Then, he began by orienting her to their location.

"We're here," he said, pointing to the small spot on the map just south of Calgary. "We can cross here, at the Piegan-Carway crossing. They open at seven in the morning. I checked," he said. "If it doesn't look safe, we can detour either east or west. The closer of the two is west, at the Chief Mountain crossing, but they're only open in the summer and the hours vary. Plus, we'd be farther west than we need to go for the Lords. It would add a little time to our ride, but not too bad. If we went east, we would be in Canada a lot longer, but we'd be better positioned to get to the Lords by taking the Sweetgrass-Coutts crossing." Again, he pointed to the spot on the map and noted that she followed with interest.

"What are the odds that, if they're watching that first

crossing, they could have allies watching all the others?" she asked, her question making him hesitate. She'd hit on the one flaw he saw in detouring the long way through Canada.

"You've got a good point, which is why I'm leaning toward taking the direct route and, if that's being watched, going up into the mountains to try the closer crossing to the west. If that's also being watched, then there are ways we shifters can get across the border without any trouble, but it might be a little rough on you," he told her. "Having bikes rather than a car will make it a lot easier, but there is still some potential danger involved and a long trek on foot, rolling the bike alongside over rough terrain."

"Better that than those mages," she said, resignation in her tone. He had to admire her grit.

"That's why I insisted you get a pair of soft boots in addition to the ass-kickers for riding," he told her.

At first, she'd resisted his suggestion in the store, but Sabrina had eventually gone along with his request to find some light boots that were comfortable. She also had the sneakers she'd been wearing when they left town, which were broken in and hopefully comfortable. Having a few options could only help on their journey, because if a human had hurt feet, they couldn't go far. Bears were different, but he tried to take into account her frailer nature in his planning.

"You're good at this," she said, surprising him into looking up from his perusal of the map. "I mean, you planned all this stuff ahead of time. Like, you take it in stride."

"This isn't my first rodeo," he told her, trying to make light of her compliment, which touched him deep inside.

"I guess you see a lot of action working for the Lords," she observed.

"Actually, I don't." He shook his head. "I mean, I don't work for the Lords. I only met them a few days ago, though I'm friendly with a bear who is one of their top people. I went to Montana to visit him. He introduced me to the Lords, and the next thing I knew, I had a mission. Normally,

I make my living as a mechanic these days, and I usually work with my brothers."

"So, where are they, now?" Her tone was gentle, as if she feared something amiss.

"I'm not sure, but we all agreed on taking a little break from each other. Most bears are solitary—especially at our age—but we've traveled the road together for a long time. Recently, we all felt a call in a different direction. Nothing solid, but enough to make our inner bears want to take off on their own, following that elusive scent that wasn't exactly a scent, but more a feeling." He shrugged, not really able to put it into words. "We stay in touch, but we agreed to have our own individual adventures. I guess, this is mine. Or, at least, it's the start of it. I'm not sure how long we're going to roam alone, but I figure, at some point, we'll meet up, again."

"Bears are solitary except for family groups, right?" She *had* been listening. He nodded, smiling at her.

"For the most part," he agreed. "But, in the past couple of years, a group of unrelated bear shifters have started a community on the Washington coast. It's a unique situation, but they seem to be making it work. I have a friend there and a few acquaintances. I was thinking of visiting those guys after I get you to the Lords."

She looked down at the map, seemingly dejected, though he couldn't fathom why. Was she feeling the same pang about the end of their journey together as he was? No. That was ridiculous. He wasn't even sure why he was feeling that strange separation anxiety. No reason she should be feeling it, too. No, for her, the end of their travels meant the protection of the Lords. She should be looking forward to getting there with relief, not regret.

Ace cleared his throat. "I'm really curious to see their town," he said, hoping for a neutral topic. "It's rare to get so many of us grouped together in one place who aren't related by blood."

"What makes it work? Do you have any theories?" She looked, for all the world, like someone who was trying to put on a brave face, but he still couldn't figure out why. Instead, he went with the direction of the conversation, hoping to find a way to make her smile, again.

"The core group of men who came up with the plan were long-time coworkers. They served in the Special Forces together, as a single unit." He paused a moment to think about it. "A family, you might say. Though they aren't related by blood, they're brothers of a different kind, but no less close. Even though they're not even all the same kind of bear."

"What other kinds of bear shifters are there?" she asked, clearly curious. "You're a grizzly. Are there black bear shifters?"

He nodded. "Smaller than us, but wiry. And there are some big Kodiak bear shifters from Alaska. Polar bears. Kamchatka bears from Siberia. Pandas from China. Even koala bears from Australia, though they aren't really bears. They tell me the one that settled in town always smells like cough drops from all the eucalyptus he eats."

That got a laugh out of her, and Ace felt like he'd won the lottery. Thank goodness. He didn't like seeing her sad or worried, and she'd been a little of both ever since they met.

"I can't even imagine panda shifters," she admitted.

"There are only two in town, from what I hear. A widow and her child. Everyone is really protective of them, and the child is supposed to be really cute," he told her.

"Like a baby panda?" Sabrina's eyes lit up at the idea, and he nodded. "That must be totally adorable."

"That's what they say. I've never seen it myself, of course, but I'm intrigued enough to want to visit."

"I wonder if they'd let me visit. After all this other stuff is settled, of course. When it's safe," she added quickly.

"I don't see why not. The town is set up as a tourist stop. Lots of art galleries and shops for tourists on their way down the coast. But, if someone wants to move there, they have to be granted permission by the town council, which means the core group of bear shifters that set up the town. They don't let just anyone stay, but there are a few witches and some Others." He didn't go into too much detail because he wasn't sure how much was more or less public knowledge in the magical world, and how much was meant only for shifters. He probably shouldn't have said as much as he had, but instinct told him Sabrina could be trusted.

They talked a bit more as he folded the map and handed it to her. "I want you to keep this in your saddlebags," he told her. "I don't anticipate getting separated, but if the worst should happen, I want you to be fully prepared."

Her expression was grave as she accepted the map. "I really appreciate everything you've done for me," she said quietly. "You're really good at planning ahead. That's not something I've ever done, and it's landed me in trouble more than a few times. Thanks for helping me stay alive and free of those goons."

"It's my honor to help you, Sabrina," he replied softly. "Besides, I like doing heroic stuff from time to time." He chuckled to lighten the mood, and she joined him.

"Well, you're definitely my hero today," she told him, making his inner bear bask in her praise.

The moment dragged a bit, but then, he shook himself to attention. There were still things to do. She cleared the table the rest of the way, and he moved it back to the side of the room, clearing the space.

"I'm going to wash up real quick," he said, grabbing a pair of shorts out of his saddlebags. "Don't open the door to anyone and stay away from the window, just in case." He'd already closed the curtains, but he wasn't sure she understood it was to hide their presence. "I'll be out in five minutes, tops. You need me before then, just yell, and I'll come running."

She nodded, and he went into the tiny bathroom. He took a quick shower and was out in the promised five minutes to find her sitting on the edge of the single bed, flipping through the channels on the TV using the remote control.

CHAPTER 6

Sabrina tried really hard not to stare as Ace came back into the room wearing nothing but a pair of shorts that went about halfway down his trunk-like legs. The man had muscles that wouldn't quit. She'd been attracted to him from the start but had tried to ignore it for the most part. Things were too mixed up, right now, in her life. She couldn't really see herself getting involved with a guy under the present circumstances.

But who said they had to be *involved*? Maybe she could just enjoy the moments she had with Ace and leave it at that. Possibly. Though, if she were honest with herself, she wasn't really the kind of woman who had ever been able to just live for today and not worry about tomorrow's consequences. In this case, to her heart.

She could easily fall in love with Ace. She was already in lust with him, that was for sure. She was in so much trouble here. Her life was in danger. She was on the run with a man she barely knew but wanted to know a lot better...in the physical sense if nothing else. But there was something else. Something that drew her to him like she'd never been drawn before.

She didn't understand it. She was even a little afraid of it. This attraction could all be some sinister byproduct of the danger she was facing. She didn't know, for sure. In fact, she didn't really know anything, at this point, except how much she wanted his touch.

Maybe she was seeking the comfort of physical closeness. Or, maybe, she was just horny. Sabrina had to stifle a laugh as that thought occurred to her. Ace was busy digging through his saddlebags, organizing things, and she knew she was staring at his butt rather than the television screen, but really, how could a woman help herself when faced with such a tantalizing sight?

Ace stowed his bags in the corner then straightened. He glanced at the TV screen, and a faint smile lifted one corner of his lips. "You're watching the weather?"

Sabrina shrugged. "It's an occupational hazard. I like to see if the scientists are puzzled about something I might've done."

He sat beside her on the foot of the bed, facing the TV. "That happen a lot?"

"In the past, not often. I really wasn't that much of a witch until a few weeks ago. I could help steer really bad stuff so that it wasn't quite as bad over populated areas or farms where crops might be in danger, but other than that?" She shrugged, making a face.

How many times had she wished to be able to do more? To really help. Well, she'd gotten her wish, not quite in the way she had intended. She sighed heavily and shut off the television.

"The weather is supposed to be good for tomorrow, and nobody noticed anything odd, so I'm in the clear for the time being." She offered him the remote control, unable to meet his eyes with him sitting so close and her emotions running so high. "If you want to watch something, go for it. Otherwise..." She tried to get up, but he placed one big hand gently on her forearm, forestalling her.

He took the remote control with his free hand and placed it on the console that held the TV, just a short distance away. The hotel room wasn't the most spacious of places, and he had a long reach. When that was done, he turned back to her, and she felt almost compelled to slowly raise her gaze to meet his.

"I know this has all been kind of jarring," he began softly, his understanding tone touching her deeply. "How are you holding up?"

She shrugged. "As well as can be expected, under the circumstances, I guess." She couldn't hold his gaze. Not this close. Not without giving away how deeply attracted she was to him and how much that attraction was on her mind at the moment, with him so near.

"Sabrina." His tone was coaxing and a little disappointed. "I hope you'll let me know if something is wrong. Absolutely anything. I'm here to help you, remember?"

"You have helped," she was quick to reply. "You've done so much for me. A total stranger..." Her words trailed off, and she couldn't help herself. She met his gaze, again, knowing he might read something in her eyes that they probably weren't ready to acknowledge.

"In my experience, shared danger forges strong bonds more rapidly than usual. I've seen you under fire, Sabrina. That told me a lot about you. And, everything I've seen, I like," he said, his voice dropping to low, intimate tones that made her tummy wobble.

"I like you, too," she told him, unable to keep from speaking the truth when he was being so nice to her. "I mean," she backpedaled when she realized how that must have sounded, "I like how you handled everything today. Most people would have gotten really mad at me for causing them to crash, but you were different. I'm still really sorry about that." She knew she was babbling a bit, but she couldn't seem to help herself. "Then, you went all grizzly bear in the middle of Main Street, and I've never seen anything like it. You were so brave, and so willing to put yourself between me and danger. I'm not sure I like that aspect of this, but I do thank you for your help. I just wish whoever it is that's hunting me wouldn't try to hurt everyone in their path. I can't believe you're here voluntarily, helping me, when you didn't even know me before this morning."

"Like I said, danger heightens awareness. You've got a good heart, Sabrina. I knew that within moments of meeting you." His smile melted that good heart of hers right into a puddle of womanly desire. Damn. He was potent up close. All that bear shifter strength, moderated when he was in human form but no less alluring. Bears where hot.

Or, maybe, it was just this particular bear that got her all hot and bothered. She wasn't sure because she'd never met a bear shifter before. Maybe that was a good thing for her sanity, though, because if they were all as attractive as Ace was, she would have been a goner.

"Thanks," she said, feeling her cheeks heat with a flush. She hadn't been on the receiving end of male compliments in far too long. She didn't quite know how to react. "But you're the hero. You saved me today, and I'll never forget your kindness. I think you have a sense of honor unlike anyone I've ever known."

He looked down, clearly somewhat uncomfortable with her praise. Good. The shoe was on the other foot for a change, she thought. Then, all thinking ceased as he lifted his hand to her cheek, cupping it gently as he looked deep into her eyes.

"You're a very special woman, Sabrina."

Time seemed to stand still. Was he leaning closer? Was she leaning toward him?

One or the other must have happened, because the next thing she knew, his lips were touching hers, kissing her in a gentle salute that lasted a few seconds before evolving into something a lot more tempestuous. His mouth was hot and demanding as she opened for him, sighing into the kiss she'd wanted for hours.

His arms were around her and hers around him. She didn't remember moving them, but she enjoyed the exploration— the sensory input of her fingers as she learned his muscular shoulders and arms. He was like a warm, velvety marble statue. Hot and hard and almost unyielding.

His hands circled her waist, one pausing at her back while the other stole under her shirt, inching upward as their kiss went on and on. She was mentally cheering that mobile hand on as the rest of her mind was blown by the sexiest kiss she'd ever known. He was growling...deep in his throat. It didn't scare her. It turned her on like nobody's business!

Then, his hand reached the band of her bra and paused. Was that as far as he would go? No! Please, no. She wanted more.

As if hearing her thoughts, he cupped her breast, fabric and all, his palm overflowing with her generous curves. He seemed to like her shape, molding and fondling in ways that made her gasp. Then, he peeled the cup downward, freeing her nipple, and she knew she was getting wet...eager...ready for his possession.

But could she? Would he? She'd never been one to sleep with a guy she'd only just met, but if she was going to break her own rule about not having sex on a first date, Ace would be the guy. He was so far out of her experience. So far out of her league.

Damn. That thought started to sober her up a bit, even as his fingers plucked at her nipple, causing her abdomen to clench in excitement. Ace must have sensed something, because he drew back, releasing her lips and searching her gaze.

"You're so beautiful," he whispered, a slight growl present in his voice that made her want to lick him all over. He was so damned sexy.

"I'm glad you think so," she replied shakily.

He shook his head as if to clear it. "I didn't mean for this to happen," he assured her. She wasn't sure whether to be insulted or pleased. What, exactly, did he mean by that comment?

The mood began to lift. More sober thoughts chasing the stupor of desire away from her silly head. Ace removed his hand from under her shirt. She took some solace in the fact that he seemed very reluctant to stop touching her.

"I don't usually…" she told him shakily. Though why she felt compelled to reveal such things, she wasn't sure. "Not so fast, anyway," she added, shrugging and looking away.

"Then, that's all the more reason to stop, now, though I'd just as soon make love to you all night and into tomorrow."

His words stole her breath and shocked her into looking at him. There was a devilish smile on his face that made her feel warm, again. He was teasing her. The sexy beast. Somehow, that made her feel better.

"Well, that isn't going to happen," she assured him. Though, if she was being honest with herself, she'd admit that she wanted just that. Long, leisurely love making with Ace. Only Ace had ever inspired such scandalous thoughts.

He chuckled. "Yeah, I really know how to kill a mood, don't I?"

She placed the tip of her finger on the tip of her nose and winked, telling him without words that he'd hit that one on the nose. Then, she got up and turned out the light on the far side of the bed from where he was seated. There was one easy chair in the room and one bed.

He was being chivalrous, letting her have the bed, but it sure looked like he was in for an uncomfortable night. She sighed.

"Would it do any good for me to point out that you don't really fit in that chair, whereas I could be comfortable enough on it?"

He grinned and scratched his chest. "Well, I'd then have to point out that I don't really fit in that little bed, either."

She looked from him to the double bed and had to laugh. He was right. When the Goddess made bear shifters—or, at least, this particular bear shifter—She'd created them on the massive side. He was probably in for an uncomfortable night no matter where he bedded down.

Sabrina shook her head, wished him a good night and climbed into the bed on the far side. A few minutes later, she heard him moving around, then the other light switched off, and there were no more noises from the other side of the room. At least, nothing she could hear.

And that was all she knew until she woke up hours later.

*

The next morning, as they were heading down the highway, Ace was feeling good. Sabrina had surprised him last night. She'd been amazing, really. She'd given him a tiny glimpse of what it might be like if they became lovers, and he couldn't wait to go back and learn more about how good they could be together. She'd been soft and womanly in his arms, and her kiss had been the sweetest wine he'd ever sipped. He wanted more.

First, though, he had to get her across the border and to the safety of the Lords. After that, he planned to stick around for a while. He had no pressing plans, and her safety and wellbeing were quickly becoming central to his peace of mind. He had no easy explanation for it. She was just...incredible.

He cared what happened to her. He wouldn't abandon her to the Lords the moment he got her to their mountain top in Montana. No way.

Getting there was going to be the tough part. They weren't even that close to the larger crossing he'd planned to try first when he felt the first wave of searching magic reaching out to sweep over him. As a bear, he was able to shrug off most magic, and he was glad to note that they were far enough away from the magical probe that it skipped right over him—and Sabrina, because she was riding right next to him—but he'd definitely felt it, and it wasn't good.

Blood magic. Once felt, never to be forgotten. He would recognize the taint anywhere.

Signaling to her, he pulled off the highway and onto the shoulder, dismounting and walking the bikes into the trees a way so they couldn't be easily seen from the road. Sabrina followed his lead without question, which was both gratifying and a little scary. Her safety depended entirely on him. For a bear used to traveling as part of a trio, flying solo on this mission—which could easily turn out to be one of the most important of his life—was becoming a little terrifying.

"What's going on?" Sabrina wanted to know once they were stationary in a small clearing among the pines.

"Did you just feel anything?" he asked, wondering how acute her power was. He had to know her limitations if he was going to protect her.

Sabrina shook her head. "Not really. Something made my shoulder blades itch just before you signaled to stop, but I don't know—"

"Somebody was scrying for you," he said shortly, cutting her off, fear making him impatient. "It reeked of blood magic, and it was coming from the direction of the border. I suspect, if it's not the two you blew down the street, it's friends of theirs, waiting for us to show up at the crossing." He frowned. "Luckily, they seem a bit impatient. They're using magic to scry for your presence, but it's distant, and it rolled off my natural shielding, blocking them from seeing you."

Sabrina's brow furrowed, and her eyes grew fierce. That was better than fear. He'd take a determined Sabrina over a scared one any day of the week.

"What do you think we should do?" she asked him.

"Well, we can't keep going this way. I felt enough of the direction to know that the magic came from where we're headed, now. We could go west a bit, cutting over on Highway 5 to meet up with Highway 6 to the Chief Mountain crossing. It'll take a little extra time, and the terrain is more challenging," he told her.

"But they could be waiting for us there, too, right?" she asked.

He nodded, unwilling to lie to her. "The other option is to go native and do an illegal crossing. It'll be easier for me. Though, if I go bear, I'll have to ditch my bike."

He would regret that. He really liked this bike. But, if he hid it well enough, he could probably come back for it later, after things settled down.

"Is it impossible to get across with the bikes? Like…with you in human form?" She hesitated a bit before spelling out what she meant.

"More difficult, but not impossible," he said. "There is one other possibility, but it's a long shot. Still, it could solve our problem handily, if I can make it happen."

"What's that?"

"If I can find a trustworthy bush pilot willing to cross the border illegally, hopefully with a large enough plane that he can fit both us and our bikes in it…" He rubbed the handlebar of his beloved Harley. He really didn't want to leave it behind, but if there was no other way, he would. Sabrina's safety came first.

"Do you know anybody like that?" She seemed impressed that he might have such contacts.

"Not in this part of the country, but I do have a friend in Washington State who might. Let me call him and see what we can arrange."

CHAPTER 7

Once Ace made the decision to ask for help, things started happening rapidly. He'd called both the Lords and his friend, Ezra Tate, in Grizzly Cove, looking for an easier way across the border. The Lords, of course, knew a pilot, but he wasn't available, which left Ezra's contact as the best option. Ez put Ace in touch with a bush pilot who was already in Canada, though he was a bit farther north.

They caught up with the man—a fellow named Lucien— by phone. He was on the ground, doing a refueling stop, and was willing to detour to do their little job, for a premium. Since the Lords were paying, money was available, but once Lucien heard who would be footing the bill, he became a bit friendlier. He was on the right side of the coming conflict, even if he wasn't always operating on the right side of human law.

Better for them that he was knowledgeable in ways to circumvent human authority. They needed to get across the border, and they needed to do it quickly, before the *Venifucus* could call in even more operatives. The last thing Ace wanted was to be caught in some kind of standoff—or worse, a pitched battle. Especially without his brothers to back him up.

Lucien had a small cargo plane that was large enough to

carry their bikes, which was a relief. He gave Ace detailed directions that led them to a grassy meadow, deep in the mountains. He claimed he could easily land his plane there and pick them up. In fact, he was willing to hop down there and meet them just before dusk that very same day.

Flying across the border in the dark of night at an obscure location was, he assured Ace, the best way to go. All they had to do was avoid the *Venifucus* and get to the landing strip on time. Piece of cake.

Until Ace saw the back-country roads they'd have to traverse. It could be done, but it would take every last minute of their allotted time. And every last ounce of skill Sabrina had at riding. Ace knew he could handle the rough ride, but he wasn't so sure about her. He hadn't seen enough of her skill set on the motorcycle to know for certain whether or not she would be able to handle it. He just had to hope for the best. He'd be there to pick her up if she fell, and encourage her every step along their path.

She was a trooper, that was for sure. She'd been a steadfast companion all along their journey. He couldn't have hoped for anything better from a woman he'd only just met. A human, at that.

Sabrina felt that uncomfortable feeling of her magic building up to a critical point. Being around Ace had helped dissipate the static charge somewhat, but it was still there, just building more slowly. She could feel it gathering, just below her skin. This was a new thing that had started happening since her power had morphed into something that refused to remain under her control. The charge would build until it drove her crazy—an itchy feeling all over her body—and she just had to release it.

Ace kept turning them onto increasingly difficult roads. Switchbacks, tight corners, rough road surfaces and narrow lanes kept her on her toes. They didn't stop, but their pace was kept to a crawl, at times, by the challenging roads. She wondered if they would make the rendezvous. Ace had explained to her about the pilot that would meet them, the timing and location. He'd kept her well informed once the plan was set in motion. She appreciated that.

He always looked out for her, making sure she understood what they were doing and that she would be prepared in case they got separated, somehow. He wasn't just leading her somewhere blindly. He was making her part of the mission. Allowing her to participate in her own rescue, as much as possible. He was teaching her things, planning for every contingency, including the worst-case scenarios that her own mind shied away from.

They stopped for lunch in a copse of trees just off the side of the road, where nobody could see them. He'd packed food in both their saddlebags, and they pulled out what they wanted and had an al fresco picnic. Neither spoke much, but the silences were companionable, even if she was still worried about what was to come.

"Do the roads get any better up ahead?" she asked around a sip of water from one of the bottles that had been in her bags.

"Not really," he told her. "At least, they look pretty much the same on the map. We're in a part of the world people don't regularly travel. There are locals, here and there, but this valley that we're heading toward is part of a large, privately owned reserve. We have permission to use the landing strip. The Lords cleared the way with the Clan that owns the territory."

"Shifters?" she asked, surprised, though she probably shouldn't have been.

This wild country was perfect for many different species of shifter. It was quiet and rugged, without a lot of people or human impact. It was easy to see why shifters would gravitate toward this part of the world.

"Yeah, there are a few different Clans, Tribes and Packs that own a lot of the land around here. The Lords have influence with all of them and have been making calls on our behalf. That's why we're not really seeing any of the sentries.

They're there, but they're not objecting to my presence in their territory as they normally could. Instead, the Lords have gotten us free passage and scouts to watch our back trail. If anybody is following us, we'll find out sooner or later. The scouts will report to their leaders, and the leaders will report to the Lords. One of them will call me if there's anything we need to know."

"You make it sound so easy," she said, impressed.

Ace shrugged. "We're pretty resourceful," he teased. "We've been doing this sort of thing a long time."

Just at that moment, his phone rang. Ace reached for it, checking the screen with a bit of a frown when he saw whoever it was that was calling. He moved off a few paces to accept the call, and she cleared up the little debris they'd created, readying both of them to take to the road, again, while trying to give him at least the illusion of privacy.

As it turned out, he didn't say much, but his expression had changed to something closer to a grin with more than a bit of bemusement thrown in when he walked back to her, tucking his phone into his pocket. He thanked her with a nod for cleaning up and secured his saddlebags before mounting his bike. Damn, he looked sexy doing that.

Of course, he looked sexy doing just about anything. Her little heart went pitter-pat every time he looked at her with those deep chocolatey brown eyes.

"Looks like we're going to pick up some additional help," Ace told her as she mounted her bike, beside his. "That was my contact in Washington. He's called in a favor from a mutual friend who happens to be working on a case up this way. He's going to detour and give us a hand. I've worked with him before. Good man. Hawk shifter."

Sabrina gasped. "You mean, there really are bird shifters? I thought that was just a myth."

Ace smiled at her. "Not a myth, though they're somewhat rare. The man you're going to meet is a private detective, and his ability to fly gives him certain advantages when it comes to aerial surveillance."

"I bet." She thought about the implications. "Is he already ahead of us or is he flying in to meet us?"

"Not sure, but I'd bet on flying in. There's really nothing where we're headed but a big flat meadow high enough in the mountains and deep enough in shifter territory that nobody else should be around to bother us."

That sounded ideal to Sabrina. Deep inside shifter territory, strangers should stick out like sore thumbs. With any luck, the bad guys wouldn't be able to stop them before they got to the landing strip.

They got back on the road—though, at this point, it was more of a trail. The path was only wide enough for one car and was laid with gravel, not pavement. The going was slow, but the towering trees all around and the deep forest made her feel...sort of...welcome. She didn't know how else to describe it. It felt like, if bad guys found them, the forest itself would try to help her...somehow.

When the road ended in a small clearing, Ace halted, and she stopped beside him. What now?

Then, a man stepped out from behind a large tree. His chest was bare, and he had the most amazing set of shoulders she'd ever seen. He wasn't massively built like Ace. He was more on the slender side. He had a body shaped like the famous Olympic swimmer she'd watched on television the previous summer. All shoulders and back. Long and streamlined.

Could this be the hawk shifter Ace had mentioned? He was dressed only in a pair of baggy grey sweatpants. He didn't even have shoes on his feet. He had to be a shifter, newly emerged from his animal form. But where'd he get the pants? A giant hawk with a pair of grey sweatpants in its beak flying overhead was bound to be noticed, right?

During her musings, she caught the barest flicker of Ace's hands making some kind of motion. The man in the sweatpants made an answering gesture, and Ace seemed to relax. He got off the Harley and went to meet the other man a few feet away. They exchanged a bro hug and some low-voiced words that she couldn't hear before they both turned to look at her. Caught staring, she suddenly felt very conspicuous.

"Sabrina, come meet Collin," Ace invited, smiling in such a way that made her tummy flip. He really was the most attractive man she'd ever known.

And that included the good-looking hawk shifter she was about to meet. Though he had sandy hair and a unique profile, the hawk man did nothing for her. Not the way Ace did. He was bigger, more approachable, if a bear could actually *be* approachable. He soothed her where the hawk man made her feel as if he was studying her like a bug.

"Sabrina, this is Collin Hastings, Private Eye," Ace introduced them. She held out her hand, and there were no tingles when she touched Collin's hand. Not like the way she tingled all over whenever her skin made contact with Ace's. "Collin, this is Sabrina."

His smile was handsome. It transformed his face from striking to downright sexy, but it was nowhere near as warm as Ace's toothy grin. Yeah, she was ruined for all other men, just as she'd feared, but Ace was really something special, even among shifters.

"Thank you for helping, Mr. Hastings," she said politely, retrieving her hand after a quick shake.

"Call me Collin, please. I'm just glad I was in the area. I was following a lead on a cold case that didn't pan out, but at least, now, my trip up here wasn't wasted. I flew recon over the entire area, and there's nothing suspicious for miles," he told them. "There are signs of pursuit further south, but they're being led astray by the local shifters. I doubt they could get anywhere near before you guys leave."

"You're not coming with us?" Sabrina asked, unsure of the plan at this point.

Collin laughed. "I have my own transportation. Lucien's plane is larger than most bush planes, but with the bikes, it's still going to be a tight squeeze."

"You know the pilot?" Ace asked.

"Yes, top man. I've used him before. He's a little funny about staying in Canada these days, so chances are he'll drop you just on the other side of the border and head back, right away. Don't be surprised if that's his plan," Collin warned.

"That's okay. Just as long as we can get across without anyone seeing us, I can take it from there," Ace assured the other man.

The sound of an engine in the distance made them pause. "That sounds like him," Collin offered. "You best get down to the landing strip. It's just through these trees. I'll fly recon after I return these loaner pants." He made a gesture toward the grey sweats and grinned.

"Thanks for making the effort. Sabrina's not used to being around shifters, and I'd have had to claw you if you showed up swinging in the breeze in front of her," Ace put in with a growling laugh.

Was he serious? He sounded a little serious there, to Sabrina's ears. She didn't know what to make of that.

"We'll walk the bikes in," he told her, putting action to words as he nodded a goodbye to the hawk shifter.

Sabrina smiled and thanked the man as she passed him. He grinned and waved back, watching them go with a bemused smile.

The little plane that landed a few minutes later had fat wheels and bounced along until it came to a rolling stop not too far from them. The man who got out of the tiny cockpit looked like a lumberjack, but maybe that was just because of the red and black check wool jacket and fur-lined hat with the ear flaps down that he wore.

"Lucien," Ace said, stepping forward. "I'm Ace." He offered his hand and was rewarded with a handshake and a tight smile.

"Nice to meet you," the man replied, his words faintly accented with a French tone. "And you, miss," he said, nodding politely to Sabrina. "I don't want to stay on the ground long," he said. "So, we'll just load up your wheels in the back and get you both settled in, and we can be off."

"Just one last thing," Ace told Lucien, stalling him a moment while Ace turned to gaze at the tree line. Sabrina turned, too, just noticing Collin striding closer. "You remember Collin Hastings, don't you?"

"*Mon ami!*" Lucien's face lit up as Collin approached and they shared a warmer greeting than she and Ace had received. "You have more work for me?"

"Actually, I do," Collin replied with a smile. "When you get back from dropping these two off, we should talk."

Collin moved back and gave Ace a quick nod. Sabrina realized Ace had been reluctant to board the plane until he was certain of the pilot's identity. Ace knew Collin, and Collin knew Lucien, so as long as Collin gave the nod, Ace would go with Lucien. That's how shifters did things, she'd learned, all based on who knew who.

Ace began to move toward the plane with his Harley while Lucien and Collin made plans to meet up the next day. She followed Ace, and a moment later, Lucien was there, opening the hatch to allow them to roll the bikes aboard, using a small ramp he pulled out from the hold. Lucien took charge of Sabrina's bike, thankfully. It was a little too heavy for her to roll up the steeply inclined ramp herself, but the shifters made it look easy.

When she looked around for Collin, he was gone. A few minutes later, while the men were still fussing with securing the bikes just so, she saw the flash of an impossibly large wing, and then, the rest of the giant hawk came into view. He perched for a moment, as if posing, in a tall tree just ahead, and she got a good look. It had to be Collin. The sheer size of the bird was astounding. It had to be a shifter.

Then, he took to the air, and his wingspan almost made her jaw drop. Now, *that* was a sight. She'd never seen—and would probably never see, again—a hawk that huge. She blinked, and he was gone, flying high, out of sight. Wow.

She was still straining to see where he'd gone when the men returned. Lucien opened another door—this one closer to the front of the small plane—and climbed in. Ace motioned for her to go next, and then, he joined her in the small passenger area. Lucien supervised the closing of the hatch and then turned back to his instruments while Ace helped Sabrina figure out the various seatbelts. It was a bit more complicated than on a commercial jet, but the shoulder harness made her feel a little safer, for some reason, so it wasn't that bad.

Then, the little plane's propeller started turning, and Lucien taxied the aircraft around to face the length of the mountain meadow he'd just landed on. He started it rolling down the grassy clearing, and the bumpiness just about jarred her teeth out of her head. She started to worry about whether or not they were going to crash into the line of trees at the other end just about the time she started feeling the plane lift off the ground.

Lucien pulled back on the stick, and they made a steep ascent, just barely clearing the tops of the trees. Sabrina cringed, but they made it. They were airborne.

Now to get over the border.

Ace was glad to get off the ground. The sun was setting, and within moments, it would be dark. A perfect time to slip across the border without anyone being the wiser. Or so he hoped.

Lucien seemed like a competent pilot. He'd asked Ace a few pointed questions about just how much trouble Sabrina was in while they were tying down the bikes. Ace hadn't liked the questions at first, until Lucien told him that the kind of trouble would dictate at which airstrip they landed. He'd explained in detail, and Ace had understood his reasoning, even if he didn't like giving out too much information about Sabrina and her problems.

He had a choice of a few different places to land. Some were closer to human cities and towns and brought with them the risk of magic users in the vicinity—and no way to guarantee those folks were on the right side. Some of the landing sites were in purely shifter territory, which made them a little safer, but also more remote, which meant they'd have to travel farther over rougher terrain to get to highways where they could make better time.

Lucien didn't want to spend too much time in U.S. airspace for reasons of his own, so the landing site had to be within a certain range of the spot he chose for crossing the border—high in the mountains, hugging the steep valleys in order to avoid radar and other ways they could be caught. Not only did they have to avoid *Venifucus* mages, but also human authorities who might object to them breaking the law by sneaking back into the country.

After hearing what they were up against, Lucien suggested, and Ace agreed, to stick to shifter-controlled areas for their entire flight, as much as possible. Different shifter groups owned or patrolled these rugged parts of the border. Some worked for various agencies and took responsibility for noting border incursions. With a bit of prior notice, the shifters who worked border patrol on both sides of the line would be willing to forego reporting their flight.

Ace had placed the call to Tim and Rafe before they left the ground, and the Lords had promised to take care of it. Ace got the impression this was something they'd done before, and Lucien didn't seem all that worried. Apparently, his plane was well known in these mountains, especially among shifters.

Ace was able to discern that Lucien was some kind of cat, but other than that, the man was a bit of mystery. Of course, cats loved being mysterious, so that was to be expected. Bears were more straightforward. They liked playing, but they didn't like games in the human sense of the word. Not like cats.

Cats excelled at keeping people guessing in all their forms and took delight in their own cleverness. Ace just let it go. It wasn't that important to know exactly what kind of cat they were dealing with. It was enough to scent the feline and just accept the man's sly humor. It was easier on the nerves that way, even if his inner bear wanted to swat the guy from time to time.

Sabrina had grabbed Ace's hand as the small plane rumbled into the air. He had done his share of flying in little planes, so he wasn't all that concerned. Everything seemed normal to him, and the engine was purring like a well-tended pet. Lucien probably spent more time pampering the airplane than anything else. It was clear he loved the winged cargo hauler. He wouldn't let anything happen to it...not if he could help it.

CHAPTER 8

Sabrina felt her power building and was very much afraid it was going to let loose unexpectedly. What would happen, considering they were in the air? She shuddered to think of the consequences of her power going rogue when Lucien was flying so close to the tops of the trees.

"You all right?" Ace asked.

Lucien had given them both a set of earphones with an attached microphone so they could communicate over the noise of the engine. He explained that all three of them were on the same loop, so they were all part of any conversation. That made her a little wary to share, since she didn't know the pilot and wasn't sure what he'd do if he knew she had an unstable talent.

"Um…" She didn't know how to tell him what she was feeling with Lucien listening in. "There's a bit of pressure."

Ace frowned then seemed to figure out what she meant. "Can you hold it?"

She shrugged, totally unsure. Ever since her magic had decided to misbehave, she was the last one able to tell how it would react. She'd tried using it. She'd tried squelching it. Either way, things had happened. Some of them had been really bad things—like the mini-tornado that had blown down the middle of Main Street. Thankfully, nothing had been too badly damaged.

"Okay, well, can you give me a warning if something's going to happen?" Ace asked. She appreciated that he was trying to stay calm about this, but inwardly, she was starting to panic.

"I'll try," she promised, not really sure if she could keep that promise or not. Sometimes, when the magic let loose, she was more its victim than its wielder.

"Problem?" Lucien asked, his gaze on Ace, though he'd heard every word of the exchange.

"Possible erratic winds. Could be powerful. Sabrina will try to warn us if they're coming. Be prepared." Ace sounded confidant, which helped calm her a little, but she couldn't help but wonder if it was all just a big show for her benefit.

"I'm sorry," she whispered over the headset, meaning her apology for both men, just as her magic tore loose. She shut her eyes tight and tried really hard to control it. "Wind gust behind us in three…two…one…"

The wind hit them, and the plane responded like a bucking bronco. Lucien swore and fought the stick while Sabrina cringed and held on for dear life. She'd grabbed Ace's hand, again, and he was kind enough to let her squeeze the circulation out of his fingers in her panic.

The plane bounced on the currents of air, eventually finding a smoother path. Lucien seemed to enjoy the challenge after the first moments of unexpected terror. He'd stopped swearing, at least. Then, he started letting out whoops of what sounded like enjoyment. Apparently, he got his jollies wrestling rogue air currents and coming out alive.

Sabrina was just trying to hold it together. Ace's touch helped. He let her clutch at his hand, and he'd put his arm around her shoulders when the plane started bouncing around, holding her tight to his side. She felt warm and safe in his embrace as her power started to settle down.

She was able to rein it in, and eventually, the wind from the north died out, leaving the little plane in peace. Lucien was checking his GPS and other instrumentation, and for the first time, Sabrina realized her unplanned use of magic might have blown them completely off course.

"Where are we?" Ace asked Lucien, clearly thinking the same thing.

"Well, we're over the border for one thing," Lucien said, still checking his instruments. "We're over Idaho. I know you wanted to be more toward the middle of Montana, but the wind and the mountains combined to send us west. Can you work with that?"

"Yeah, we'll be fine. I have friends all over the Northwest," Ace replied. "We can figure something out. Question is, do you know of a safe place for us to land?"

"No problem there. We're over the edge of Kaniksu National Forest, right now. There's a lynx Clan just north of McArthur that has a landing strip. They'll let me land there," Lucien said confidently.

"Friends of yours?" Ace asked.

"Better than friends," Lucien replied, a smug tone to his voice. "Family." He chuckled. "It'll be good to see my sister and her kids, again. I don't get over the border much, and I miss them. Your little windstorm helped me get here for a visit, and for that, I thank you." He tipped an imaginary hat toward Sabrina.

"I'm sorry about that," she said, but he waved her off.

"Most fun I've had in ages," Lucien said. "And now, I get to see my nieces and nephews, so it's all good on my end. That tailwind saved a lot of fuel, too."

He sounded happy, so Sabrina decided to let it go. She'd made the apology, and she felt ridiculous not being able to control her magic. She could've just gotten them all killed, but it had worked out after all. At least the pilot was thrilled with the results, even if it did put them on the wrong side of the mountains.

"I'm glad it worked out," she told him, sitting back in her seat, very conscious that Ace hadn't removed his arm from around her shoulders.

Lucien put in a brief coded radio call to the landing strip, and a few minutes later, they saw a few beacons light up. It wasn't much. Certainly not enough light for a commercial airport or a human pilot to land by, but it seemed to be more than enough for the shifter at the helm. Sabrina hardly dared to look as the laughing lunatic made his approach to the small field that passed for a runway.

Ace's arm around her shoulders tightened. She was certain he could feel her terror and was offering what support he could in this situation. She took comfort both from his touch and from the fact that he seemed calm and confident in their pilot. His steadfast presence helped her not to scream when the big rubber tires made uncertain first contact with the ground then bounced them down hard before rolling them at increasing levels of bounciness into the darkness between two tall stands of trees that was all she could see of the runway.

When they finally started to slow, she started breathing, again, realizing only then that she'd been holding her breath from the moment the wheels first touched ground. She'd never been so scared on a flight in her life. Hands down. She was tempted to kiss the ground when they finally got off the plane, but refrained.

She was glad she had when she realized they had a welcoming committee. A smiling woman tugged Lucien into her arms for a bone-crushing hug before he was let up to exchange another hug with the man who stood at her side. Then, he was passed down the line of younger people who called him uncle, and Sabrina realized his sister and her family had come out to greet him.

She followed Ace around to the cargo door and tried to help him, but she could barely see in the dark at the back of the plane. Only the faint light from the small building at the end of the runway had allowed her to make out the family that was still greeting Lucien. At the back of the plane, all bets were off. Still, she had to offer.

"Can I help?" she asked quietly, her voice just barely above a whisper. She'd grown used to speaking softly around the werewolves up north and knew that shifter hearing was way better than her own.

"Can you actually see anything?" came Ace's amused reply.

"Not much," she admitted. "But I'm here if there's something I can do to assist."

She heard a few metallic clanks and then rolling tires as a dark shape that was probably Ace pushing one of the bikes came down the ramp toward her. He moved the bike past her and into the faint light at the front of the plane.

"Can you see me, now?" he asked, and she just made out the wide grin on his face as she walked toward him.

"I see you," she replied, grudgingly, though she smiled at his teasing mood. "You don't have to rub it in. I know I'm just a measly human."

He surprised her by touching her shoulder. "Nothing wrong with being human, but don't forget, you're more than that. You handled that power surge really well before. If it had hit us from the side, we could easily have smacked into the wall of a canyon. Guiding it in from behind was a stroke of genius."

She shook her head. "I wish I could take credit for being a genius, but it was all instinct."

He squeezed her shoulder. "Every shifter knows that instinct is one of our best teachers. You were right to follow it and not to try to force the magic into some other path. Following your instincts probably saved our lives. You did good, Sabrina. Real good."

He leaned down to place a soft kiss on her lips, and she leaned into him. Stars! She'd needed that all day long. Touching him last night—holding him and being held by him—had stirred a need in her. She'd been like a starving woman all day, longing for a time when they could be alone, standing still and having the freedom to touch again.

He'd given her casual touches during the day, spawned from the new intimacy between them, but they'd essentially been on the run. There had been no time for hanky-panky, much as she could have wished for it. But it was dark, now, and their pilot was still busy with his extended family. For this short moment out of time, she could press against Ace and drink in his kiss.

Ace nearly lost his head. He'd been wanting to take her in his arms all day and kiss the heck out of her, but circumstances had prevented him from giving in to his desires. Her safety had to come first. But, now that they were on the other side of the border, he figured he could take a moment and give her the kiss he'd been dying for all day.

They weren't out of danger. Not by a long shot. But he hoped things would get simpler from here on out. At least they were in the same country as the Lords, now, and Ace's own contacts were more numerous in the States than farther north. They were on the wrong side of the mountains, thanks to Sabrina's loss of control, but they'd figure it out. For tonight, they would find a place to stay, and if the Goddess was kind, he would make love to Sabrina late into the night and wake with her in his arms.

He heard Lucien approaching through the grass and knew he had to end the kiss. She clung to him as he drew back, and the dazed look in her eyes made him feel like a titan. He'd done that to her. He'd given her the moment of respite in the chaos of their day. He felt good about that and hoped to continue as soon as he got her alone again. For now, though, they had things to do.

"You want to have dinner at my sister's?" Lucien asked heartily, coming into view around the wing of his plane. "She's invited us all to join the family for a meal, and if you two need a place to stay for the night, they have a cabin on their land that they use for guests. I'll stay up at the house since I need to leave before dawn, and we'll probably stay up all night talking, anyway."

Lucien looked like a cat just served a very large bowl of cream. He was happy to see his sister and family, that was easy to see.

"We do need a safe place to spend the night," Ace replied,

looking at Sabrina to see what she thought of the idea.

"That's very kind of your sister, Lucien," Sabrina said politely. "If Ace thinks it's a good idea, I'm very happy to accept the invitation. Thank you."

Lucien's sister was lovely and welcomed them into her home with kindness and gracious hospitality. Sabrina had never been around cat shifters before, and she found them charming. The children were sweet, and the meal they shared delicious and plentiful. Even though they hadn't been expected, it felt like the whole family had rolled out the welcome mat.

Later that night, as they settled into the guest cabin, having left the family up at the house, Sabrina asked Ace about it. He said cats were usually welcoming if you had the right introduction.

"In this case, we were not only the reason Lucien came to visit his family after a long absence, but we were sent here by the Lords, in a roundabout fashion. Lucien got the job of transporting us from Tim and Rafe, and most shifters would do anything for those two. Just being asked to help out was a sign of their confidence, and an honor," Ace told her. "Knowing all that, the family was definitely more willing to welcome us than it would have been otherwise."

"Well, whatever the reason, I think they were really nice," Sabrina replied, opening her saddlebags and fishing out the few toiletries she had with her.

"They were," he agreed, moving closer. He took her into his arms, swinging her around so that they were face to face, chest to chest, heartbeat to heartbeat. "But you won them over with your kind heart, Sabrina."

His head dipped, and he kissed her. Thank goodness! She'd been waiting for hours to be in his arms, again. There was no one here but the two of them and no reason anybody should come around until the morning at the earliest, so this time was all for them.

Sabrina sank into his kiss, wrapping her arms around him

and snuggling up tight to his hard body. He felt so good.

She was aware of the feel of motion, but she didn't know what he was doing until the backs of her legs hit the foot of the large bed. This was a bed big enough for a shifter—even one as large as Ace. It would fit them both, as a matter of fact, which suited her right down to the ground. She had come to a decision as she ran for her life that day.

She wanted to know what it was like to make love with Ace, and it didn't matter to her that they'd only known each other a couple of days. Screw the waiting period. She wanted to have sex with him, now. After the day she'd had, she wasn't sure she'd even be alive tomorrow. Her enemies could find her at any time. She'd rather enjoy herself—enjoy *him*—while she still had the ability and freedom to do so.

Tomorrow would take care of itself. Tonight was for passion. Lots and lots of passion.

That decision firmly in mind, she sank onto the bed, sitting down in front of him. When he would have moved to join her, she stopped him by the simple expedient of moving her hands to his belt. *That* got his attention.

She rubbed the long, hard length of him through his trousers and felt her insides quiver with excitement as she learned the shape and size of the hardness she would soon be enjoying. He'd done so much for her these past two days. It was time for her to do something strictly for his enjoyment. Though, of course, she would enjoy it, too, she was sure.

She teased him a bit, but he didn't seem to mind. He didn't rush her. He didn't prod her. He just let her explore as she wished, which made her feel in control. Powerful.

Heaven knew, she'd had enough of feeling lost and out of control these past few weeks. Today, especially. Perhaps he knew she needed this time where she could be the one in charge. And, perhaps, he was the most empathic man she'd ever been with. He certainly seemed to be able to read her like a book, even after such a short time.

She didn't want to wait, though. Not for long. She wanted to feel his flesh in her hands. Against her lips. To that end, she reached for the zipper, undoing the button at the top of his pants, first. His breath rumbled in his chest, a barely suppressed growl that she found incredibly sexy. The sounds he made were animalistic, at times. Wild, yet contained. Sort of how he moved in the world, wearing his human guise, but sharing his soul with an untamed spirit.

She lowered the zipper and set him free, immediately wrapping his hardness in her hands, learning the shape and feel of him. He growled, then. A real, hearty, low growl that sounded like pure need. And, when she put her mouth on him, the sound from his chest rumbled through the room. She swore she could feel the vibrations of sound against her own body.

Then, she didn't think for a few minutes as she sucked on him, wanting to pull that sexy sound from him again. When he'd given her the satisfaction of that earthy growl two more times, she pulled back, and he seemed to take that as his cue to take over. She didn't mind. She'd given him something and received a massive boost to her confidence in return. He really was the most amazing man. And, right now, she was so turned on that she would jump his bones in a second, given half a chance.

He seemed to realize how urgent her need was. She suspected he was feeling the same himself. He lifted her to her feet, only to take her into his arms and kiss her senseless. It was wild. Tempestuous. A no-holding-back kiss, unlike those he'd given her before. This one spoke of need and fierce, animal longing.

When he released her from the near-bruising kiss, he lifted her onto the bed and turned her, positioning her body just so, according to his plans. It soon became apparent that he wanted to mount her from behind. Instead of scaring her, the thought of it made her moan.

"You like it this way, Sabrina?" he asked, his breath coming in hot puffs against her ear as he bent over her on the bed. "I don't want to frighten you."

"You're not scary, Ace," she managed to say, smiling as

his hands shaped her hips, rubbing her ass and caressing her spine. She arched into him, like some sort of needy she-cat. "You're a teddy bear," she teased him, receiving a playful nip to her ear and a short growl in return.

She looked back over her shoulder at him, and he was smiling right along with her. She'd been right. There was nothing scary about making love with Ace—no matter what position he wanted to take. And then, it dawned on her. This choice had been some kind of test. He'd put them in this position, probably wanting to know if the beast half of his nature frightened her. She shook her head and almost laughed. If he only knew! She saw his massive grizzly not as a threat, but as a protector. The fact that the grizzly was also a hunky, tall, handsome man was what counted here. And that man was proving to be the most unique individual she had ever known.

He caressed her a bit more, but she was needy. She moaned, again, and was about to beg when he seemed to get the message and began a slow, deliberate penetration from behind.

Oh, yeah. That's just what she needed. He was long and thick...and patient. He didn't rush her. He took his time and let her enjoy this moment of discovery. He touched her, bringing her to higher levels of excitement even as he completed his possession.

In her to the hilt, he stilled.

"Okay?" he asked, his breaths coming short and hard against the nape of her neck. Damn. She hadn't known how much of a turn on that could be.

"Almost perfect," she whispered back, her voice rough. "Move, please. Make it sublime," she instructed him, and his chuckle was felt as well as heard, so close were their bodies.

Then, he followed her directive. He began a slow, pulsing motion that started out easy and quickly worked its way into a frenzied state. She thought he rose to his knees behind her, his big hands anchoring her hips in just the right position for his thrusts. Then, he went to town, making her come once, twice, three times before he joined her in ecstasy.

She cried out his name, glad the guest house was far enough away from the main house that, even with shifter hearing, the family of lynx shifters couldn't hear her. Ace's growl as he joined her in climax probably shook the rafters of the little house. It certainly shook her world. She had never imagined that she'd be so drawn to the sounds a bear shifter made while in human form, but she felt like they were a peek into the wild soul shared by both bear and man.

It pleased her that she could make him lose control to the point where he'd let his bear side show through. She knew he was careful not to do that, lest he give himself away. That he felt free to be who he really was with her meant a lot.

When the storm wound down, he cuddled her into his arms as they rested for a while. The next time they made love, he took a more traditional position, but the passion still ran just as hot. The ecstasy was just as explosive. And the man was just as sublime as she'd asked him to be.

All night long.

CHAPTER 9

Ace's cell phone rang before dawn, waking them both. He answered on the second ring, wiping the sleep from his eyes with his free hand as he sat up in the disheveled bed. It was Tim, and his tone was brusque.

"Don't come to Montana," he said, right off the bat. "We have reports of *Venifucus* activity all around our location. They seem to have sent a huge force of their operatives to Montana, though it appears they haven't been able to figure out exactly where we are. But we've been fielding reports from shifters, shaman, and the occasional priestess, all over the state. There's a witch hunt going on, and the object of it is Sabrina."

"Shit." Ace ran a hand through his hair. "We'll go west, then, I guess. Trying to get to my friends in Phoenix would be just too damned far if she's as hot as you think." He paused a moment. "Why *are* they so eager? Do you have any idea why they're so keen on finding her?"

"We have some suspicions, but until another high-level magic user can examine her brand of power, it's all just conjecture," Tim said, his tone somber.

Ace told him about the incident with the wind gust during their flight down from Canada. Suddenly, it seemed more important to reveal all than to save Sabrina a bit of embarrassment over her loss of control.

"She could be some kind of wind elemental," Tim offered, confirming thoughts that were just forming in Ace's mind.

"Not full-blooded," Ace agreed, "but she definitely has that sort of flavor to her power. And it's still evolving."

"You've got a contact in Grizzly Cove, right?" Tim asked.

Ace sighed. "Yeah. I'll give my buddy a call and see if we can go there. I hear there are some powerful mages in town that have proven to be on the right side of all this. Maybe they can help."

"I'll call John Marshall on your behalf, as well," Tim volunteered. "Whatever is going on with Sabrina, we can't let her fall into the hands of the *Venifucus*. For one thing, she's an innocent. For another, whatever power she has, it must be something the *Venifucus* want really bad. We can't let them have it." They were both silent for a moment, thinking about that. Then, Tim spoke, again, more quietly. "Do you want me to send backup?"

"Not yet," Ace told him. "We're traveling light and fast, and we're not too far from the coast, as long as the guys in Grizzly Cove let us in."

"They will," Tim promised. "Big John owes me a favor, and if I have to call it in, I will. This is too important. Though, I'd rather have his willing agreement to help, of course."

"I don't think we'll have a problem. Bears love a challenge," Ace reminded the werewolf Lord. Both men chuckled. "I'll call my friend, now. If I encounter any problems, I'll let you know. Otherwise, I'll check in later tonight."

"Sooner, if you have problems," Tim reminded him unnecessarily. Ace agreed, and they said goodbye and ended the call.

"What's happening?" Sabrina asked, concerned by what she'd heard of Ace's side of the conversation.

"Change of plan," Ace told her, and she just knew he was

trying to sound cheerful for her benefit. "We're going to head for the coast, not the Lords."

"But I thought they could help me," she said, confused by the sudden change in destination.

"Lucky for us, they're not the only ones who can," Ace replied. "I have a good friend and colleague on the Washington coast. That little town I told you about? We're going to head there, just as soon as I clear it with my friend." He tugged on a pair of pants as he headed for the door of the cabin, taking his phone with him.

She didn't like the fact that he went outside to make the phone call. He was hiding something from her. The danger level had ramped up since the night before, she just knew it. Though, what had caused the change, she had no idea.

Sabrina knew she had blown them off course, and they were on the wrong side of the majority of the mountains, but at least they were now in the right country. Surely, they could make it over land to the Lords from here? Something must have changed in the overnight hours. Some new threat had been discovered, or some confrontation had occurred. She wasn't sure what had happened exactly, but to cause them to change their destination entirely, it had to be something big. That worried her.

When they headed out later that morning, Lucien's plane was already long gone, and his sister's family were asleep, having stayed up all night with him. Ace left the key to the cabin under their front door mat, as they'd arranged the previous evening. Sabrina had done her best to clean up after them, leaving the place in as close to the condition they'd found it in as possible. She'd also left a note of thanks on the table for their hostess to find later.

"I feel strange sneaking away like this," Sabrina told Ace as they mounted their bikes in the early morning light.

"We're not sneaking. They can hear our engines, even if they're mostly asleep. They expect us to be leaving, and it's only courteous to let them sleep in after they stayed up all night visiting with Lucien," Ace told her. "From what I understand, he's got some kind of legal trouble in the States that keeps him far from his family. They were thrilled to see him, even if it was only for a few hours."

"Well, I enjoyed meeting them," Sabrina said. "Having a safe place to stay was like a miracle after the problems we faced yesterday."

"Ready to make a run for Grizzly Cove?" Ace asked, challenge in his eyes and a determined expression on his handsome face.

He'd told her a bit more about the town last night, but she still couldn't picture it. A town filled with all kinds of bears? She couldn't even imagine what they would find when they finally got there. They just had to get through Idaho and drive the entire width of the state of Washington until they hit the coast, traversing more mountains, until they finally hit the downhill stretch toward the rocky coastline.

"I guess so. You said it was about eight or nine hours away?" she asked just to be sure she knew what she was in for.

"If we ride straight through and keep to the speed limit, it's eight and a half, but we'll have to stop for breaks and to eat, of course," he told her. "We'll skirt around Spokane and the larger cities, but the best passes through the mountains are on the main highway, so we'll try to stick to it as long as it seems safe."

"And you really want to try to do this trip all in one day?" she asked again, just to be sure.

"If at all possible," he replied. "Let's just take it one step at a time and see how we do, okay? I don't want to push you too hard, but I also want you safe as soon as possible," he admitted, which made her feel sort of warm and fuzzy inside.

They set off, their engines rumbling down the drive and onto the road. The sun was playing hide and seek with puffy white clouds, and Sabrina felt a little tickle of wind teasing the back of her neck. She could sense the winds above, starting to gather. Was she causing it? No. She couldn't be. Her power levels were running at a lazy equilibrium after the night spent in Ace's arms.

So, the winds were natural. A storm gathering above them, blowing in from the northwest. She could almost taste the tang of the ocean on the air, even though there was a heck of a lot of land between their location and the coast that was their goal. Sabrina kept watch on the billowing clouds. If conditions got bad for their ride, she'd try to do something about it, but she was afraid she might make it worse. She thought about maybe talking it over with Ace before she took any action, just in case.

Sabrina rode alongside Ace as they made their way to ever-larger roads. When they neared the highway, Ace pulled over on the side of the road.

"Anything wrong?" she asked, pulling up alongside him.

"Nope. Not so far. I just wanted to stop, observe, and sniff around a bit before we hit the highway," he told her. "Tim said there was a lot of *Venifucus* activity on the roads all over Montana."

"Seriously?" Sabrina was a bit appalled. "Was that why we headed in this direction, instead of going to their place?"

He shrugged. "This'll work out better in the long run. While the Lords are good guys, I don't know many of their people. They're kind of secretive. I have a good friend in Grizzly Cove, and I know some of the other guys, and...we're all bears. I know bears. I know what we can handle and how we react. If push comes to shove, I'd rather have those bears backing us up—no offense to the Lords' people. They only have one bear I know on staff, so to speak, and I have no idea what the rest of their people are, but I think it's a mixed bag of mainly wolves, but also cats and raptors. Maybe others." He shrugged again, looking around. "Like I said, I don't know all that much about their operation."

"But there have to be more than just bears on the coast, right? You said there were mages. Witches who could help me figure out my power," she reminded him.

"Mates," he supplied, nodding as he continued to scan the

horizon. "Quite a few of my bear brethren have found mates with magical abilities. Powerful abilities, by all reckoning. They'll be able to help you. I have no doubt about that at all."

Reassured once more, Sabrina watched him for a few moments. His eyes saw all, and his nose was lifted slightly to the wind. He was engaging his shifter senses to survey what lay ahead and all around. She found it fascinating.

Finally, he nodded as if in satisfaction. "I think we're clear. You good to keep going?"

He turned those warm brown eyes on her, and she nodded. She'd say yes to anything when he looked at her with that devilish hint of a smile.

They started moving, again, and it was a couple of hours before they stopped at a roadside restaurant to grab some food, walk out their stiff muscles, and use the restrooms before hitting the road, again. He kept them to a quick pace, breaking the speed limit, but only by a few miles per hour. He didn't draw attention to them, and they were moving rapidly along the interstate, making good time.

All the while, the weather began to thicken. The sun disappeared completely around eleven in the morning, and they made their second stop shortly after. Ace went into the gas station convenience store to pay for their purchases. They topped up their tanks and took a few minutes to sit at a picnic table at the side of the building and eat lunch. They'd been on the move since dawn, and Sabrina was starting to feel it.

"Storm coming," she said quietly around a bite of sandwich. "Do you think I should try to do something about it?"

"I'd rather you didn't use your magic, if at all possible. We may have lost them, for now, but if they're scanning for your energy, any use of it could, potentially, lead them to us, again."

"Then, we may have to stop. I feel rain coming, and it won't be long before it reaches us," she told him.

Ace looked thoughtful. "I want to get us to safety today, if possible, but using your power could be a problem. On bikes, we can't really make time in rain."

"I could use just a little tendril of energy to try to nudge the storm away from the highway," she offered.

He tilted his head, considering. "Do you think you can push it away from our path without drawing too much attention?" he asked, his tone low and serious.

"I can try. Otherwise, we're going to get smacked with heavy rain." The feeling had been growing all morning. "We're going to ride into it within the next hour."

"Do you want to try this here or shall we go up the road a ways and see if we can find a more private venue for you to try your magic?"

"Private is probably better, just in case something goes wrong," she told him, trying not to cringe. He knew her power wasn't fully under her control, so there was no use in pretending it was. She'd either push the storm away or cause unanticipated problems.

If she managed to control it—as she had when they'd been in the air—then they could keep going. If not, they'd have had to stop, anyway, for the storm. So, she had a fifty-fifty shot.

About twenty minutes later, they were in a small clearing just off the side of the highway, hidden from the road, but with a relatively clear view of what lay ahead. Ace had led her to the perfect location at the top of a hill where she could see a good portion of the sky. He had also whipped out his phone and tapped up a live weather radar image so he could watch what was happening with the storm while she did her thing. She thought that was pretty ingenious.

"Okay, I'm just going to try to nudge this a little north, so it doesn't hit the highway," she told him, already thinking about how she would loose the power that was building within her.

A little blast here and little tweak there. She just had to be careful not to overdo it. Her abilities had grown, and that was the basis of all her problems—or so she now believed. She'd been over-casting when she sent her power out into the winds, and they'd responded in unexpected ways. The challenge here was to use just the right touch. Just the right amount of her own energies.

"I'm going to start really slow," she told Ace. "How long does it take before you see the updated radar image on your phone?"

"I've got a direct line to the radar the military sees, so it's basically live," he told her. She was impressed by his connections.

"Anything I do will have a ripple effect that may take a few minutes to fully resolve, so I'll just do a tiny nudge, and we can maybe watch what it does before I make my next move." That sounded like a really great plan to her, and he nodded his agreement. "Here goes nothing."

She reached out with one hand, tapping a finger in the direction she wanted the main body of the storm to go. She was using the barest bit of her power. If nothing happened, so be it. She would ramp this up slowly and, hopefully, avoid the mess she'd made, time and time again, up north. Done, she lowered her hand and stepped back to Ace to watch his phone with him.

"It's moving," he said as the next radar sweep showed modification of the storm. They watched the radar image loop around, and the storm was different, changing. "Hell, it's really moving. That's just about perfect. I bet the next radar spin will show it clearing the highway completely."

"Wow." She hadn't used much of her power at all, and the big storm was already clearing their path. No wonder she'd been having trouble. Her abilities had grown even more than she'd realized. She was a bit stunned.

"This could be a problem." Ace's somber voice came to her, and she immediately refocused on the tiny screen he was holding. The main body of the storm was moving away, but the tail end of it was curling around a bit, on a direct path to the highway.

"I can fix that, but it's going to require a more delicate

touch," she told him. "I didn't realize until just now how big my gift had gotten." She was almost afraid of it, right now, and she was trembling a bit with shock.

Ace must've seen her distress. He moved closer, putting his big arms around her from behind, hugging her close to his warm body. He rested his head on top of hers. He was so tall. She hadn't ever been with such a large guy before, and she found she liked feeling delicate compared to his mass. He touched her with the utmost care and treated her like she was some kind of rare treasure. She liked that, too.

And his energy seemed to stabilize hers. He was a delicious sort of magic. Big, furry, fierce magic.

Feeling more balanced than ever, she reached out one hand and gave the lightest tap of her power toward the tail of the storm, to put it back on track with the main body of the clouds, wind and rain. Ace held his phone out in front of them both, and they watched together as the little line of fierce storms got back in line with the rest of them.

Loop after loop, the storm straightened out and flew northward, away from their path. She'd done it. With his help and support. Sabrina turned in his arms and reached up to kiss him soundly.

"Thank you," she whispered against his lips. "I couldn't have done that without you."

They kissed passionately, but when she wanted to take it further, he let her down gently. "We need to get back on the road," he told her. "Much as I'd like to stay here for a bit and ravish you, your safety comes first." He placed a gentle kiss on her forehead before stepping away.

She was disappointed but also touched. He was such a good man. She wondered how many other guys would have put her safety before their own pleasure. Not many, she was sure.

They rode for another two hours then made another pit stop. They were just mounting up, again, when Ace's phone rang. He took the call, his expression growing concerned before a frown spread over his face. He hung up with a terse word of thanks and turned to her.

"We'd better get moving."

"What's wrong? Who was that on the phone?" she asked, unable to keep her curiosity to herself.

"That was my friend, Ezra. Apparently, he and some buddies decided to ride out to meet us. They're not too far away, but not too close, either, and they've noted an increase in surveillance along the highway. They smell like blood magic, too. Bad stuff." Ace shook his head. "I think your weather working alerted the enemy, and they're somehow homing in on us. Ezra thinks they know we're on this road, and they're actively searching along here, now."

She wanted to rail against the unfairness. Why in the world was anybody searching that hard for her? She was nothing special. Sure, her gift had changed a bit—make that *a lot*—over the past few weeks, but she still only had the one ability. She wasn't mage material. She was just a weather witch.

Wasn't she?

They got underway, again, and this time, she was keeping her eyes peeled for anything that might look suspicious. She felt fear rise and, along with it, her power. She did her best to tamp it down, but at some point in the next few hours, she was very much afraid it would let loose. Chaotic emotions like fear seemed to make it even more unstable.

They crested the last pass out of the mountains, and Sabrina wanted to breathe easier—until she noticed a car crashing through the divider from the other side of the road behind them. It made a highly illegal U-turn, and though she lost sight of it as they went down the other side of the pass, she knew it was following them.

They'd been found.

Ace saw the car break all kinds of laws to turn around and follow them, and he knew that, sooner or later, people in that car would alert any of their allies in the area, and the chase would well and truly be on. As it was, they were being followed at high speed. They had gravity to work with as the road took a steep downhill pitch coming down out of the last of the mountains, but speed wasn't the only answer in this situation.

Ezra and some of the guys from Grizzly Cove were on their way. Ezra had detailed a plan they'd come up with to set up a roadblock, of sorts—the magical kind that wouldn't interfere with ordinary humans who happened to be driving along the road with them. It was more like a temporary ward, with a bunch of bears watching over it. All Ace had to do was get Sabrina there in one piece, and they'd have a formidable escort all the way to Grizzly Cove.

He wasn't as familiar with this road as he could be, but he thought maybe the spot Ezra had talked about was nearby. He'd said it was after the last pass, near a runaway truck ramp. They had these gravel-filled ramps that led off the side of the road specifically for trucks that were going way too fast and couldn't slow down the normal way. Ace had seen them in only a few places around the country, but he'd heard stories from truckers about how well they functioned when necessary.

Today, if all went as planned, that runaway truck ramp would mark the spot of a totally different kind of save—this one magical in nature. Ace kept an eye on his rearview mirrors. He was acutely aware of the car jockeying for position among the others behind them. He could've wished there were no innocent people driving on the highway with them, but then again, the other cars made it more difficult for the bad guys to move up on them quickly.

Ace dropped back to keep Sabrina slightly in front of him. He waved her on, hoping she understood that he wanted her to go as fast as she felt comfortable with on the steep downhill. She took off, easily breaking the posted limit, but he didn't care. A few dozen cop cars, right about now, would be a good thing.

Of course, when you needed a police presence, there was none to be found. No matter. Ace had something better up his sleeve...if they could just get to them.

The road switched back, long curves attempting to smooth out the downhill run, and then, Ace saw it. The runaway truck ramp he'd been promised. And sitting at the entrance was his friend, Ezra, astride his old Harley. They had just enough time to slow down and pull off to the side.

Unfortunately, that meant the car—make that cars, plural—behind them also had enough time to slow. The only good thing about this whole scenario was that the innocent humans driving with them on the road could just keep going, and thanks to the angle of the runaway truck ramp, whatever was going to happen would be mostly out of sight of any passersby.

Ezra was revving his motor when they met up with him. "We've got a strong ward across the road and a truck full of bears just itching for a fight behind me. We can keep going and let the showdown happen while we get your lady to safety."

Sabrina hated the sound of their plan. She was supposed to run for her life while people she didn't even know risked theirs to keep her safe? No way. That's not how she was made. She wouldn't allow these good men—bears—to risk their lives for her and not even participate in her own rescue.

"No." Sabrina made herself heard, getting off her bike and rolling it to a safe spot while she peeked around the side of the truck ramp to see a passel of huge men lying in wait for whatever might come their way. She waved to them then turned back to see Ace heading toward her, his face set in a grim line. His friend was right behind him.

"What are you doing?" He was shouting, but she understood. Tensions were high, and time was short.

"I'm ending this. I don't want any of your friends hurt because of me. Just let me do my thing and stand back." She braced her feet apart and watched the oncoming cars. There were at least half a dozen of them with more than one person visible in each. Too many for the handful of bear shifters hidden behind the embankment. "Tell your men to stay where they are. This could get messy," she warned before she tapped into the power that had been building right along with her fear. No way could she hold back the tempest this time.

CHAPTER 10

Sabrina lifted her hand, and the wind started to whip up around them. No, scratch that. Not around them. In front of them. In a very tight pattern that left the normal traffic on the road alone but affected the half dozen cars that had pulled off to the side by the runaway truck ramp.

When the wind brought their scent to him, Ace had a hard time controlling his recoil. Blood magic...and death. Lots and lots of death. These people didn't deserve mercy, and he hoped, in that moment, that Sabrina's power was enough to stop them. Because, if it wasn't, the small group of shifters that had made the trip from Grizzly Cove to help out were going to have a tough time taking them all on.

"We seriously underestimated the amount of firepower we'd need here." Ezra shouted to be heard above the wind. He was at Ace's side, just behind Sabrina.

"So did I," Ace admitted. "But I think Sabrina's powers have grown in just a few hours, so maybe our miscalculations will cancel each other out."

"What do you mean?" Ezra strained to be heard above the escalating wind.

"Just watch!" Ace shouted back.

Then, the cars started to move—backward. A few of the men jumped out, but the wind swept them off their feet and into the trees. A few hugged whatever trees they landed in, trying to stop the unplanned motion, but the wind ratcheted up another notch as Sabrina crooked her finger. And then, she used her whole hand, and the cars started to flip, end over end, smashing their way through the trees behind the runaway truck ramp and down the steep mountainside, out of sight.

The heaviest of the vehicles—a military surplus Humvee—resisted. Sabrina narrowed her eyes and twirled one little finger. The next thing he knew, that massive vehicle was caught in a tiny whirlwind created just for it, and the men inside were bailing out, taking their chances with the winds and the distance to the ground.

A few were armed, but they couldn't get their bearings after being whirled around inside their vehicle and then tumbling to the ground. There were a few obvious broken bones, but it wasn't stopping them. They kept trying to run toward Sabrina until she finally flicked their vehicle over the tops of the trees to crash down the mountainside. Then, she turned her full attention on the men.

She took one step forward and screamed at them. "Leave me alone!"

The force of her voice seemed to carry its own power. The men flew backwards, their guns torn from their hands to land on the ground while the men flew into the trees.

And then, it was over. Sabrina slumped as she released the winds she had called to her aid. Ace was there to catch her, and he hugged her to his side, even as he marveled at what she had done.

"I didn't know you could do that," he said, stunned and proud of her abilities. "I didn't know you'd perfected such control."

"Neither did I," she admitted.

"Well, hell," Ezra said, coming up beside Sabrina. "I'm glad you're on our side."

Ace introduced his friend, Ezra, and then, they were no

longer alone. The group of men who'd been behind the elevated runaway truck ramp came out and gave her varying looks. Some seemed impressed. Some were blasé. None were scared, which was a relief to her tense feelings. A big man in the center of the action whistled sharply and gestured toward the trees, at which point, most of the guys peeled off with big grins on their faces.

"Where are they all going?" Sabrina asked, knowing her voice sounded a bit groggy.

"Hunting," the big man answered with a smile. "You did a great job, ma'am, but we're just going to make sure any stragglers are dealt with. We don't want that kind of evil near our homes."

Sabrina's jaw dropped. These guys were actually going looking for trouble. She was just glad the bad guys were gone. It would never have occurred to her to go after them. Nor would she have sent anyone to collect the weapons that had been dropped by that last group of paramilitary guys in the big Hummer. Yet, that's what one of the bear shifters was doing. He'd already collected an armful of gear and was heading back with a look of joy on his face.

"Some great equipment here," he called out to them as he passed on his way back to where the good guys had parked their vehicles out of sight—and out of the wind, thank goodness. "Fancy stuff, worth a lot, even if we can't use it ourselves. Nice work, ma'am, getting them to drop it all."

He nodded his thanks at Sabrina, and she wanted to explain that she hadn't really been thinking that far ahead at the time, but he seemed too happy. She didn't want to spoil his fun. Plus, it was too much effort to have a long conversation, right now. All she really wanted to do was sleep.

She lost track of what happened next, but at some point, Ace picked her up and was carrying her. She saw someone rolling her bike onto a trailer that had been positioned behind the earthworks of the runaway truck ramp. Her bike was strapped in place next to Ace's Harley, which was already on the trailer. Then, she saw the inside of a big SUV as Ace put her into the backseat.

Sabrina must have dozed because she was vaguely aware of Ace outside the open door of the SUV, talking with some of the men as they came and went. There was a bustle of activity that she only saw in a peripheral way. Then, at some later time, she felt Ace get into the SUV next to her and take her in his arms.

They started moving, and she snuggled into Ace's embrace and knew no more until she woke up an hour or two later. They were just pulling into a picturesque coastal town. Grizzly Cove. Had to be.

The SUV was being driven by the man who'd been scooping up the bad guys' discarded guns with such joy. Her eyes met his in the rearview mirror, and he smiled.

"Welcome to Grizzly Cove, ma'am. I'm Zak. Former deputy sheriff and current owner of the best restaurant in town." He tipped a non-existent hat to her and smiled. Oh, this guy was a charmer, all right, with those flashing dark eyes and lazy drawl.

But his mention of a restaurant seemed to bring her empty stomach to life. It growled loud enough for her to hear, and she was certain the shifters in the vehicle heard it, too. She felt her cheeks heat with embarrassment.

"Don't talk about food unless you're prepared to feed us, Zak," Ace joked easily with the other man.

"You know I called ahead," Zak replied. "There'll be something waiting for you in your rooms at the hotel. The ladies know what it means when someone exerts that much magical energy."

"Does it mean I could eat a buffalo? On the hoof?" Sabrina quipped, sitting up a little straighter but remaining close to Ace. "Or a horse. Or a cow. Anything! I'd settle for cold pizza and chips, right now. I'm starving."

Both men laughed. "Yeah, that sounds about right," Zak told her. "We have a few magic users in town, now, and they all get sleepy and ravenous after exerting their magical muscles like you did today. By the way, in case I don't get to talk to you later, what you did was damned impressive. We didn't know what to expect, but it certainly wasn't what you did. Thanks for the weapons and the show." His grin was contagious, and she smiled back at him.

"Will it disappoint you if I say I didn't intentionally make them drop their weapons?" she asked. "I just didn't want them to point the muzzles at anyone, and when I had that thought, suddenly, they fell to the ground. I'm not sure how that happened."

"Doesn't matter how, really," Zak said magnanimously. "Just that it did. Your actions saved us a whole lot of bother. Not that we don't enjoy a good fight, now and then, but sometimes, the best fights are the ones you don't have to engage in, if you know what I mean." He winked at her in the rearview mirror as he drove through town. "I'm ashamed to admit, we woefully underestimated how many operatives they would send after you, but after seeing what you did, I guess they're the ones who underestimated you, eh?"

"I honestly didn't know I had it in me until the power started to build, and then, I saw you all waiting, and I realized you intended to fight my battle for me and just let me ride away to safety." The words were tumbling out as she held onto Ace's hand. "I couldn't let you do that. You didn't even know me. I mean, it was such a noble gesture, but then, I felt all this power gathering, and I knew I had to let it loose. Then, there wasn't any time to think, anymore. I just had to act. I had to protect you guys as you were prepared to protect me. A total stranger." She felt tears gather in her eyes as her words tumbled to a halt. She didn't want to start crying in front of the men.

Zak stopped the big vehicle at the other end of town after pulling into a parking lot. He turned in his seat to look at her, his expression solemn. She got the impression he didn't get solemn very often.

"Not sure what Ace here has told you about us, but you should know the core group that set up this town—of which

I am one—are all retired Special Forces soldiers. Protecting people we don't know from evil bastards intent on screwing up the world is sort of our *raison d'être*. I can count on one hand the number of times we've had the tables turned on us as they were today, where we were the ones being protected rather than the other way around. It made a deep impression on every last one of us who witnessed what you did." He paused a moment, then went on. "I haven't had a chance to talk with the others yet, but for my part, I sensed a kindred warrior spirit in you. Our shaman, Gus, might be able to verify that." Zak tilted his head, humor returning slightly. "Or not. I'll go get you checked in."

Zak got out of the vehicle and went ahead, giving Ace and Sabrina a moment of privacy.

"You okay?" Ace asked her in a tender tone.

She looked up at him and felt the impact of his warm brown gaze. He was such a handsome man. So compassionate and sweet under that gruff exterior.

"I'm good. Just really hungry. Sorry I conked out on you. Not sure what that was about." She sat up a little straighter. "Thanks for taking care of me."

"It's my honor and privilege," he said, his tone serious. She felt something... And then, the moment snapped as the back hatch of the giant SUV was opened from outside.

"Sorry, folks. Gotta get these weapons secured ASAP," Zak told them in too peppy a voice. "There are a lot of folk waiting out here to see you, ma'am. He winked at her again, as she met his gaze over the top of the backseat. "You too, Ace."

"You don't have to call me ma'am. My name is Sabrina," she told him, smiling at his lazy charm.

"Yes, ma'am. Sabrina. Duly noted." Zak grabbed two cases from the back of the SUV that looked really heavy. There were a few more like it. Somehow, they'd put the scavenged weapons in those cases, though she had no idea where they'd come from. Zak walked away before she could ask.

"We didn't leave right away from the truck ramp," Ace told her, somehow intuiting her questions. "A few of the guys went furry and followed the paths of the vehicles through the trees just to see what became of them. They found the Hummer down the slope, and those cases were inside, strapped down to what was left of the truck. They build those things tough," he commented, giving a low whistle as he opened the door and began the process of extricating his large form from the backseat of the SUV.

Ace held out a hand for her, helping her down. She stumbled a bit when her feet hit the ground, her knees more wobbly than she had expected.

"Sorry," she whispered, her hands against his chest while his arms were around her, supporting her. "Just let me get my bearings."

"Take your time. We're safe here, and I love having you in my arms. As you know." He dipped his head and placed a little kiss on the tip of her nose. In public. In front of all the men who were piling out of vehicles or pulling up on bikes all around.

Ace's friend, Ezra, pulled his Harley right up next to them, in fact. He cut the motor and grinned at them both as he dismounted the large motorcycle.

"Damned fine work back there, ma'am," Ezra said to Sabrina before even greeting Ace.

"Uh…" Sabrina didn't really know what to say. She'd always been a one-hit wonder with just a little weather witchery and nobody much who cared either way about what she did or didn't do with the clouds.

Ace could tell Sabrina wasn't really comfortable with all the attention. The men were staring at her, talking about her power out in the open in a way he was sure she'd never been subject to before. It all probably made her uncomfortable, judging by the panic in her eyes and the little tremor in her limbs.

Ace did the only thing he could think of. He lifted her in

his arms and strode through the crowd, heading for the hotel. Ezra was at his side.

"Zak said something about a room?" Ace prompted his friend.

"Sure thing," Ezra replied, opening the outer door and holding it for them.

He led the way to a suite of rooms in the hotel. Luckily, the door was already open, a trio of women inside setting up a small feast. When they saw Sabrina in Ace's arms, they immediately started issuing orders. Ace was told, in no uncertain terms, to put Sabrina on the couch. Then, the women—the sisters—set to work. One made a plate for Sabrina and brought it over while another helped her with her jacket. The third helped her out of her boots, all three women cooing over her and helping her get comfortable. Ace stood back and watched, amazed at the welcome.

Ezra came over to stand next to him. "Those three sisters own the bakery in town. The eldest is mated to the sheriff. The middle sister is mated to the town lawyer, and the youngest is Zak's mate."

"Magical?" Ace asked.

Ezra shook his head. "Nope. But they're all excellent additions to the community. They bring some much needed balance, I think."

It was an astute observation for a deep-thinking bear shifter. Ezra had always been a man of few words, but he'd finally settled down, and Ace thought his inner bear was just beaming with contentment. Ezra's mate was also a shifter, and they'd settled here in the cove after a serious show-down with bad guys who'd been trying to capture his mate.

Now, that sounded familiar.

"By the way, Zak was really impressed by what Sabrina did out there," Ezra told Ace. "He's telling anyone who'll listen that he's never seen anything like it before. And, uh, there's a little quirk you should know about Zak. He *sees* magic. More than any of the other guys in town, except maybe the shaman. He was the deputy around here until he opened his restaurant. Cajun. If you like spicy stuff, you'll find no better."

"He from Cajun country?" Ace asked. He'd crossed paths with most of the guys in Grizzly Cove over the years, but he didn't know them that well.

"Louisiana," Ezra replied. "Born and raised in the bayous. He knows a lot about human magic and voodoo."

Their private conversation ended just then, because the three human sisters finished fussing over Sabrina and started making a move toward the door near where Ezra and Ace were standing. The eldest seemed to be the leader, and she smiled at Ace, marching right up to him and sticking out her hand.

"I'm Nell," she said. "These are my sisters. We're going back to our shop for more supplies. You take care of her until we come back."

Bemused, Ace shook the woman's hand and gave her a strict, "Yes, ma'am." It seemed there was no other acceptable response in this situation.

"I'm Ashley." The middle sister also offered her hand to Ace, and he shook it dutifully. "Urse wanted me to tell you that she'll be over with Big John as soon as you're settled in and comfortable. Urse is the Alpha's mate," she clarified, passing Ace to the final sister, who stuck out her hand and grinned at him.

"I'm Tina. You've already met my husband, Zak. We'll bring more food later. Hope you like spicy!"

And with that, the whirlwind of women left the room, taking their busy energy with them. Ace was a little dumbfounded. He hadn't known human women could be that bossy, but then again, they'd have to be of strong character to stand up to a bear shifter mate.

"Nice ladies," Ace commented as Ezra followed their path toward the door.

Ezra nodded. "We'll give you two some alone time to recover, but don't get up to any mischief. Big John wants to meet your lady ASAP. I suspect he'll be here with his mate sooner rather than later. The sisters are probably already talking to Urse. The grapevine around here is highly efficient." Ezra winked and went out the door, closing it behind him.

Sabrina felt a bit overwhelmed by the attention of the three sisters, but they left her with a big sandwich, which quickly grabbed her full attention. She had already eaten a quarter of it when the door closed. She looked up to find only Ace with her. They were alone. Finally.

Ace came over to sit beside her on the couch. "How are you feeling?"

"Hungry," she replied around a bite of the most delicious sandwich she'd ever had. At least, that's what it felt like. Maybe hunger made everything taste better.

"Well, eat up. It'll make you feel better, and we're probably going to have another set of visitors in a few minutes—the Alpha bear and his mate."

"I thought bears didn't really do the whole Alpha thing," she said, pausing only to say the words before chomping on another huge bite of the sandwich.

"Normally, we don't. I mean, we have Alphas, but they're not like wolf Alphas. They're not supreme leaders of all they survey. They're more like rulers by consensus, if anything. Bears don't go in for the whole Pack structure. We're too independent for that. But Big John has earned a lot of respect from all his men, and many others besides. He's a tactician without peer, and this whole town was originally his vision."

Sabrina could hear the admiration in his voice when Ace spoke about the man he called Big John. She looked forward to meeting the Alpha bear, but she also felt a bit of trepidation. If this Alpha was anything like Tobias, the wolf Alpha, she might have a problem.

"Do you think he'll want me to leave?" She couldn't forget the hostility of the wolf Alpha as her gift started to go awry. He'd been welcoming—grudgingly so—at first, but when she started to have problems, he'd become a nightmare.

"Not at all," Ace was quick to assure her. "Big John may look scary, but he's a big old teddy bear at heart. Just don't tell him I said so. He's more the fatherly type who tries to solve everybody's problems," Ace told her. "From all accounts, he does a pretty good job at it, too. You'll like him. And, more importantly, he's not going to kick you out of town for a little wayward magic. We're bears. We don't frighten easy like those sissy wolves up north." She grinned at his teasing, just a little. It was good of him to try to cheer her up. She was still feeling a bit shell-shocked, to be honest. "Also, his mate is a mage. I think she'll have a lot of sympathy for your problem and will be able to offer some help."

Sabrina thought hard about what he'd said while she gulped down the rest of her sandwich. There were chips, too. They disappeared in quick order. As did two bottles of iced tea the sisters had left for her. Around about the time she was considering looking for seconds, there was a knock on the door.

CHAPTER 11

Ace opened the door to reveal a couple. Well, the first thing Sabrina could see was a very large man taking up most of the doorway space. Behind him, she could just make out a woman, trying to get past. The men greeted each other in a friendly way, and Ace stepped back to allow them entrance. This, Sabrina figured, had to be the Alpha couple Ace had told her would be visiting.

She noted the way the man held the woman back as best he could. She seemed a little frustrated with his over-protectiveness, but Sabrina understood how things were when shifter males mated. She'd seen it in action in the werewolf Pack. The men always put the safety of their mates and children first, no matter the situation. Bears seemed to be the same in that respect, at least.

"Alpha, this is Sabrina," Ace made the introductions. "Sabrina, this is John Marshall and his mate, Ursula."

Sabrina stood, straightening her clothes as best she could. She must look pretty ragged after what they'd been through, and she regretted not cleaning up first, before she met such important people. Her only excuse was that she hadn't really been thinking clearly since the confrontation on the highway.

"I'm honored to meet you both," Sabrina said politely, unsure of her welcome, despite Ace's reassurances. "Forgive my appearance. I haven't really had a chance to freshen up, yet." She knew she was blushing from the heat infusing her cheeks, but she couldn't help it.

Ursula stepped closer, despite her mate's attempts to block her. She just grinned and ignored the big man, sidestepping him indulgently.

"Just call me Urse. And we don't worry much about appearances, Sabrina. We're just glad you made it here in one piece. The guys have been talking about what you did nonstop since they got back. What I want to know is, are you okay? I got the impression you might never have expended such great amounts of magical energy before, is that right?" Urse came right up to Sabrina and guided her back to her seat, taking the one next to it so naturally, Sabrina hardly realized she was being ushered exactly where the Alpha female wanted her to go.

"Yes, that's right. I've always been a low-level weather worker. That was my only gift, and not really much of one, at that," Sabrina explained. "But, a little while ago, something started to change. I don't know what caused it, and I didn't know how to control it. I kept causing strange things to happen whenever I tried to steer weather away from particular areas. I'd always been so good at that before, and suddenly, I was causing miniature tornadoes all over the place. I was so afraid somebody was going to get hurt, and then, the Alpha started yelling at me all the time and shaking his head." Sabrina paused to catch her breath. "Sorry. It was getting pretty awful there, before Ace came."

"Well, you're safe here. At least as safe as the rest of us are." Urse made a face that Sabrina didn't quite understand, but her tone sounded a little sarcastic. "We've got some problems of our own, but part of my calling as a *strega* is to help sister witches in need...as long as they are servants of the Light." She paused a moment to look deeply into Sabrina's eyes. "I know you serve the Light because the permanent wards I put up around the town would never have let you through if you weren't one of the good ones."

Permanent wards? This witch could cast permanent wards? Even a no-talent like Sabrina knew that was the kind of power that came around only once every few generations. She was in the presence of one of the greats. She was so overwhelmed by the idea, she didn't know what to say. But that was okay. Urse seemed to understand, giving Sabrina the compassionate look and a pat on the back of her hand.

Their magic met and tingled in recognition. Oddly, Sabrina's little power wasn't completely overwhelmed by the immense strength Urse represented. Instead, the tingle was of recognition. Of the possibility of working together in harmony. Of friendship.

Sabrina felt a sense of wonder. She'd never been welcomed by any magic user of consequence, before. This Urse was something special, indeed.

"What's a *strega*?" Sabrina asked, her dazed mind coming back to the point.

Urse smiled warmly, her dark eyes shining. "It's a kind of hereditary witch from Italy, where my family comes from. Both me and my sister inherited the gift. I do spells, and she does potions. We each have our strengths." She shrugged and smiled. "If we can't help you, we have a few other people in town, and resources we can call on, to help figure things out."

"I really appreciate everything you all have done for me," Sabrina said, feeling surprisingly close to tears, still unsteady from what had happened earlier in the day. "I can't thank you enough, and I'm sorry to have brought my troubles to your town."

"Oh, honey." Urse laughed. "Don't be sorry. You may start running the other way once you realize everything that's been happening here. This isn't quite the idyllic paradise John had hoped to build. At least, not yet. First, we have to get rid of the sea monsters prowling just offshore."

"Sea monsters?" Sabrina's eyes widened as the Alpha female chuckled.

"A tale for another time. Right now, I suspect my mate wants to say a few words, then we'll get out of your hair, so you can rest and recover." Urse stood and rejoined her mate, who had been standing only a few feet away, watching over them.

The big man stepped up. "First of all, welcome to Grizzly Cove," he said, his deep voice both warm and authoritative. He had a sort of impressive command presence, and Sabrina began to understand why the men who knew him would follow him, even though bears were usually solitary creatures. "Ace tells us—as do the men who went up to meet you on the highway—that you have some control over wind power." He didn't pause, but she nodded, anyway. "My only question is, do you feel able to control it while you're in town? If you say no, I won't ask you to leave, but I might ask you to begin working right away with some of our magic folk, so we can keep a lid on it."

He stopped talking, waiting for her response. She was so relieved by what he'd just said, she felt a little tongue-tied, at first.

"Uh… I think… I can keep control. Ace has been helping me. I feel it build up, and there's time before I have to release the power, so I can keep an eye on it." She tried to gather her thoughts and speak intelligently. "What happened on the road was a result of anger and fear on my part. Once I knew they were chasing us, I felt the power build and build until it had to be released, and I figured releasing it at them would save a lot of trouble for your people. I couldn't let them fight for me. They didn't even know me." She paused, again, trying to find the right words. John's patient presence encouraged her to say what she felt. "I can't tell you how much that means to me—that they were willing to put themselves in harm's way for me. For someone they don't even know. Ace explained that's what you guys do, but still…"

John nodded gently. "It's all right." His reassuring presence—and Ace standing right beside him—somehow made her feel that everything really was going to be all right, now. Even though she knew she was still being hunted. "I'm just glad you made it here in one piece. Now, I've got a phone call to make. Rafe and Tim were worried about your progress, and they'll want an update. You rest up, and we can start figuring out how to help you once you're recovered."

She sniffled. They were being so nice to her when she'd brought such trouble practically to their doorstep. This was very different from the way she'd been treated by the wolf Pack.

"You'll find we have a mix of Others in town. Mostly, we've got a booming mer population," John said, bemusement clear in his tone. "Once Urse and Mellie made the cove waters safe, a whole pod of mer moved in, so don't be surprised by anything you might see going in or coming out of the water, though they're actually pretty covert about it. The cove, and most of the coastline, is absolutely safe, now. The leviathan and its creepy little friends are out at sea, but they still try to bother us all the time. We're working on that problem as well." John scratched his head. "I can't say I expected all of this when I came up with the idea for this town, but we'll figure it out. We always do."

He smiled, and she had to smile back at him. He was such a warm, almost fatherly figure. She could easily see how his charisma had attracted so many to follow him in creating this community.

"I hear Zak is cooking up a storm for everybody who went out to the highway," Urse put in as the Alpha couple prepared to take their leave. "I suspect he'll be sending a picnic over for you two, but if you need anything else, just ask, okay?"

"Thank you," Sabrina replied. "Thank you both, so much." She might've said more, but her emotions were tricky at the moment, threatening to spill out in tears. She'd never felt so much relief in her life. These people had been so welcoming. She felt as if she'd finally come home after a long time out in the cold.

It was ridiculous, she knew. This town was built for bears. She wasn't a shifter, and she had already experienced being the outsider in a town full of werewolves. It had started off okay, but the moment she had problems, it had become clear that she couldn't count on the people she thought had been her friends—or at least friendly—for any kind of support. Only Marilee had stood by her, out of the entire Pack.

Sabrina wasn't entirely sure what would happen here. She figured the bears had already shown themselves to be way more tolerant than the werewolves had been, but there was probably some point at which they would cut their losses with her. She had to be cautious. She didn't want to get hurt that way, again, if they all turned on her.

John and Urse left, and Sabrina was alone, again, with Ace. He was quiet. He probably sensed she was close to her breaking point. Sabrina got up and headed for the bathroom.

"I'm going to get cleaned up," she told him, taking her saddlebags with her.

Ace nodded, watching her go with concern in his expression, but she couldn't talk to him, just then. Things were too unsettled inside her. She had to regroup a bit. A nice hot shower would be just the thing to help.

Sabrina soaked under the hot spray for a while. She wasn't really sure how long she stood there, shaking, after she'd washed her hair and soaped up her body. It all just got to her, all of a sudden. The relief of being in Grizzly Cove. Being *safe*. It overwhelmed her.

Time had lost its meaning when, suddenly, Ace was there. He was standing in the large shower stall with her, tugging her away from the wall against which she'd pressed her forehead, allowing the hot water to beat down over her back. Ace turned her and took her into his embrace, enveloping her in his warmth. His security. His caring.

She let go, then, allowing her tears to mingle with the water drops as they rolled down over her cheeks onto Ace's bare chest. She stood there a long time. Again, she had no idea just how long. This place seemed to have an endless supply of hot water, so there was no need to hurry.

Ace held her through the storm, his presence the one solid thing in her world. He was her rock. Her port in the tempest of her fate. He was real.

And, as she started to regroup, she realized he was also very much naked. Correction. Wet and naked. Slippery and hard against her own bare skin.

Just like that, the last of the shakes fled and, suddenly, she was more concerned with more…um…carnal matters. From the looks of things—and the feel of his hardness rising against her—so was Ace.

"How are you doing?" he asked her, speaking for the first time since he'd entered the bathroom.

"A lot better, now, thanks." She moved slightly away from him so she could dunk her head under the water, allowing her hair to stream back away from her face and the last of her tears to wash away. She opened her eyes to meet his soft brown gaze. He was such a special man.

"Do you want me to leave so you can finish your shower?" The slightest note of uncertainty entered his tone.

"No," she told him quickly. "I'd already finished washing my hair. I guess it all just got to me. Thanks for the save. Yet again." She smiled at him, moving the few inches back into his arms. "Is there anything I can do to show you how much I appreciate everything you've done for me these past days?" She had never been much of a siren, but she tried her best to put her unpracticed moves on him.

She'd never had really good shower sex, and she suspected Ace would be the one man to show her what it was really all about. Just the thought of his hot, hard, slippery skin next to hers as he made love to her in the wide shower stall made her breath catch. Suddenly, she wanted that more than anything. She just had to make him aware of her desires.

Sabrina trailed her hand downward, between their bodies, over his washboard abdomen, and then lower, to the long, hard staff that rested against her. She put her hand around him and squeezed gently, loving the low growl that sounded deep within his chest, rumbling against hers. He was definitely interested. Thank the Goddess.

Feeling very daring, she reached for the bar of soap with

her free hand. "While you're here, do you want me to help you get clean?"

He growled and thrust gently into her hand. "What if what I have in mind is dirty?"

"Hm. Well, then. I'd say, let's do that first, and we can always get clean again afterwards."

She smiled at him as he took the soap from her hands and worked up a bit of lather between his fingers before putting it back on the little ledge built into the side of the tiled enclosure. His soapy hands sought her breasts, cupping and shaping, sliding deliciously as the soap made her slippery. She pretended to pout as he fondled her.

"I wanted to make you all slick," she told him softly.

"Later," he promised. "If you do that to me, now, this could be over before it begins. I need you too bad."

Her breath caught. Really? He sounded like a starving man, which flattered her battered ego. No man had ever sounded quite so desperate to be with her. That the man saying it was Ace made it all that much more appealing. Damn. She liked being needed sexually. It made her feel like a femme fatale. And *that* was something she'd never felt before.

"Then, let's not wait. I'm ready. I'm willing. Take me, Ace." She reached up and dragged his head down so she could match her lips to his.

She felt bold. Almost invincible. Ace had done that. He'd given this gift to her. Moments ago, she'd been shattered. Now, she was high on the passion that rose whenever they touched. Whenever they kissed. Just like that, she was raring to go. Wanting him beyond all reason, because of the things he made her feel that she'd never experienced before with any other man. Ace was special. And, he made her feel special.

Sabrina might have instigated the kiss, but Ace took it to new heights. She felt his arms come around her waist as he deepened the kiss, their bodies sliding together deliciously. The soap on her breasts made her slick against his chest. Her nipples quickly became hard little peaks, excited beyond all reason and sensitive to his every move.

Then, he dipped, scooping his big hands under her butt, lifting her and turning her so that her back was to the tiled wall. It was a little cold, at first, but she barely noticed. She'd had to let go of her prize when he'd lifted her up, but he was aligning that glorious cock with her opening. She willed him to push deep, taking her hard against that wall and finally giving her what she wanted. What she needed. Him. Only him.

As if he heard her desires, Ace slid home within her, allowing her body to slide just slightly down the wall so that she rested at the perfect height for his penetration. He stilled, watching her carefully, as if gauging her reactions. Sabrina placed her arms over his shoulders, loosely around his neck, one hand reaching into the damp strands of short hair at the base of his neck, the other feeling his shoulder muscles ripple as he held her in place, his body hard in all the ways designed to drive her senses into orbit.

"Okay?" he asked, his breath coming hard as if holding back was difficult.

"Better than okay," she told him truthfully. "Do me now, Ace. Take me hard."

In answer to her request, he began to move. The growl was back, low and intense, as he moved slowly, at first. He was holding back. Probably, he was trying to make sure she had time to adjust, to build up to a crescendo. What he didn't know was that she was already halfway there. They'd only just begun, and already, this was one of the sexiest, most earth-shattering experiences of her life.

"Go faster," she begged him. "Feels so good." The word was too weak to describe what she was really feeling, but communication was quickly moving beyond her capabilities as he gave her what she wanted. She moaned as he moved faster and harder, just as she desired.

She keened as he took the pace up another notch. She couldn't take much more. He was pounding into her, now, giving her everything she wanted. Taking her and making her feel wanted, needed…cherished. It was what she needed, right now. Hard, fast, intense lovemaking that only Ace could give her.

When her climax hit, she blanked out for a moment, her eyes closing, her muscles clenching against the onslaught. It swept her away and brought her back as Ace stiffened against her, his own release happening in time with hers. They were in tune. One, for that brief moment out of time.

The water rained down around them, steaming up the room and misting their bodies with cleansing hot water. She'd cried out as she'd come, and her throat was raw now from the strain, but she felt oh-so-good. Her bear-man had growled in that sexy way that she was completely addicted to, now, after only a short time together.

The thought crossed her mind—would she ever have another lover like Ace? Nope. Not in a million years. When the Goddess had made him, She'd broken the mold after. There was only one Ace, and for right now, he was all Sabrina's. She was going to enjoy every moment she had with him for as long as this lasted.

They ended up eating dinner sometime in the middle of the night in between even more pleasurable sessions on the wide, comfy bed. After the intense joining in the shower, she had, indeed, helped him wash off. They'd laughed and played with the soap suds, exploring each other's bodies and probably using way more water than they should have. They enjoyed drying each other off just as much as they'd enjoyed soaping up and rinsing off. Then, they moved the party to the bed and spent a long, leisurely night making love in many inventive ways.

When the food had arrived, Ace had accepted the delivery and then parked the tray on the table, returning to bed to pick up where he'd left off. It was some time later before they started investigating the contents of the tray, feeding each other tidbits and acting silly.

Laughter and sex filled their night, helping Sabrina come down from the anxiety of the past days. Ace was the best medicine of all, and he seemed to know just what she needed to bring her back to Earth. They slept, finally, entangled in each other's arms, and knew nothing more until morning.

CHAPTER 12

The next day, Sabrina and Ace walked down Main Street to have breakfast at the bustling bakery where the sisters had set up tables for the folks who wanted to eat on premises. When they got there, the place was mostly empty, except for a few people picking up orders to go, so they claimed a table near the window.

The selection of pastries and the freshly cooked egg sandwiches Nell brought over a few minutes later were fantastic, and Sabrina dug in with renewed hunger. It felt like her system was running a little hotter than usual, and she was burning a lot of calories. Of course, that might just be because of the sexy bear shifter in her bed, driving her to distraction and firing her hormones on all cylinders every minute of the day. Or, it could be magic. Or, maybe, a little of both.

They were about halfway through the mountain of food when the little bell above the door signaled a new arrival. Sabrina looked up to see two women enter. She recognized the Alpha female immediately, but the second woman seemed to light up when she saw Ace sitting with Sabrina. She came right over and called his name.

A little tendril of jealousy sent a twisting breeze stirring around Sabrina's body. The moment she realized she had lost a bit of control, she squelched the power, but it was too late. Urse had noticed. As had Ace, if his smug smile was anything to go by. He was returning the greeting of the strange woman when he turned to introduce Sabrina.

"This is Thea, Ezra's mate," he said. "Thea, this is Sabrina."

"It's good to meet you," Thea said enthusiastically.

She seemed genuinely friendly, and Sabrina realized her jealousy had been misplaced. Thea felt like a bear to Sabrina's magical senses, and she was mated to another bear—Ace's friend. Mates were for life among shifters. There was no question that Thea had any designs on Ace, so Sabrina's fit of jealousy was ridiculous, given the facts.

"Ezra told me you were in town. You have to come over for dinner one night, if you can," she told Ace. "Both of you," she added, including Sabrina in the invitation.

"Thanks, I'd like that," Ace replied politely. "Sabrina needs to see how we bears live," he chided, apparently on easy terms with this woman, though there were no possible romantic leanings because Thea was mated.

Thea smiled at Sabrina. "We just finished our new place, and I'd love a chance to show it off," she enthused. "Ace and his brothers were so helpful to Ez and me," she explained to Sabrina. "How are King and Jack?"

Ace started talking about his brothers, and Sabrina was intrigued, but Urse came over to speak with her while Ace was talking with Thea on the other side of the table. The Alpha female seemed intent on speaking with her privately, so Sabrina couldn't be rude. Hearing about Ace's brothers was interesting, but she would be foolish to disrespect a woman with so much power in this town. Plus, she'd liked Urse when they first met, last night, and wanted to talk more with the powerful witch.

"How are you feeling? Fully recovered?" Urse smiled at her over the cup of coffee she'd secured from the bakery counter while Thea had been talking to Ace.

"Much better, thanks. The sleep helped a lot," Sabrina told

her. "I'm sorry I was so dazed yesterday."

"Don't worry about it," Urse told her kindly. "We've all been there. Using strong magic takes it out of you, sometimes." She smiled and shook her head. "Speaking of which—are you free today? I'd like to take you up to the stone circle. We have a local shaman, and he is the caretaker of the sacred space. I've invited a few others to meet you, and it's probably safest to explore what you can do up there, away from the town. The circle can help contain your energies if things go awry," she explained. "Maybe we can figure out a little bit more about what you are and what you can do."

Sabrina liked the idea and said as much. "Ace hasn't really said what we're supposed to be doing today. Probably because he figured you all would fill up our dance cards quick enough." Sabrina chuckled and looked over at Thea still talking with Ace. "Looks like you're doing that, right on schedule."

"Don't worry. I've got a message for Ace from my mate. The guys want to talk to him while we do our magic thing in the circle." Sabrina felt a little pang at the idea of separating from Ace, even for just a short while. "I assure you, it's nothing bad," Urse was quick to say, probably misunderstanding whatever look passed over Sabrina's face, betraying her thoughts. "He'll be okay."

"I have great confidence that Ace can handle whatever comes his way," Sabrina said in support of her escort. "I'm just being chicken because I've somehow gotten used to having him around." She shook her head. "I shouldn't be. I've always been alone. Before I met him, I mean. And we've only been traveling together a couple of days, but…"

"But you've come to depend on him," Urse whispered, her smile kind as she shook her head ruefully. "These bears. They have a way of insinuating themselves into your life, and before you know it, you can't live without them." She winked, even as she chuckled. "But, like I said, don't worry. He'll be okay with the guys, and you'll be well taken care of by the folks I've invited. Two grannies, me and my sister, and the local shaman. Some of the mer might show up, as well, but I can't be sure about that. They tend to keep to themselves more than I expected they would when they moved into the cove, except for the few who've found mates here."

*

An hour later, Ace was sitting at a conference table in the town hall, looking out the window at a magnificent view of the cove. A meeting, of sorts, was just getting started, at which he seemed to be the star attraction. Ezra was sitting next to him, with Zak on the other side. Arrayed around the table was the core group of badass retired Spec Ops soldiers that made up the so-called Town Council.

Bear shifters, one and all, these guys were the brain trust that had followed John Marshall's dream, creating this town from the ground up. Ezra was a calming presence, but Ace couldn't help but feel a bit odd about this command appearance before the group that effectively ran the town. Were they about to read him the riot act or something? Were they going to grill him? Or maybe ask him to leave town? Only one way to find out.

Ace did his best to appear calm, but inside, his bear felt like someone had stroked his fur the wrong way. He wanted to scratch the itchy feeling away, but he repressed the urge. He was a grown man. He didn't need to feel like he'd been called into the principal's office—even if that was exactly what it felt like.

"Thanks for coming down here on short notice," John Marshall said, taking his seat at the table. The low conversations that had been going on while they were waiting for him ceased, and the room came to order. "Thing is, Ace, you've been to see the Lords recently, and we'd like to pick your brains about that, and what you encountered up north."

Ace was surprised by the statement but willing to humor the Alpha bear—as long as he didn't ask Ace to betray any confidences. He didn't see how that might happen, so he felt relatively comfortable in nodding his agreement.

"None of us have been to the Lords' compound in recent years. Some, not at all," John said, looking around at his men, some of whom were nodding. "And contact with Rocky— our main grizzly contact with the Lords—has dropped considerably in the past year. Did you get to see him when you were there?"

"I saw him when I rode in," Ace told him. "But he passed me on to the Lords pretty quickly, and I didn't really see him after that much."

"But you did see him," Zak asked.

Ace nodded. "Yeah, he looks good. Happily mated, with that same smug look a lot of you mated guys have on your faces," Ace joked. "But he did seem a little preoccupied. I figured the Lords keep him busy, and I know they'd asked him to send me over to them, so I didn't think it was too strange."

"They wanted to see you about the job up north?" John looked very interested in Ace's report.

"Yes," he replied. "I didn't go there looking for a mission, but they were happy enough to give me one. I think this was the kind of thing they normally would've sent Rocky to take care of, but I suppose he was busy with whatever they had him working on in Montana, so they asked me to fill in, seeing as I was a bear, and a friend of Rocky's."

"They specifically wanted a bear shifter on this job?" one of the other men asked.

"Seemed like it. They wanted someone who could withstand Sabrina's magic. When I got there, she was chasing a snow squall she'd spawned down Main Street." He knew the corner of his mouth hitched up in a small grin, but he couldn't help it. "I suppose they wanted someone both big enough to take a buffeting and magical enough to help her get back to them—or, at least, someplace she could get better help."

"Can you give debrief us on what happened after you got to her?" John requested, and Ace knew this was the old commander speaking, wanting to gather all the intel he could regarding possible threats to his people.

Ace was happy to comply. He filled the group in on the entire story from the time he first saw Sabrina to the moment they all met up on the highway. He didn't leave out any details pertaining to the enemy that he had observed. He got asked a few pointed questions, and he gave them what information he could from what he had observed. He didn't feel the need to tell them every last thing that had passed between himself and Sabrina. Some things, these busy-body bears didn't need to know.

When he was done telling them everything he knew about the enemy he and Sabrina had just faced, the town council thanked him for his time and sent him on his way. The meeting went on behind him as he left, and he felt like a man who had just given testimony in a court case—both relieved it was over and intrigued to know what the verdict would be.

The men of the unit had always impressed Ace. They might seem like easygoing bears on the outside, but their questions had been focused to laser precision. They were deep thinkers and strategists, though it was Big John who had the reputation of being the ultimate strategist. Undoubtedly, his way of looking at things had rubbed off on his subordinates.

It had been the other guys who had done most of the questioning while Big John remained silent, taking a few notes on the pad of paper in front of him and basically absorbing everything that was said. His men knew just the right questions to ask. It was clear this group had done this many times before. They knew how to work together as a team to get the results they wanted. Ace was just glad this had been a friendly questioning session. He'd hate to see what they could do in an honest-to-goodness interrogation.

He checked his phone for the time and realized he'd spent hours in that debriefing. No wonder he felt as if he'd been put through the wringer. He wondered what Sabrina had been up to all this time. Was she okay? Had they deliberately separated him from Sabrina so they could subject her to a similar kind of intense scrutiny?

He thought maybe the answer to that question was a resounding yes. It worried him on one level, but he also knew that the people of Grizzly Cove had a right to be cautious. He and Sabrina had both passed the test of the wards, and she'd more than proven herself on the right side of things all along their journey, and particularly at that road block on the highway, but he supposed the mages of the town were concerned about her power being let loose in an unplanned way. After all, the Lords had been called for exactly that reason.

If there was a design behind splitting them up, it was probably so that she could receive some magical instruction. At least, he hoped that was the case. But he wasn't going to just sit still now that he had met the requirements of the town council. He was going to find her.

*

While Ace was being interviewed, Sabrina was with Urse and her sister, Amelia, down at the most wondrous spot Sabrina had ever seen. An honest-to-Goddess circle of standing stones that looked like a natural formation, complete with an altar stone in the center. It was wild. On the southern tip of the cove, jutting out just the tiniest bit into the Pacific Ocean, the place pulsed with magic in time with the rolling waves that crashed nearby.

Amelia—who insisted that Sabrina should call her Mellie—took Sabrina around the outside of the ring, stopping at the closest point to the ocean and pointing out a disturbance in the water some distance away. "That's the leviathan," Mellie said, a little catch in her voice. "That's what we're up against."

Sabrina squinted to try and see more of what was out there, but it was very far away. "What is it?"

"A creature from another realm. It feeds off anything

magical, including people. The guys believe it was drawn here because of the high concentration of bear shifters. They're very magical, you know, and they don't often gather in such great numbers. Then, me and my sister moved in, and the mer showed up. All in all, we've got a lot of tasty magic here in town, and that tentacled monster wants it." Mellie shivered.

"It looks like it can't come any closer. Did you guys do that?" Sabrina asked, trying to figure out what was keeping the sea monster at bay.

"I crafted a potion that extended a magical barrier up and down the coast," Mellie told her. "It was really something. Before that, we had the leviathan and all its mini-me's patrolling the mouth of the cove. My sister had been able to encircle the town in one of her most powerful wards."

"I felt it on the way in," Sabrina mentioned. The ward had been a tingle of intense magic that momentarily surged through her entire being, then was gone. It had felt like both a welcome and a warning. If Sabrina hadn't passed its test, she would have been repelled in a most violent fashion. As it was, the ward had let her pass, thank goodness.

"Well, before that, the darn creatures were in the cove itself," Mellie told her as they started walking again. "It tried to drag Tina right off the beach and into the water."

Sabrina imagined something straight out of a horror movie. "That's really scary." She shivered, again.

"It really was," Mellie agreed.

They completed their circuit around the outside of the standing stones, and Sabrina noticed that more people had arrived and were standing just inside the circle, talking with Urse. The magic of the place meant that Sabrina couldn't hear anything of their conversation. The circle contained whatever happened within.

So, maybe if she accidentally spawned a tornado, it wouldn't destroy the town. Always a plus, she thought with grim humor.

"Good," Mellie said, at her side. "Looks like everyone's

here." Following the younger sister's lead, Sabrina stepped into the circle of stones and felt the surge of power right down to her bones.

"Wow," she whispered, stopping for a moment just inside the ring. She put one hand out and touched one of the stones. She was a little dizzy at all the power this circle contained.

The moment her hand made contact with the stone, another surge blasted through her. It was as if the stones were trying to communicate with her in some way she didn't fully understand. It wasn't scary, though. Not really. It felt…right? As if the earth—represented by the stones—was welcoming her as a kindred spirit. No. That couldn't be right. Could it?

"You okay?" Mellie asked, turning back to look at Sabrina, her face showing concern.

"Yeah," Sabrina told her, trying to catch her breath. "It just took me by surprise."

"The circle speaks to you," a male voice rang out, strong and sure. Sabrina had no trouble identifying the speaker. There was only one man present, and he stepped forward, Urse at his side. "Perhaps more than it speaks to me," he mused, tilting his head to one side as he seemed to study Sabrina's hand and her continued connection to the warm stone. Could he *see* the flow of magic happening?

"It's sending me images," she confirmed, feeling more than seeing what the stones were trying to show her. "The four elements," she said, closing her eyes to comprehend better. "Earth, water, fire, wind. The stones and bears. The ocean and mermaids." She was more than a little puzzled. She'd heard some of the people in town talk about the mer, but she hadn't seen any, yet, and the very idea that mermaids were real totally intrigued her. "Flames and…a dragon?" She tilted her head in surprise as the final images came to her. "The whirlwind and…me? I'm wind?" The stones seemed to answer in the affirmative, which kind of blew her mind. The living rock was talking to her—not in words—but definitely communicating.

"Shifters are of the earth, mer the water." Urse moved forward to stand next to the man. "I thought the dragon was both fire and wind?"

"We need the best representative of each element, and he was all we had...until now." The man nodded at Sabrina in a knowing way, his smile kind, even if his words were confusing. "I'm betting she's at least part sylph."

Sabrina removed her hand from the stone once the images had stopped flowing. "What's a sylph?" She wasn't sure she liked the sound of this.

"A sylph is a creature of air, most closely related to man, according to the alchemist Paracelsus." An older woman came forward, her words heavily accented. She sounded Italian to Sabrina's ears. "It has not been unheard of through the centuries, for them to walk among mortals—even mate with mortals. The males are ruggedly handsome, from all accounts."

Sabrina shook her head. Who were all these people? And what in the world were they talking about?

Urse came closer, taking Sabrina's hand. She must have seen the distress on her face.

"Sabrina, I'd like you to meet my Nonna. Grandmother, this is Sabrina." Urse presented her like a prize, but oddly, Sabrina didn't mind. Urse's grandmother had a kindly look about her, and a sharp-eyed glance. She saw way more than the average person. Of that, Sabrina was certain.

Sabrina offered her hand to the older woman in greeting, and it was immediately clasped between her two wrinkled hands. The older woman seemed to be testing Sabrina's power...subtly. It wasn't anything intrusive—or anything Sabrina would have objected to. It was just a tiny tickle of energy, flowing from the old woman's hands to hers, feeling her out, magically. The old woman nodded then released Sabrina's hand. She felt like she'd just passed yet another test.

"Call me Nonna," the old woman told her. "Everybody does." She shrugged as if it didn't matter, but Sabrina got the sense that she liked being *everybody's* grandmother. "You, my dear, are part-sylph. I met a full-blooded sylph once, and you feel like that, only diluted. Though, not by much. Your power is strengthening, even as we speak."

Sabrina cringed. "It does tend to build up throughout the day," she admitted. "It never did that before."

"If you need to release the magic, do it toward the creatures." Another heavily accented voice came from Sabrina's side. She hadn't heard the woman come over, but suddenly, there was another older woman standing at her side.

How Sabrina had missed the other woman's approach was a mystery. Where Nonna was small of stature and wrinkled with age, this woman was tall and strong-looking. Older, for certain, but still statuesque.

Was this what shifters looked like when they got really old? Maybe that's why she'd been able to sneak up on Sabrina. She had shifter stealth. And a really thick Russian-sounding accent.

"The dragon you saw in your vision is of my family," the woman proclaimed. "Dragons are very, very rare."

"You're..." Sabrina gulped, "...a dragon?"

The woman laughed, thank goodness. "No, no. I am Kamchatka bear. From Siberia. But one of my ancestors was dragon shifter, and recently, I have found—or, rather, he found us—a young dragon, who is related. He promised to help us defeat leviathan." Her expression was fierce and proud. "You may call me Babushka. Everybody does," she said, sending a teasing shrug towards her contemporary, Nonna.

The town had two grandmothers? One Italian and one Russian. Sabrina had to grin. This place was fun.

"This is the local shaman, Gus," Urse introduced the man who had spoken before. "He guards the ring of stones and is part of our growing magic circle."

"So...I'm part-sylph? Can you tell me anything more about sylphs?" Sabrina asked, puzzled as she went over what the Italian granny had said.

"Sylphs are a type of elemental creature," Mellie said. "I've read about them and the others. There are water sprites and something the old books call salamanders for fire and gnomes for earth."

"Shifters are also of the earth, so we're well covered there, and mer are of the water. I'm not really sure what a salamander is," Urse put in, "but the animal salamanders are a type of reptile, right? So, maybe dragons...?" She let her thought trail off as she looked around the group.

"Are you intending to do some major magical working?" Sabrina asked. That could be the only real reason they were so interested in gathering representation for every element. "I have to tell you, I'm not much of a witch. All I've ever been able to do is influence the weather, and just lately, I've been screwing up left and right. The werewolves in the last town I lived in called the Lords to take me away because I kept spawning tornadoes accidentally."

She didn't like admitting it, but these people had to know the truth about her. Especially if they intended to ask her to be part of some complicated spell work. She'd heard about that kind of thing, but she'd never been part of it. She'd never had the power.

Things had changed for her, of course, but it was all still so new. She didn't really have any control yet. She was very much afraid that if she tried to help, she would only mess things up. Again. As usual.

CHAPTER 13

"We're preparing our defenses, as well as strategies, to deal with the creature once and for all," Urse said gently, but with a hint of steel in her tone. "We managed to push it back that far, already." She pointed to the creature just visible in the distance by the turmoil in the water. "Our ultimate goal is to send it back to where it came from, but until then, we're trying to prepare for all contingencies."

"You don't want to kill it?" Sabrina asked. She would have thought those who lived with bear shifters wouldn't shy away from killing.

Nonna shook her head. "It cannot be killed in this realm. It must go back."

Sabrina had never heard of such a thing, but these people knew a lot more about magic than she did. If they said it couldn't be killed, then it couldn't be killed. She had no reason to doubt their beliefs.

"Sabrina," Urse spoke, again, after a moment of silence. "You said your power builds up until it has to be released. Is that what happened on the highway?"

Sabrina nodded slowly. "Yes...and no. That was a bit of an extreme case because my anger and fear was feeding it into a frenzy. We'd been chased for an hour or more to that point, and even before that, there was a lot of anxiety about watching everything around us. We had been told there were people coming for me. It was kind of a terrible day, and the emotions roiled up and brought out more energy, somehow. I don't know how it all works, but I can definitely say, my emotions are tied to it. If I'm having a calm day, like today, the energy buildup is nothing like it was on the highway. And..." She hesitated, ducking her head in a bit of embarrassment, but these people were trying to help her. They needed to know. "When I'm with Ace... You know... Alone. Then, he seems to be able to help me stabilize. I guess the energy gets channeled into...um...other things."

"Sex," Babushka said in such a loud tone Sabrina flinched. "It is powerful magic in itself. My people have always known this." The old lady nodded as if that was all that needed to be said on the matter.

"How are you feeling, now? Is the magic too much, or are you good for a little experimentation? We'd like to assess your abilities so we can help you refine your control," Urse explained. "Sound good?"

Sabrina nodded. "Yeah, that sounds really good." She felt a bit of her old spark returning. These were kind people who knew a lot more about magic than she did. "I'm stable, for now. No need to blow off any steam at the moment. Maybe later." She shrugged. Her power wasn't all that predictable and hadn't been for weeks.

What followed was the most intense magical training Sabrina had ever had. First, they tested her abilities. They actually wanted her to create whirlwinds. Just small ones, within the protective circle of stones. Dust devils, Gus called them, daring to walk into the middle of the smaller ones, to see just how strong they were. When she lifted him off the ground with her mini-tornadoes, he actually laughed like a kid on a carnival ride.

Crazy bears. Sabrina had to shake her head, even as she found amusement in his antics.

Ace watched Sabrina and the odd assortment of women

141

plus one guy. It looked to Ace like they were trying to help her as he kept an eye on things from outside the stone circle. He couldn't hear any of what went on inside, nor could he feel the magic she was stirring up in there. He could see it, though. When she sent the guy airborne with a mini-tornado, it was pretty obvious they were testing her powers.

He'd come in search of Sabrina as soon as the town council had gotten through with him. He'd almost expected even more of a grilling than the one he'd received, but apparently, being sent by the Lords had helped pave the way for him a bit. Still, it was pretty clear the bears of Grizzly Cove had done their own investigation about him and his prior life history.

Of course, he knew a bunch of them, having become acquainted with them years ago while he and his brothers had still been in the service. The three bear brothers had never served under John Marshall, nor had they been part of his unit, but their paths had crossed, from time to time, with some of the men in the group, and Ace had a lot of respect for those guys.

They had been particularly interested in his experience as a mechanic, which had surprised him. Mechanics were a dime a dozen, and most of the guys in town probably knew one end of an engine from another. But, on his drive through after the meeting, he realized there was no garage in town. None at all.

Oh, there was one gas pump next to the town hall that seemed to be self-service for official vehicles—and he'd bet that any vehicle owned by anyone in the community would qualify as official, when necessary—but there was no gas station. No garage. No place for a broken bike, car or truck to get fixed.

If the town was open to tourists—and judging by all the art galleries lining Main Street, he was pretty sure it was—then where did they get gas or get their vehicles fixed if they broke down? This was a pretty rugged part of the coastline, which was why it hadn't been settled before. If someone had a mechanical failure out here, it was a long way to another town. He wasn't sure what the folks had been doing about the problem until now, but Ace smelled a business opportunity here, if he was interested in staying in Grizzly Cove.

It became apparent by their questions that the town council was interested, too, though they hadn't come out and said anything, yet. It felt like they were still gauging whether or not he'd fit into their community. He wondered idly if they were going to vote on him or something, after he'd been in town for a while and they'd gotten to know him better. He had no idea what it might take to win their confidence and the invitation to stay, but he wasn't sure whether he wanted it or not, just yet.

He wanted to see how things worked out for Sabrina, first. And he wanted to be sure this place was still going to be here. That big fucker out in the water looked pissed, if Ace was any judge, and right now, Grizzly Cove seemed to have a big fat bulls-eye all over it. Maybe this wasn't the safest place to be… Or, maybe it was.

To Ace's admittedly spotty knowledge of history, nothing like this town had ever been attempted before. Concentrating so much magic here—so many bears, and now, mer and mages—well, it made the place a juicy target for their enemies, but it also really concentrated the power in one place. And the knowledge. Maybe they invited attack here, but they were also better able to defend from this position of strength in numbers than any smaller group would be alone.

The town had also been designed by warriors. They'd taken every advantage of terrain, elevation and landscape into account. The town itself was surrounded by homesteads, which were placed strategically for defense from outside. He'd bet his bottom dollar that the outer perimeter of every property was patrolled and marked. Probably also under high-tech surveillance, at all times. These military bears knew what they were doing, after all. They'd been highly-trained and vastly experienced Special Operatives for too many years to go soft in civilian life.

Then, there were the witches. And the mer.

So much magic here.

Just as Ace had that thought, he saw Sabrina make a gesture, and the now-familiar power of hers reached outside the circle and blew strong toward the ocean. Whitecaps appeared suddenly, in a straight line headed straight for the sea monsters he could just make out by their disturbance in the ocean far, far out. Sabrina's winds were pushing the creatures even farther away.

Ace stood to watch. He hadn't expected them to unleash her winds on anything, but it was truly a sight to behold. And, he noted with pride, it was much more controlled than anything he'd seen from her before. Maybe they were making progress here. In just a few hours, it sure looked like they'd been able to help her channel her energies in just the one direction, in a controlled burst, unlike the more chaotic release on the highway but still quite impressive.

When the winds died down, Ace's attention focused on Sabrina. He wasn't sure what he'd expected. After the highway incident, she'd pretty much collapsed from the power drain. Would she be as drained, now? He was almost afraid to check her condition, but she looked okay. She was standing on her own two feet without support from anyone, and she was smiling. Beaming, actually. She looked really happy and proud of herself.

Ace felt happy for her, as well. She'd controlled that power, and she'd withstood the release of it without draining herself too much. He wanted to pick her up and twirl her around. She'd done so well!

Ace looked back at the ocean and tried to gauge how far the leviathan had been pushed by Sabrina's power. The creature certainly looked a lot smaller and farther away now, but it was hard to gauge exact distances from this angle. He wondered if the mages or the bears would have some way to quantify it, and what they would glean about Sabrina's power from it.

It sure looked like they'd been able to help her gain a bit

of control over her whirlwinds, which he counted as a step in the right direction. Apart from the fact that he'd wanted to visit Ezra and Thea, and see Grizzly Cove for himself, he was really glad they'd come here because there really were people here who could help Sabrina figure out her new powers. And she could direct her energy at something that really needed fixing here. The leviathan was a real threat, and Ace knew Sabrina well enough by now to know that she enjoyed helping people. Using her talent in this way probably gave her a great sense of satisfaction, which would go a long way toward rebuilding her confidence.

The wolves up north had knocked her down. They hadn't supported her in her time of crisis, and their lack of faith had badly interfered with her own sense of self. It would take time, and good work like she'd done here today, to bring back her faith in her own abilities. And, judging by the smiles on the faces of the people inside the circle with Sabrina, these magic users were encouraging and supportive. They would be able to help her both magically, and in regaining her self-esteem.

It looked to Ace like they were wrapping up for the day, so he waited for the group to exit the stone circle. He did not want to mess with whatever residual magic might be hanging around inside the ring. Magic that powerful would not have dissipated so quickly. Any bear worth the name knew that.

Sabrina caught sight of him, and her whole face lit up in a smile. He found himself answering with what was probably an equally goofy grin, but he didn't care. She made a beeline for him the moment she stepped outside the circle, and he opened his arms and gave her a hug of welcome. If anyone raised their eyebrows, he didn't really care. Bears were known huggers. Let them think he was just allowing his inner fur ball to dictate his actions.

Unless, of course, Sabrina didn't mind. He hadn't really talked to her about their relationship, and how public or private she wanted to keep it. He'd abide by whatever she decided, but they had to have a conversation about it, first.

He wasn't a guy who exactly *liked* talking about his feelings, but his inner bear was pushing him to figure out a few things about his relationship with Sabrina. The bear wanted answers, and the man was starting to crave them, too. Both sides of his being wanted to know exactly where he stood with her and how far they could take this. He might've only known her a couple of days, but she felt...important. Like someone he wanted to be with...possibly...forever.

It hit him while he held her in his arms, hugging her close. She could very well be his mate.

Stunned, he opened his eyes to find two very old ladies looking at him with knowing, indulgent smiles. They grasped each other's arms and giggled like schoolgirls, despite their advanced ages, then walked off, arm in arm, probably planning some sort of conspiracy of grannies. Ace found the whole thing amusing. Hell, everything was butterflies and unicorns when he had Sabrina in his arms.

Where she belonged.

Sabrina felt triumphant after her morning within the magic circle. She'd learned a lot about control and centering herself and her power. These were the things mages were taught by their mentors, but Sabrina had never had a mentor. No one had been interested in teaching someone with only a little weather magic to call her own, before now.

Ace took her to the bakery for lunch. She was really hungry, as the others had warned her might happen. Apparently, the expenditure of magical energy took something out of the mage that had to be replaced with both rest and calories. She wasn't so fried that she needed to go to sleep immediately, but she was definitely hungry, and the giant sandwich Ace brought over from the counter to their small table was a welcome sight.

They ate while she told him about her discoveries and how nice the other magic users were. She told him about the bear shifter granny from Russia and the Italian granny who was Urse and Mellie's relation. She also told him what she'd observed about Gus, but the male bear was a bit of a mystery to her. A shaman, he'd said, though she wasn't exactly sure what that meant in the context of shifters.

Ace told her a little about his meeting with the town council, and she wondered if they would allow him to stay in town on a more permanent basis, if that's what he wanted. Everything she'd seen of the town so far made her want to stay, and she wasn't even a bear.

"Whoa, you hear that?" Ace's head was cocked toward the glass window they were sitting near. "Sorry. Give me a couple of minutes. I think someone's going to need a hand."

"What's wrong?" she asked, puzzled.

"Sorry," Ace looked sheepish, even as he stood up. "I keep forgetting you don't have shifter hearing." She wasn't sure whether to be delighted or insulted. "The vehicle that just pulled up isn't going to start, again. Not with that rattle coming from the engine. I'm going to see if I can prevent further damage."

Sabrina looked out the window to see a Sheriff's Department SUV parked at the curb. She saw Ace walk over to the man who was just getting out of the vehicle. They shook hands and exchanged a few words, then they went around to the hood of the big car and opened it. Ace leaned in and did something, then straightened. Both men went around to the back of the large vehicle, and the driver opened the back door.

When Ace reappeared, he had a few tools in his hands. He and the other man then spent a few minutes working on the engine. It looked like Ace did the work while the other man handed him tools and asked questions. Sabrina kept eating her sandwich while she watched the show. The man in the SUV was wearing a uniform, so he had to be a deputy or maybe even the actual sheriff, and from the way they were talking, it sure looked like Ace knew the man already.

When Ace finished, the uniformed man went to the driver's door and cranked the starter at Ace's urging, and then, Ace cocked his head and listened to the engine for a moment. His smile was clear to read. Whatever had bothered him about the way the engine had sounded before had been fixed.

The officer shut off the engine, again, and got out of the vehicle. He and Ace shook hands after Ace shut the hood, and then, they walked into the bakery together. Since their table was near the door, Ace brought the other man over and introduced him.

"Sabrina, this is Sheriff Brody. Nell is his mate," Ace said, indicating the woman behind the counter who had taken their order and prepared their food.

Sabrina said hello to the man, smiling. "Nell is a doll," she said, truthfully. "It's nice to meet you." She gestured toward the window and the vehicle beyond. "Car trouble?"

"Not anymore, thanks to Ace," Brody said, slapping Ace on the back. "We've been talking a bit about how there's no real mechanical expertise in town, yet, and Ace would certainly fit the bill, judging by what I just witnessed." Brody grinned. "I mean, all of us like to think we can take anything apart and put it back together, but most of us are better with weapons systems than with motor vehicles. A couple of the guys tried to figure out what's been making that whirring sound in the old wagon, but none of us could find it. Give Ace five minutes and a couple of basic tools, and it's fixed."

Sabrina could tell the sheriff was pleased. It was like he'd just administered a test, and his star pupil had come through with flying colors. Come to think of it, this probably had been a set up—a test—all along. Shifters were crafty, that way.

"He's a wonder, that's for sure," she said, giving Ace her vote of confidence. "He knows motorcycles really well, too. He did all the negotiating and picking out when it came time to buy my bike, and he got me a really good one." He'd paid for it, too, which was something she'd have to talk to him about if she wanted to keep the bike—which she did. But that was a topic for another time.

Nell came over with a platter of cookies and handed them to Ace before snuggling under the outstretched arm of her bear shifter mate. "Thanks for looking at old Bessie," she said to Ace. "I know some noise she's been making lately has been driving Brody nuts, but of course, I can't hear it."

"Noise is gone," Brody reported, kissing his mate on the temple.

"Really?" Nell looked impressed. "Then, the cookies are on the house," she said, grinning at Ace.

"Thanks, ma'am," Ace told her, looking a bit embarrassed. "It wasn't that big a deal."

"Maybe not to you," she said, "but it is to me. Now, I don't have to humor him by trying to listen for something that's completely out of the range of my hearing." She laughed, patting her mate's chest as she reached up to kiss him quickly, then ducked away to go back to work.

"I'd be happy to assist with any repairs you all may need while I'm in town, if it's really something you need help with," Ace offered.

Brody reached out to shake on Ace's offer, seeming truly glad. "That's kind of you, and we'll definitely take you up on that. Drop by the sheriff's office anytime, and I'll show you around to the motors that need expert attention. I'm sorry to say, there are more than a few in town at the moment."

Brody took his leave then went over to the counter where his mate waited with a large shopping bag she'd filled with food. They talked for a while, exchanging a few steamy kisses Sabrina pretended not to see, and then, he left, taking the large bag with him. He flashed Ace a thumbs up through the window when the engine turned over—apparently without the annoying sound it had sported before. He drove away while Ace and Sabrina lingered over the remains of their meal and the bonus cookies Nell had given them.

"So, are you thinking of staying in Grizzly Cove?" Sabrina asked, breaking into his thoughts as Ace munched on a cookie and mused over what had just happened with the sheriff.

"Maybe, though I'd have to be invited. The core group

controls who they allow to settle here," he told her.

"Well, it looked like the sheriff was giving you an audition as a mechanic. Maybe they'll like your skill set enough to offer the invite," she said, shrugging as if her observations were nothing special.

Ace looked at her speculatively. Few other people would have picked up on the *audition*, as she called it, so easily. She was not only powerful, but perceptive. The more he got to know Sabrina, the more she fascinated him.

He especially liked the way she had seemed to blossom under the care of those people in the circle this morning. They had treated her well. As an equal, judging by her positive response to them. They had taught her and helped her, unlike the werewolves up in Canada. The Lords would be getting the full report about Tobias and the way he ran his group, that was for sure.

Sabrina had been very enthusiastic in her response to both the *strega* sisters, Urse and Mellie, as she now called them, and the two grannies, Nonna and Babushka. As far as Ace knew, those were just two foreign words that meant the same thing—grandmother. The two old ladies had really made an impression on Sabrina. She said less about the male, which was probably good for Ace's sanity. His inner grizzly had been getting too easily riled when Sabrina was around single males.

The mated men were okay, but the bachelors had better mind their manners, or Ace might just take a swipe at one and start a minor war. The last thing he really wanted was to fight any of the bears in Grizzly Cove, but he was becoming increasingly irrational when it came to Sabrina. He knew that had to mean something, but he didn't want to think about it, just then. No, he'd rather look into her pretty blue eyes and ponder the ways he'd make her scream his name in pleasure later...when they were alone.

"But, if they do invite you to stay, what about your brothers?" she asked as she snagged another cookie off the plate. "I thought you said it was rare that you three were traveling separately. Do you think they'd like to join you here, if you stay? And would they be welcome?"

Ace sat back in his chair and stretched a little. "All good questions, to which I have few answers. I can't imagine settling down anywhere without my brothers. If that was a condition of staying, that would make it really hard to say yes. But, I do have to say, my bear feels a lot more stable here than I expected. It's like we're all one big Clan, not a bunch of solo bears competing for territory. It's a lot different than what I'm used to, and that's all down to the core group that founded the place. They're a true family, even if they're not all related by blood."

"I have to say, these people are night and day different from the werewolves I knew up north," she agreed.

"Bears rule. Wolves drool," he replied, grinning as he smoothed down his shirt. She laughed, and he tried to capture the joyful sound in his memory to take out on rainy days and bring a bit of sunshine to his heart. "The climate would take some adjusting to, though," he observed as clouds moved in over the cove. "It's very different than Phoenix."

"You live in Phoenix?" She sounded surprised, and he realized again that they hadn't really known each other that long, even if it seemed like his soul recognized her on a much deeper level than most folks he knew.

"We do—or, maybe at this point, I should say, we *did*. Until Ezra called for help, we worked for a very exclusive custom shop, but then, Ezra needed some backup, so we went to Sturgis for the motorcycle rally and gave him a hand," Ace revealed. He wanted her to know about him and his brothers. He didn't want to be a mystery to her. He wanted her to know it all and like him, anyway. "We originally planned to go back to Phoenix after, but all three of us felt pulled in different directions, so we sat down and talked it over. We decided to do a little solo adventuring, which is something we've done in the past, on occasion. We always get back together after our walkabouts, but I'm not sure what will happen, this time. Things have gotten more complicated than

I expected."

"Because of me?" She suddenly smelled both nervous and sad.

He reached across the small table and placed his hand over hers. "Not like you think," he was quick to tell her. "It started when I tried to visit my old friend, Rocky, and got sent straight to the Lords. I didn't expect that—or anything that came after—but I don't regret a moment of it. I'm glad I got to be the one to help you. No, scratch that. I'm *thrilled* I got to be the one to help you, and I'm hoping we can do a lot more to help resolve your situation." He pitched his voice lower, using a more intimate tone. "I don't want our relationship to end anytime soon. I'm in no hurry to leave." He met her gaze and tried to see into her mind to get at what she was thinking. "I hope that's okay with you."

Her smile was his answer. It lit the dim places in his soul. "It's more than okay," she told him. "I've kind of gotten used to having you around."

CHAPTER 14

Sabrina's heart was fluttering madly at the near-declaration. Too bad they were in a public place, or she'd jump his bones and nail down just how long he wanted their relationship— and she was thrilled to hear him use that word in reference to them—to last. She was starting to dream about what it would be like to live here, in this idyllic place with these amazing, accepting people...and Ace, of course. He was the main draw.

Grizzly Cove had its attractions, but she really couldn't imagine making a life here without Ace. He was the one that made it all possible. He'd become so important to her over the past few days, it hardly seemed real, at times. Yet, there it was. She was finding it hard to contemplate her future without him in it.

Too serious. She knew she was getting in way over her head, but her heart didn't care what her head thought. Her heart wanted to follow these feelings wherever they led. Ace was at the center of everything, and if he wanted to stay in Grizzly Cove, she just hoped he invited her along.

And, if he didn't want to stay here, that was okay, too. As long as he wanted them to be together, she would go wherever he did. It was just that simple. And that staggering. She'd never had these kinds of thoughts—permanent thoughts—about a guy she'd only really just met. Heck, she'd barely had daydreams of forever with her last serious boyfriend, and they'd dated for more than a year, on and off.

Then, her power had shown up in earnest, and her life had gotten weird. She'd been rolling along fine as just another regular human woman with no magic for most of her life, when suddenly, in the middle of what should have been her college years, her strange affinity for the weather had become obvious, and she finally realized that she could actually control it to some extent.

A girl in one of her classes had been the daughter of a highly-ranked mage family, and she had looked down on Sabrina. It was that snobby girl who had finally clued Sabrina in.

Magic. The girl had uttered that word when they were alone in the hall one day, and something had clicked into place in Sabrina's mind. Magic was her problem, and the obnoxious girl obviously had a lot more knowledge than Sabrina did about it.

Sabrina braved the other girl's scorn to ask a few questions. It had been worth the insults to finally learn that there really was such a thing as magic and witches…and wizards, mages, magic users, sorcerers…whatever they were called.

The girl had admonished Sabrina to get her act together and stop leaking magic all over the place, where just anybody could sense it. Apparently, she'd been wreaking havoc with the girl's concentration all semester, and that was probably a large part of the reason she was so hostile. Of course, she was the first of many to disparage the fact that Sabrina only had a small amount of power—and all of it was directed towards weather working.

A one-trick pony. That's what she'd been, magically. And it wasn't really much of a trick, at that. Just a little weather-witchery. Nothing special, and certainly nothing to garner enough attention to attract a teacher. The girl had grudgingly told her how to stop broadcasting her power, but that was more for the girl's benefit than Sabrina's. After that brief, nastily-worded exchange, Sabrina had never spoken to the other girl, again.

Sabrina had left school soon after. Her heart just wasn't in it, and frankly, she'd run out of money. Loans were available, but she didn't feel comfortable going into debt when she didn't really have any clear idea of what she wanted to do with the rest of her life. She just couldn't see herself working in an office, watching the clouds roll by through a tiny window. That sounded like torture, in fact.

So, instead, Sabrina had traveled wherever the wind had taken her. Eventually, she'd discovered the town in Canada and learned about werewolves. She'd bartered her small gift for a safe haven, though it hadn't lasted all that long before her power ratcheted up unexpectedly.

And that's how she'd ended up here. With Ace. A man who could very easily be the love of her life. Strange, how things worked out. It was enough to make her believe in magic, all over again.

And, speaking of magic… Urse walked into the bakery, greeting Sabrina and Ace with a friendly smile.

"Glad you two are still here," Urse said brightly, coming right over to their table. "I thought maybe this afternoon would be a good time to introduce you, Sabrina, to some of the mer."

"Seriously?" Sabrina lit up. She was really intrigued by the idea of honest-to-goodness mermaids living in the cove.

"You bet. And Ace," she looked at him, "John wanted me to ask if you had time, maybe you could have a look at some of the town vehicles? He said he'd count it as a personal favor. Apparently, Brody's been singing your praises all over the office."

Sabrina spent the afternoon with Urse, meeting some representatives of the mer pod that lived in the cove, while Ace took a look at the small fleet of vehicles parked at the town hall. He knew damned well that he was being checked out by the guys. Several of the core group of ex-military bear shifters came up to talk with him while he was working on the cars and trucks. A few offered to help for a while, subtly grilling him while they worked.

Ace didn't mind. He knew acceptance here would have to be earned. Most of these guys didn't know him, but they seemed to come to respect his skills by the end of a very productive afternoon of automotive repair. He had taken care of all the easy fixes, right away, and left a few more complicated jobs for later. He'd started an overhaul on one engine that was badly in need of it and was already making mental plans on how he would go about fixing the others.

He would need to order a few parts, and he'd made up a list, intending to talk to John about it at dinner. He figured he'd go right to the top—to the Alpha bear. Few things happened in this town without his say so. At least, that's the very strong impression Ace had. He'd do a bit of evaluating of his own. He was on display for the guys who'd built this town, but they were also on trial with him. If Ace was going to even start thinking about staying here, he'd have to know more about the population. He'd need to make friends, which wasn't something he did easily.

Honestly, he felt a bit like a fish out of water without his brothers around. They made friends as a group, usually. It was odd to not have Jack and King there to get their opinions on the people he met. He wondered if they were having the same issues, but he still had a few days until the agreed-upon call time.

Wherever his brothers were, he wouldn't impinge on their time away. They'd agreed to a schedule of check-ins, and he would abide by it. Only a dire emergency would make one of them break the schedule and call early.

The Alpha's home was really nice. John and Ace stood outside on the deck while John presided over the grill. The girls were inside, talking like old friends. Apparently, the day spent together had helped create the beginnings of a bond between them. Ace was glad. Sabrina could use a few allies in her corner, and these two were powerful—each in their own ways.

"So, have you heard from your brothers lately?" John asked as he turned the steaks on the grill. The Alpha's tone might be casual, but Ace knew the question was anything but.

"We agreed on a timetable for check-ins," Ace explained to the Alpha bear. "It'll be a few days yet before we call each other."

"Must be difficult for you, being away from them like this," John said, clearly fishing.

Ace shrugged. "It's good for our mental health to get out and do things on our own once in a while. We usually spend so much time together, I'll admit, it feels strange not to have them around, but we've separated before a few times, and it always turned out to be a good thing. It makes us that much closer when we get back together."

"You know we've been scouting you." John turned, pinning Ace with his intent gaze. Ace nodded. "The thing is… We've all met you, and pretty much everyone who's interacted with you has a good report, but we don't know your brothers. The background we've been able to establish makes it pretty clear—in addition to what you just told me—that in all likelihood, you three come as a package deal. That's where we have reservations."

Ace nodded. "I appreciate your honesty, and I'll be just as blunt. I like your town. I think you've done a really great thing here. Everything I've seen tells me I'd be a fool to leave, but by the same token, I have a life and friends—and, yes, my family—to consider. Our original plan was to meet back in Phoenix when we were done with our travels."

John held Ace's gaze for another long moment before turning back to the grill and giving a philosophical shrug of his shoulders. "Well, nothing needs to be decided, right now. You're more than welcome to stay in town for a while. Who knows? Maybe one or both of your brothers will wander through in their travels, and we can get to know all three of you." John started serving up the steaks, the two men working together to juggle the plates. "Stranger things have happened."

Dinner was lovely, and Sabrina had seldom enjoyed an evening with friends more. Urse was someone she could both respect and like. Given half a chance, Sabrina thought Urse could become a really good friend. It all depended on how long Sabrina got to stay in Grizzly Cove. Right now, she wished she could stay here forever. She had a little fantasy about working in one of the galleries on Main Street and helping keep the place safe from the worst of the weather. Maybe the people here would appreciate her efforts in a way nobody else really ever had.

She could even do as some other weather witches she'd heard of did and hire out to local communities of Others to help them keep their areas free from damaging storms. Some magical folk who had interests in agricultural activities hired weather witches to steer rain to their crops or away, depending on need. Sabrina could do that. She'd been able to do that even before her power had taken a massive spike.

She'd bet, with her increase in ability and the control she was learning from the mages here, she could do it from a much longer distance. She could probably stay here, safe in Grizzly Cove, and steer weather within several hundred miles. She'd have to ask the magic circle if they thought her hunch on that was right. Maybe they could even do a few controlled experiments.

But that was a daydream for another time. For now, she still had to work on her control and understanding of her newly increased abilities. She pulled her bike up next to Ace's in the hotel parking lot and parked. She liked riding the bike because it gave her time to think, but being with Ace was even better.

They walked into the hotel room together, speaking softly about the dinner they'd just shared with the Alpha couple, and she had a warm glow in the region of her heart. After all the turmoil of the past few days, to have such a calming, enjoyable evening was a treasure.

The hotel room was just as inviting as it had been when she'd first arrived. She just could appreciate it more, now that she was way calmer. The rooms were built for shifters. Everything was large and durable, and there was actually space to move around, unlike most other hotel rooms, which were built for economies of scale.

After checking the suite for safety—something Ace did as a matter of course, it seemed—he plunked himself down on the sofa in the main room. They'd been given a suite that had a main room with a seating area and large television with separate bedroom and bathroom attached. Compared to the rinky-dink place they'd stayed that one night on the way here, this suite was a mansion.

Ace looked like he wanted to talk. Or decompress. He didn't turn on the TV, but he sat on the couch, looking like a man with a lot on his mind. Sabrina went to the small fridge in the suite and took out two cold drinks—beer for him and bottled water for herself—and joined him on the couch.

"Penny for your thoughts," she said. "Or, rather, how about a beer, instead of a penny?" She handed him the bottle and was glad to see him smile faintly. He looked tired. Or, maybe, contemplative.

"Thanks." He opened the bottle and took a long pull of the imported brew before speaking. "John told me they'd been scouting me."

"For what?" She wasn't sure exactly what he meant by the term. Were the bears putting together some sort of team? Or was he talking about being checked out for residency in the cove?

"They don't have a mechanic shop in town. Seems they think it'd be a nice addition," he replied. "Makes sense," he added. "They've set the place up for tourists to pass through and spend money. Those tourists will need a place to get things checked out if their vehicles decide to misbehave. Fastest way to get them on their way is to have someone in town qualified to fix them up and move them along."

"So…they're open to tourists, they just don't want them to hang around that long?" Sabrina had to chuckle at the way the bears thought.

"That's about the size of it. Blending in, but also not allowing folks to stay too long. I bet Urse will ask for your help with that if they ever have a problem. Bad weather will usually get tourists to leave a place and go somewhere sunnier."

"You've got a point there, but I have no idea if they're willing to let me stay." Sabrina took a sip of her water. It felt cool against her throat. Clean. Pure. Like almost everything about this magical place.

"Would you want to, if they let you?" Ace asked in a soft voice.

Sabrina didn't really have to think about it. "Yes," she answered immediately, her tone wistful. "I'm not sure they'll let me, but if they did, I'd want to do it. I've never been any place as…accepting…as this."

Ace sighed. "You got a really raw deal up north. Most wolf Alphas are a lot better than Tobias. He basically hung you out to dry." Ace's gaze met hers. "Don't worry. I'm making a full report to the Lords. They will have a little talk with Tobias, I'm certain of it. They're werewolves themselves, and they don't tolerate that kind of insensitivity."

"It's okay. Don't sweat it. I'm done with that place, now." She thought about that for a moment. "Except for Marilee. I'd like to stay in touch with her, if at all possible. She was the best thing about that town. My one true friend up there." Sabrina smiled. "And, she's got my stuff. She said she'd pack it up and send it for me. I'm going to have to give her a call soon and make arrangements. Once I figure out where I'm actually going to land, that is. I'm hoping it's here, but I should probably wait to make sure."

"No need to rush anything. Marilee seemed like a good friend. She'll take care of your things until you figure out where you're going to end up settling," Ace advised.

He had a way of making everything seem so simple. She

liked his calm manner and had really needed his quiet determination when they were in jeopardy. He was a good man to have around in all sorts of circumstances.

"So, you never said if you'd stay or not. Do you like Grizzly Cove?" she asked him.

"This place..." He seemed to search for words. "I've never felt more at home in a new place so quickly," he finally admitted. "But there's more than just me to consider," he added.

For a split second, she thought he might be hinting at something more permanent between them, but then, she remembered his family. She'd never met them, but apparently, the three brothers were more together than apart.

"Have you talked to either of your brothers, yet?"

Ace shook his head. "We agreed on a strict schedule for calls. I don't want to interfere in their journeys, so we have a few days yet before we call each other. By then, maybe, things will settle out, and I can be more definite about what's going on. We have jobs waiting for us in Phoenix. We liked working there and the people we worked with. But, I guess, we were all feeling sort of antsy to be on the road. When Ezra called and asked for help, we were out of there like a shot, headed for South Dakota. And, then, when we probably should have headed back to Arizona, we decided to go walkabout." Ace shrugged. "I expect all three of us felt it was time for a change. Whether that means just having a little adventure before returning to Arizona or relocating completely, I still don't know."

"But, if you get the invitation to stay here and your brothers are willing, would you?" she insisted.

Ace looked at her, meeting her gaze with an unreadable expression on his face. "Yeah," he finally answered, "I would. I like the people and the place. There are just a lot of variables to work through, right now."

Sabrina nodded, feeling the weight of her own uncertainties pressing down. "Yeah. I know what you mean."

"Come here," he said gently, holding one arm out. She

scooted under his arm and snuggled into his side, enjoying the quiet and the man. He placed a tender kiss on the crown of her head as she settled against him. "It'll all work out. I promise."

Sabrina must have dozed, because sometime later, she felt herself being lifted into the air by Ace's strong arms. He treated her so gently. How could she not enjoy her time with this special man?

"What time is it?" she asked, her voice rough with sleep.

"Sorry," he said immediately. "I was trying not to wake you. It's after eleven. I was just going to put you in bed."

He crossed the threshold into the separate bedroom of the suite and placed her on the bed. She looked up at him, and suddenly, she didn't want him going anywhere. She had no idea what he'd had planned when he brought her in here, but she had definite ideas about what was going to happen next. Starting with getting rid of all the clothes between them.

"Don't go," she whispered, touching his cheek as he bent over her.

His eyes flared with awareness as he sat on the side of the wide bed. She sat up and moved closer, putting her hands on his shoulders in a caress as she angled in for a kiss. He picked up on her intent and met her halfway, his arm going around her waist and pulling her in closer.

The kiss started out steamy and ended up downright scandalous. She pushed at his clothing, wanting it gone. Luckily, he seemed to get the idea, and he helped her remove his shirt. When she was able to touch his skin, she settled in for a nice long exploration of his shoulders and arms. She loved his broad, muscular shoulders so damned much. Just watching him move made her want to touch him, and touching him... Well, that was just the beginning. Touching led to wanting other things. Much more wicked things that she already knew would send her right up to the stars and back, again.

Being with Ace was an addictive thing. The more she touched him, the more she wanted to touch him. The more they made love, the more she wanted to make love with him. It just kept getting better.

Which hadn't always been the case with the few men she'd shared intimacies with in the past. Only a couple had rated a return performance after a disappointing start. And those hadn't lasted very long. Her longest relationship had been an on-again-off-again year of drama during her ill-fated college career. After that, she'd met a couple of guys she tried on for size, but none were keepers, and they never really made it past the audition into the role of boyfriend.

Ace, though… He was something altogether different. She didn't know if they were seeing each other or what. So much had been compressed into such a short time. She wasn't really sure what others might call what they had going on. An affair? A fling? Something more serious? For sure, it was the most intense relationship she'd ever had. Just like Ace was the most intensely masculine male she had ever had the pleasure of knowing…in the Biblical sense.

Maybe it was because he was a shifter. But…none of the wolves up in her last town had affected her like Ace. And none of the bears she'd met so far in Grizzly Cove had attracted her. Not like Ace. Maybe it was less a shifter thing and more an *Ace* kind of thing.

She smiled as that thought crossed her mind and dipped her head so she could lick his chest. He shuddered, and a soft growl sounded deep in his throat. She moved upward and licked the corded muscles of his throat, kissing her way upward to his jaw, where a five o'clock stubble was just rough enough to tease her senses.

"Mm," she murmured against his lips. "I want more."

"Your wish…" he kissed her briefly, then continued, "…is my command." With one motion, he lifted her top off over her head, leaving her breathless and a little stunned, but more than ready to see where he would lead her this time.

Her bra followed in short order, and he wasted no time spreading her out on the bed, removing her pants and panties in one fell swoop. She was naked, stretched out before him.

He still had his jeans on, but as she watched, he toed off his boots and began inching down his zipper.

Sabrina was salivating as his fingers move so damned slow over the zipper. Was he teasing her? A quick glance up to his eyes told her yes. He was definitely teasing her. Getting into the spirit of things, she licked her lips, reminding him subtly about things that had passed between them. When he growled, she knew her message had been received. Still, he took his time.

If there had been music, he probably would have strutted. As it was, he revealed himself one slow inch at a time. Her very own personal male stripper, doing all he could to please his audience. Sabrina was very, very appreciative.

By the time he kicked off his jeans and stepped closer to the bed, she was ready to accept whatever he had in mind to give her. He came down over her, making room for himself between her legs. He spread them, stroking up her inner thighs with gentle hands, making her shiver in anticipation.

He'd barely touched her and already her body was weeping, wanting to be filled. Possessed. Conquered and released. She would willingly be his slave.

"Do you want me?" he whispered as he moved over her, his head near hers, his lips by her ear. His chest brushed her nipples, and she had to stifle a moan.

"Yes," she whispered back, unable to speak too loudly. Unwilling to break the mood with harsh tones. This was a magical time. A hushed silence surrounded them, waiting for what would come. What he would give her.

He rose up, settling between her wide-spread thighs, and then, he started stroking her body with his hands. Those big, warm, talented hands. They paused here and there on her skin, pinching, plumping and caressing every inch of her torso on his way to his ultimate goal. He spent a lot of time on her breasts, bending to lick and suck at the pointed nipples. Then, he kissed his way down to her belly button, then lower.

When he licked her clit, her hips jerked, but his big hands

were there, holding her, taming her. He made her dance to his tune and brought her a delicious bit of pleasure on the way to something even better.

This time, when he rose over her, she was more than ready. She was eager, willing and oh-so-receptive. She accepted him into her body in one long, steady thrust. She gazed into his eyes as he filled her, loving the look of primal possession deep in his brown eyes.

Then, he began to move. Slow, at first, his motion was deep and penetrating, smooth and seductive. He took her along on a journey of discovery as each and every thrust brought her some new rapture, all leading up to an ultimate high that only Ace had ever shown her.

The intimacy was intense. She knew she should be feeling vulnerable, but not with Ace. There was nothing she couldn't give him. Nothing she couldn't show him about her fear. He'd seen her at her worst and seen her through some incredibly dangerous scenarios. After all that, sex was easy. At least, sex with Ace had always been easy. Never had she known a man who made her feel like that.

He was special. Unique in every way. An original in her admittedly limited experience, but that didn't matter. What mattered was him. And her. Together. Skin to skin. His cock inside her body, bringing her to new heights of pleasure. New avenues of discovery. He was with her and in her. He was her guide and her guest. And, together, they were unstoppable.

His motions lost their smooth glide and took on a more urgent tone as their passions rose together. She clutched at his shoulders as he pumped his hips in increasingly out-of-control motions. They were going to explode, and it was going to be together. Her passion rising in time with his.

"Sabrina!" He growled her name. So sexy. Pushing her to a new height of satisfaction as she climaxed amid a sea of stars, out in the stratosphere somewhere, floating on a cloud of near-painful bliss.

"Ace," she whispered as she felt him join her. She held onto him throughout, encouraging, accepting, wanting to be with him always…

CHAPTER 15

A loud banging on the hotel room door woke Sabrina the next morning. Ace jumped out of bed, ready for anything, it seemed, as he stalked towards the door, apparently not caring that he was naked.

"Who is it?" Ace demanded in a loud voice.

"Ezra," came the voice, shouting back. "Open up, man. There's a big problem, and we need your help."

Ace opened the door, pushing forward to make sure the other man stayed in the hallway. Sabrina got up and wrapped the sheet around herself like a toga. She could easily hear their conversation. She glanced at the clock, alarmed to see how early it was. Judging by the soft glow around the edges of the curtains, it was just barely dawn.

"What is it?" Ace demanded.

"One of the guys took his fishing boat out a little too far. He just *had* to go out and see how much the beast had been pushed back yesterday." Ezra sounded pissed. "Only problem is, the leviathan's little helpers have cut off the boat, and our boy can't get back to shore. The big boy was last spotted heading straight for him, though it was still a ways out. John sent me to get you two. Urse thinks your lady might be able to help push the creatures back long enough for the boat to get through."

Sabrina gasped. Someone was in danger of their life, and she had to help. A tiny frisson of fear made her wonder if she really could or if her magic was going to go all wonky, again, but she pushed those thoughts aside. She could do this. The work she'd done yesterday with that odd group of magic coaches had helped. She just needed to recreate that, and she could definitely help.

Ace looked back at her, and she nodded. "We'll be right out," he told Ezra and shut the door.

Neither of them wasted any time getting dressed. Sabrina threw on the first clothing she found and didn't really care that her T-shirt was on backwards. There would be time to fix it after they saved the man who was in danger.

Ezra met them in the hall and escorted them out the nearest door on the side of the building. A truck was waiting there for them with its doors open and engine running. All three of them piled in and took off without a word being spoken. Ezra drove at top speed down the now-familiar dirt road that took them to the circle of stones on the southern point of the cove.

Urse was already there, as was the shaman, Gus. He was chanting something, his eyes focused steadily on the little boat Sabrina could just see, far out on the water. When Urse saw them, she came right over, meeting them halfway between the truck and the stones. Everyone was jogging, urgency in the air.

"Thanks for coming. Gus is holding a protective barrier around the boat, but I don't know how much longer he can hold it. I've tried everything I know, but it's not working," the Alpha bear's mate told Sabrina in a rush. "I was hoping maybe you could blow them back, like you did yesterday."

"The trick will be not to get the boat caught in the winds," Sabrina thought aloud, already working on the problem in her mind. She could feel the winds already gathering, coming to her call. They would be there for her when she was ready to set them free.

Sabrina paused to gather herself before entering the circle of stones. Urse paused, as well. It was important to respect the way the stones focused power. She'd learned that yesterday. Ace was right beside her, and she reached out to take his hand as she took one calming breath. Then, she tugged him into the wide circle with her. His presence went a long way toward grounding her, both physically and magically.

"I think I have it figured out," Sabrina said in a low voice, her mind more on the problem at hand than the people around her. She could feel Urse watching and worrying, splitting her attention between Sabrina, Gus—who was looking more than a little strained—and the little white boat bobbing in a sea filled with thrashing limbs that clearly wanted to crush it, just out of reach. Held there by Gus, Sabrina had no doubt. She let go of Ace's hand and took a moment to look up at him. "Help Gus, if you can. I've got this."

He smiled at her, and she felt his pride and confidence wash over her. It was like a benediction. A vote of confidence from the man her heart had chosen.

And, just like that, she knew she was deeply, truly, in love with him.

"Oh, no!" Urse sounded scared, and Sabrina looked where the other woman pointed.

The biggest of the sea monsters, the leviathan itself, was getting way too close to the boat. It had surfaced, its extra-long tentacles almost within reach of the fishing boat. The time to act had come.

A peacefulness settled over Sabrina as she prepared to loose her power. She felt Ace back off a bit, moving toward the other bear shifter in the circle. Gus would probably drop when he finally was able to release his hold on the boat. With all the stones around, it was probably best if someone could guide him safely to the ground. She trusted that Ace would do that. Ezra hovered on the shaman's other side, so she let concern for Gus's fate float away on the winds that now came to her like favored pets.

She felt the winds caressing her, lifting her hair and hugging her like an old friend. She greeted them with joy, thanked them for answering her call, and asked them to float over the little boat without harm. Then, she asked more of them. She didn't put her request into words, but rather, showed the winds what she wanted of them with images in her mind.

She wasn't sure if they were conscious or not, but something within the massive power of the sky and atmosphere seemed to understand. On her signal, it went out and sought the boat, protecting it while pushing relentlessly at the sea around it—and the monsters within the waves.

"It's working!" Urse's voice came to Sabrina as if from far away.

Sabrina opened her eyes. She hadn't realized she'd closed them. Her hair was whipping around her head, but it wasn't uncomfortable, and it didn't get in her eyes, which was kind of a miracle in itself. She giggled as she raised her arms and directed the wind energy that seemed without end. It bounced in eager joy, reflecting her happiness that what she was doing seemed to be helping the bear shifter and his little boat. The monsters were being pushed away. Far away.

The boat seemed to come alive and started to move under its own power, zipping away from the creatures that thrashed and wailed in anger as their prey moved out of range. Sabrina was aware of Gus collapsing off to her side, but she was confident the guys would see that their friend came to no harm. Gus had done his part. He'd held the creatures at bay until a solution could be found.

That Sabrina's winds had been the solution was humbling. She'd only just learned how to do this yesterday. It seemed striking that her new skill and ability would come to the rescue so soon. Maybe she would survive this massive escalation in her power, after all. And maybe—as had just happened—she would be able to use her new powers for good. To help people. To fight evil.

Wonder filled her. She'd always wanted to do important things, but her weather sense wasn't much to work with. Now, she had plenty of power to summon, but her goals hadn't changed. She still wanted to help people. She didn't want the power for her own glory, but to stop people like the ones who had attacked her on the road. To help the good people of this town. People who had helped her without expectation of recompense. People who were on the side of Light, the side of good.

At last, she'd found her calling. Here, in the center of the sacred circle, she felt as if she'd just had an epiphany. She would continue to serve the Goddess. The Mother of All. She would use her power over the winds for good alone.

Sabrina went to her knees and sent the prayer skyward, up with the winds and down over the earth and sea. She sent the prayer to the Mother of All, wherever She was, and hoped She would hear. In that moment, Sabrina made a vow to the guardian of the Light. The Goddess. The Mother of All.

And She answered. Visibly.

The stones all around began to glow with pure white Light. Urse gasped, and Gus seemed to revive as the Light coalesced above Sabrina's head, reaching downward like a benediction.

Then, it was gone. Winking out of existence as if it had never been. But the effects were there.

Gus got to his feet, his smile wide as he walked over to Sabrina. He held out a hand, and she took it, allowing the other man to help her to her feet.

"It is a good thing you have done here today, sister," he said, putting one of his big hands over the top of her head as if in blessing, just for a moment.

Gus moved back, and Ace was there, watching, a slight frown on his handsome face. She wanted to hurl herself into his arms, but it looked like she had to explain a few things. She didn't want to leave any doubt in his mind about her loyalties or feelings. She opened her mouth to explain, but Gus spoke, first.

"What you just saw…" Gus addressed himself to Ace and the others, as well, "…was Sabrina's instinctual reach for the Light, and the Mother of All deemed fit to answer, blessing the promise Sabrina made, to use her powers only for good. In other words, Sabrina just dedicated herself and her abilities to the side of Light. There can be no doubt about her allegiance, now. Not when the Goddess manifested the Light on Sabrina's behalf. I suspect that was for our benefit," Gus added, nodding to the two other bear shifters. "So, we know, for sure, she's one of the good guys."

"Oh, I already knew that," Urse said with a big grin. "Who else would get out of bed at the crack of dawn to help some idiot they don't even know?"

"I'm telling Sig you called him an idiot," Ezra said, clearly teasing the Alpha female.

"Don't worry, I'll be telling him myself when I see him," Urse promised, shaking her head. "What was he thinking?"

The three men shared an amused look, but it was Gus that answered. "He was probably thinking he's a grown bear and that makes him pretty much invincible."

"Invincible?" Urse almost shouted.

"Well, in Sig's defense, we usually are," Ezra pointed out. "It takes a lot to take one of us down. We're not used to being up against something like this." He gestured out toward the water, which was still roiling in places, far out to sea.

Urse just shook her head. "Come on," she said, her voice sounding both tired and triumphant. "Let's all go back to town. Breakfast is on me. I think the bakery is probably open by now."

Everyone agreed and piled into the trucks waiting just beyond the stone circle. Ezra turned over the wheel to Gus, surprisingly. Apparently, he'd borrowed Gus's truck to come get Sabrina and Ace. Gus drove somewhat silently, inserting a comment, here and there, as Ezra and Ace caught up a bit since they'd last seen each other. Sabrina listened with one ear, watching the terrain out the window and trying to sort out the changes that had come over her in such a short time.

That Light had been an amazing experience when it was happening, but now, given a bit of time and space from the event to think about it, she found herself a bit in awe. Had that really been a manifestation of the Mother of All's power? Had it really blessed her?

It had certainly felt that way. While her body and soul had been bathed in the Light, she'd felt pure and connected to the universe in a way she had never felt before. She'd felt...a welcoming presence within the Light. As if the Mother of All were smiling down on her in approval. It was a feeling like nothing else.

If that was what it felt like to be in the presence of the divine, Sabrina would work hard for the rest of her life for the chance to feel it, again. She thought she understood why some people devoted their lives to the endeavor. Sabrina had never felt any sort of calling, but if she had known this communion before, she probably would have given serious thought to following the priestess's path. As it was, that road was most likely closed to her. She was...well...she was something else altogether.

Exactly what, she still wasn't really sure. It had to do with the escalation of her power, and with a fine tuning and focus of it. Wind. That was her element. They'd tested her the day before and found she had no real inclinations toward any other kind of magic. Just wind. Air and the way it moved. That was her thing. Her only thing.

She would never be an all-around mage. She would never be trained or part of a fancy magic school or tradition. She was a one-trick pony. As she always had been. The only difference, now, was the scale of her power. She'd gone far and above any minor weather skills she'd had before. The winds came to her call in greater strength and number than ever before.

Sabrina had heard Urse and the grannies talk about being a sylph, but Sabrina still wasn't exactly sure what that really meant. The word had seemed to strike a chord deep down in her center, where her power lived. Her magic recognized the term in some way that she didn't fully understand. But she would. She would figure this out and make it the goal of the rest of her life, if necessary, to learn about what she could do and use it in service of that amazing Light.

The bakery was open and welcomed them with the wholesome fresh scent of newly baked bread. Ace escorted Sabrina in, along with the rest of their party, and they took over one of the larger tables by one of the front windows. Nell came over to greet them and soon had coffee and scones served while she went to work on the more complicated orders behind the counter.

Sabrina had been very quiet on the car ride back to town, but Ace figured she had a few things to think about. Heaven knew, he'd been pretty amazed at what she'd done and the spectacular Light show at the end there. He'd known instinctively that, at heart, she was a good woman, but he had never expected to see such tangible proof of the approval of the Goddess. It humbled him and made him want to wrap her in cotton wool to protect her from all the evil in the world that would try to harm her.

She'd hate that, of course. If there was one thing he'd learned about Sabrina in their time together, it was that she was an independent soul. She liked to stand on her own two feet. She welcomed assistance, when needed—she wasn't stupid—but she did more than her share when the going got tough.

This morning's incredible bravery and skill was just an extension of what she'd done on the highway to confront the evil that had been chasing her. She was a protector, at heart. She would put herself and her power forward to save others, which was a rare thing to find among non-shifters, in Ace's experience.

Such a rare soul needed protection, and Ace was just the bear for the job. Now, he just had to convince her of that. Seeing her this morning, rising to the occasion to help someone she didn't even know had only solidified his desire to join his life to hers forevermore.

His inner bear was scoffing at him for taking so long to recognize what was right in front of him. Sabrina wasn't just another woman. She was his *mate*!

Ace just sat there, stunned. The conversation flowed around him as the revelation kept echoing through his mind. Of the gathering, only Ezra seemed to notice Ace's distraction. His old friend leaned over and spoke quietly while the women's conversation went on around them.

"You okay, buddy?" Ezra asked, concern in his quiet tone.

Ace shook himself. "Yeah. I'm good." A slow smile spread across his face as he looked at Sabrina, seated across from him. She'd ended up sitting between Gus and Urse, as they discussed the magical aspect of this morning's events.

"She the one?" Ezra asked in an even lower tone.

Ace started and looked over to meet his old friend's gaze. Ezra chuckled at Ace's expression.

"Oh, man, you got it bad," Ezra told him and put one friendly paw-sized hand on Ace's shoulder.

"How did you...?" Ace had to ask.

"You look like a guy who just figured things out, that's all," Ezra assured him. "It's okay. It happens to all of us—if we're lucky enough." The hand on his shoulder lifted and slapped him on the back in a bearish version of low-key congratulations. "I'm happy for you. And, I've been in your shoes. Thea hit me like a semi-truck going ninety. She flattened me and then made me whole, again. She's the best thing that ever happened to me. I'm glad you found that for yourself, man."

Ezra turned away as Nell returned to the table with plates of food. He helped her distribute the loaded platters while Ace tried to gather his scattered wits. He had to figure out how to tell Sabrina. He wasn't sure how—or if—his declaration would be welcomed. She wasn't a shifter. He didn't really know how that worked. Would she feel the same bond? Would she understand what shifter mating was all about? What she meant to him?

She'd lived among werewolves for a while. Hopefully, she'd picked up a thing or two from watching them. Still, he'd have a lot of explaining to do, once he figured out how to tell her.

He couldn't really ask Ezra for advice. His mate was a shifter. She had, no doubt, felt the same bond pulling them together. Maybe one of the guys in Grizzly Cove who had mated with a human would be willing to give Ace some pointers, but he didn't really know most of them well enough to ask that sort of thing.

As he was puzzling that out, the door to the bakery opened with a jingle. A man rushed in, his gaze zeroing in on their table, and he came right over. Ace tensed. He didn't know this bear. Of course, there were a lot of people in town he didn't know. He watched those around him for their reactions.

Ezra laughed when he saw the man, which put Ace at ease. Urse rose from her seat and started pointing an angry finger at the guy while calling him an idiot, and it clicked that this must be the man who was on the fishing boat. Gus and Ezra laughed out loud while Urse berated the poor guy, but when Urse stopped cussing at him and pulled the newcomer into a shaky hug, they rose and piled on in the group bear hug.

This, then, was one of their close friends. Possibly, he was part of the central group that had founded the town, though Ace had never crossed paths with the blonde behemoth. Not that he remembered.

Regardless, it was clear the newcomer was one of the band of brothers who had fought side by side for so many years, in so many foreign places around the world. Ace almost envied their bond, but then, he remembered his own little band of brothers. Blood brothers. They might be pains in his ass, sometimes, but they were his closest friends. The fact that he'd had so much of an adventure without them was both surprising, and a little sad. They'd shared most of their lives together, traveling from job to job, always together, a trio of badass bear shifters who were there for each other when push came to shove.

But they all had recognized that, eventually, they would have to expand their circle if they wanted to settle down and start families. They'd been doing solo trips for years, going out and exploring on their own, from time to time, always keeping their eyes open. It was an unspoken thing that they were each looking for a mate when they went out on their solo adventures.

Ace knew his brothers would be happy for him that he'd found his mate on this trip. They'd tease him, of course. That's just what younger brothers did. But, at heart, they'd be happy for him. If he could get Sabrina to agree to be his mate, Ace knew things were going to change for both himself and his brothers. They wouldn't be a trio any longer. Now there would be three brothers, one of whom was mated and had another person in his life that meant as much, or more, than his brothers. And, in time, perhaps there would be cubs.

Just the thought of it made him catch his breath.

The bear hug broke apart, and the newcomer walked over to where Sabrina was sitting and dropped to one knee at her side. Ace bristled. What were this guy's intentions? Then, he saw the brightness of the man's eyes and knew strong emotion was driving him. Ace sat back and waited to see where this was going. He calculated he could have the guy flat on the floor with his arm across his airway in the blink of an eye if he did something stupid.

"Ma'am," the man's voice came out rough. "I'm Sig. I own the fish market, and I can't thank you enough for the rescue today. It's hard for a bear shifter to admit when we need help," he said, his mood visibly lightening as the others chuckled at his statement. "But I'll be the first to admit that I bit off more than I could chew this morning, and I really thought I was a goner. Thank you for your timely intervention."

Sabrina blushed at all the attention, making Ace love her all the more. She hadn't done what she'd done out of some need for attention or a desire to prove how great she was. Ace knew that firsthand. She was the greatest—even if she might never see that about herself. Still, her humility was endearing.

"You're welcome…um…Sig. I'm Sabrina. And this…" she motioned significantly to Ace, seated across from her, "is Ace."

Sig got up off the floor and reached across the table to shake Ace's hand. He was a friendly guy whose emotions rode close to the surface. Ace wondered if his recent brush with death was the cause, or if he was the kind of guy who always walked around with his heart on his sleeve. Only time, and further observation, would tell.

"I managed to come back with the hold full of fish. Really good fresh stuff that I haven't been able to get to since the leviathan troubles started," he told them enthusiastically. "I'm delivering the catch of the day to Zak's restaurant, and I hope you'll all be my guests tonight for dinner. We're going to have a fish feast the likes of which we haven't been able to have for months."

Sig's enthusiasm seemed contagious, and the others wholeheartedly agreed to his plan. Ace thanked the man, accepting his invitation after checking with Sabrina. She nodded, and Sig moved slightly back from the table to look at her, again.

"I'm saving the best of the best for you, ma'am. To show my thanks."

Sig's smile was kind, and Ace didn't think there was anything to object to in the gesture, but his inner bear bristled at the other man paying so much attention to Ace's mate. He tamped down a growl that wanted desperately to come out.

Sabrina blushed, again, and looked at Ace. "Thank you, Sig. Ace and I will be there, though you don't really have to go to that much trouble. I was happy to help, and I'm just glad that I was able to do so."

"You're a very modest woman, ma'am," Sig told her as he moved farther back. Then, he looked at the others and grinned. "See you all tonight!"

CHAPTER 16

Sabrina spent the rest of the day with the magic circle, as she was beginning to think of them. First, right after breakfast was over, she accompanied Urse back to the bookstore she owned with her sister, Mellie. They spent an hour over coffee, talking through what had happened that morning and the research Mellie had been doing ever since Sabrina's situation had come to their attention.

The real revelations came when the girls' grandmother showed up mid-morning. Nonna Ricoletti had tales to tell that were both eye-opening and a little scandalous.

The store was empty, so the four women sat in the reading nook they'd created in one of the windows and chatted over coffee. Nonna was served by her granddaughters and treated with all respect due her age and revered position in the family. When everyone was comfortable, Nonna began to speak.

"When I was a younger woman, I had a lover who had great power over the winds. Air was his element, I always thought," Nonna said, her aged eyes sparkling as she looked at Sabrina. "Just as I said when I saw your power."

Urse and Mellie seemed a little shocked by their granny's frank discussion of a former lover, to Sabrina's amusement. What did they think? That their granny had never had sex?

She had to have had it at least once in her life if they existed.

"My lover called himself a mage, but I always suspected he was something more." The old woman sighed heavily. "He died a long time ago, fighting evil, but I still talk to his sister, from time to time. I placed a call to her last night. After hearing your story, she also believes you may be part-sylph. She said, as such, you might be able to learn how to fly, after a fashion, given a bit of practice. You just have to direct the wind to support you and move you around in the sky."

"Fly?" Sabrina was flabbergasted by the mere thought of it.

"Power over the wind, dear," Nonna said quietly. "Think about it."

Sabrina was thinking about it, and it was scary! She didn't like heights.

"We'll table that idea, for now, if it makes you uncomfortable," Urse said, reading Sabrina's reaction accurately.

"To be a sylph is to be a spirit of the air, at one with it," Nonna went on. "I think, since you came to your power so late, you may have sylph heritage, but perhaps not too close. Do you know much about your ancestors?"

Sabrina could only shake her head. She'd been on her own a long time. She didn't know much about her origins and ancestry. She told the women as much, and they all looked sympathetic.

"My father raised me, but he died around the time I started high school, and I went into foster care. He never talked much about my mother, but I remember her a little. She was tall and willowy. With blue eyes like mine and wavy golden hair. She died when I was little, and Dad never got over losing her. After she was gone, he seldom spoke of her, and I was too young to really ask about the important stuff." Sabrina looked down, feeling the loss, all over again. "He was a great dad, but as far as I know, neither he nor my mother had family that could take me in when he was killed."

"It's a shame you don't know for sure," Mellie said quietly.

"You are part-sylph. It is the most reasonable explanation," Nonna concluded with a nod. "And armed with that knowledge, we can begin honing your skills."

The old woman's eyes narrowed as she looked at Sabrina, and she wondered if she should be worried. They'd already shown her so much in such a short time. Now that they had a plan in mind, what more could she learn from them?

"A storm is gathering," she blurted out, surprising even herself with the bald pronouncement. "I mean…"

"Go on, dear," Nonna said gently, encouraging her to speak.

"My weather sense got knocked around a bit when my power increased so quickly, but after yesterday, it's starting to become more workable, again," she told them, putting into words something she'd only just begun to realize. "Before this all started, I used to be able to forecast weather better than any meteorologist. I could tell you a week in advance if a storm was headed your way. Right now, my senses are saying we're in for a really bad storm coming from the direction of the mountains, which seems wrong." Sabrina frowned in concentration. "Nothing about the storm feels normal, in fact. It's not natural."

"Not natural?" Urse asked, her brows knit in concern. "So, it's magical? Someone is weaponizing the weather?"

"I believe our enemies are attempting to get your attention," Nonna said sagely, nodding in Sabrina's direction. "The question is, what will you do about it?"

*

Ace went to pick Sabrina up later that afternoon at the circle of stones. Apparently, the ladies had relocated there, at some point, to work on magical things that would be contained by the circle while they experimented.

When Ace pulled up on his bike, he could hardly believe his eyes. Sabrina was floating about six feet off the ground, her arms held out at her sides like a high wire act, balancing over a gorge. She looked scared, but also a bit triumphant, which made him back down from running to her aid as he'd first intended.

The more he watched, the more he realized she was up there on purpose. The people in the circle with her were spotting her. Gus was close enough to catch her should she fall, and the other women were shouting encouragement and giving her advice as they watched. This was some kind of lesson, and Ace was loath to interrupt it once he realized she wasn't in any real danger.

He sat back and watched as she rose a little higher, but ten feet was about as high as she seemed to want to go. He relaxed a bit. She wouldn't be killed from a ten-foot drop, if she lost control. As she got used to it, she seemed to get more comfortable and even tried moving around a bit, using her arms to direct her movements.

Ace didn't pretend to understand how it all worked, but it certainly looked like she was able to call air currents to support her in various ways. What he was watching was her experimentation as she learned how to shape the commands, and the power, to do what she wanted.

None of the magic leaked beyond the stone circle, but Ace was pretty sure that was some massive magical power she was wielding. Good for her. He was proud of her quick learning and aptitude and relieved that she was getting stronger and better able to defend herself. She'd been vulnerable when they'd first met, but he'd been glad to see her blossom as her power and confidence grew.

She'd done an amazing thing out on that highway, but judging by what he could see now, she was even stronger. She certainly had more skill. Working with these people had helped her develop finer control, and they had encouraged her to try new things—like flying. Ace had to shake his head. Who knew a person could actually fly under their own power without first shifting to some kind of bird form?

That she wasn't a shifter still concerned him. He grew more positive with each passing minute that she was the only woman for him. His inner bear was pushing him to declare himself. To stake his claim and hope that she would return it. His human side was just plain scared. He dreaded letting her know how he felt if she didn't return those feelings. He would die inside if she rebuffed him, but not knowing was also making him a little crazy.

He'd have to say something, but he'd have to pick exactly the right time. He didn't know when that would be, exactly, but it would come. He was certain of that. And, then, in one fell swoop, the rest of his life would be decided. Either she would accept him and claim him in return, or he'd live out his days alone. For there was no other woman for him. Sabrina was it. The One.

On that thought, Sabrina lowered herself back to the ground. The grannies clapped in delight, and the others smiled. Urse and Mellie went over to Sabrina, and an animated discussion followed as they began making their way toward the nearest edge of the circle to Ace. Sabrina saw him, their eyes meeting across the distance, and he knew her smile was just for him.

His breath caught in his chest. She was the most amazing woman. Beautiful. Smart. Brave. She made him want to be a better man. A better bear. A better being all around. Just for her.

When the group broke up, she headed straight for him. She gave him a jubilant hug, bringing her light and joy to the deepest parts of his being.

"Did you see me levitate?" she asked, her voice filled with excitement.

"I did, indeed," he confirmed as she pulled back from the quick hug. "Looked like you were flying to me."

"That's what Nonna said," Sabrina told him. "She said the elementals can actually fly that way and dared me to try it. I didn't think it would work, but it did!" She grabbed his arm as they walked the short distance to his bike. "I still can't quite believe it."

"Believe it," he said, turning her to face him as they

reached the side of his Harley. He bent down to kiss her, wanting to mark the moment and feel her warmth against him, even if only for just a moment. "You were magnificent, baby."

She smiled up at him, her eyes flaring with power as blue as the sky. That was new. And very, very sexy.

He knew they didn't have a lot of time before they were meant to be at dinner in Zak's restaurant, but oh, how he wished he could take her to bed, right now. She put her hand on his chest, and the power was back in her eyes.

"Tonight," she promised in a sultry whisper that revved his engine like nothing else ever had.

"I'll hold you to that," he agreed with a grin as he patted her bottom before letting her go.

She mounted up behind him, and they headed back toward the center of town. They had just enough time to freshen up a bit before they had to be at the restaurant. The others waved and promised to see them later. Apparently, the whole town was going to show up, at one point or another, to get in on the freshly caught fish of the day. Of course, as Ace well knew, bears seldom needed much excuse to have a party, and fresh fish was as good a reason as any.

Sig's safe return was at the heart of it, but the guys wouldn't get all mushy about it. They'd thank him for the fresh fish, give him a back-pounding hug, and then, the party would carry on. It was the way bears worked out their feelings. Gathering together and making merry when the occasion called for it. Ace was just glad Sabrina had been able to use her new powers to bring the fisherman home safe, or the mood would have been quite different.

*

Dinner was a raucous affair. Sabrina and Ace were shown to a giant table at the center of the restaurant's main dining room and found themselves sitting with the magic circle folks she knew and their spouses. Big John among them. Sabrina was still a little afraid of him because he was the Alpha, though she'd started to realize that the title in a bear Clan held a different connotation than among a wolf Pack. Still, he was the big cheese, and she didn't want to do anything that might turn him against her—like Tobias had turned on her up in Canada.

The restaurant had outdoor seating, as well. Sabrina could see colorful umbrellas through glass doors at the back and side of the huge room they were in. She frowned, thinking about the storm she thought was headed toward the town. Toward *her*, in particular. After all, she had brought the enemy to the town's doorstep, and only Urse's incredibly powerful permanent wards were keeping them from infiltrating into the town itself.

Thank the Goddess for Urse and her wards. Sabrina would never have forgiven herself if she'd brought chaos and evil into this beautiful little town. As it was, she feared the weather would get through and wreak havoc—unless she could stop it. Her stomach clenched in anxiety when she thought about it. She'd have to figure out a way to push the giant storm that she believed was brewing, away from the town.

Any way she looked at it, it would probably have to pass overhead. Meaning some damage—from rainfall and high winds at the very least—was unavoidable. She could feel it gathering, but for some reason, it was stalled at the perimeter of the town. Probably due to Urse's wards. Sabrina didn't know enough about other kinds of magic to know if that would last, but Urse was right there at the table, sitting next to her. She couldn't really enjoy the evening until she knew.

"Can your wards hold against the storm?" she asked Urse as quietly as she could.

The bear shifters seated all around could probably hear, but they were polite enough not to make a fuss—except for John. He seemed very interested in what his mate would say in reply to Sabrina's question.

"My wards hold against evil. Once the mages on the other

side realize that, they'll let the storm go without intent behind it, and it will probably drift across the ward, just like all weather does," Urse told her, taking a casual sip of her wine. "But, at that point, you can do your thing and push it out to sea."

An unexpected laugh bubbled out of Sabrina's mouth, surprising her—as much as Urse's calm expectations about what Sabrina could do surprised her. Was she serious? How could the Alpha female be so nonchalant about something so important to the safety and wellbeing of the entire town?

"I wish I had your confidence," Sabrina finally choked out after working her jaw several times in an attempt to reply.

Urse reached out and put one hand on Sabrina's shoulder. "I saw what you can do. I have faith that you are here to provide yet another avenue of protection for our people and our town. I think that's why the Mother of All sent you to us." Urse removed her hand, but the tingle of her intense power remained, as if she had tried to transfer some of her confidence to Sabrina. "In case you haven't noticed, we've been under siege here, for a while now. From the land. From the sea. Your arrival helped identify another vulnerability that I hadn't quite thought of until now—the sky. Evil couldn't get through my ward, but it was only a matter of time before our enemies thought of this new ploy. At least, this way, you're here already to help us deal with it." Urse shrugged and sipped her wine.

Sabrina was dumbfounded by the very idea, but as she thought through Urse's words, they started to make a perverse sort of sense. Though Sabrina had originally been meant to go to Montana and the Lords, she'd been diverted at every turn and wound up here. Almost as if her path had been guided by some higher power, showing her the place she needed to be.

By all accounts, they didn't particularly need her kind of magic in Montana. They didn't have the same kind of critical situation as the cove. The people of Grizzly Cove needed all the help they could get, it seemed—even a trainee wind power was better than nothing in this case, Sabrina supposed.

She blinked a few times and let that thought settle into her mind. She was getting stronger with each passing hour, and she had learned so much about control and how to cast her weather magic with a lot more precision than she'd ever known. She could probably handle almost anything they could send across the barrier of Urse's ward.

In one way, that ward helped a lot. It wasn't like the evil intent could pass through, so nobody would be wielding the storm after they let it loose. All Sabrina would have to do was push it out to sea. One way or another, she should at least be able to do that much. It might get a little scary, for a while, as the storm passed overhead, but she would do all she could to limit the time it lingered over land. Timing was going to be critical.

"Will you know if it crosses the ward?" she asked Urse, but the other woman was shaking her head.

"You'll probably feel it before I would notice anything. If there's no evil intent pushing it, the ward won't be triggered. It'll just drift in. Wouldn't your weather sense tell you when that's about to happen?"

Sabrina thought about it, for a moment, then nodded. "I think you're right. I'll keep my senses turned toward the direction of the storm, and I'll let you all know the moment I sense they've released it to head this way."

"Good plan," Urse told her. "In the meantime, let's just enjoy our dinner. If things change, let us know, and we'll spring into action." Urse chuckled and raised her glass. Sabrina toasted with her and then sipped the most delicious vintage she'd ever had the good fortune to sample.

She liked the occasional glass of wine, but her budget didn't usually extend to such fine bottles. She surreptitiously glanced at the bottle on the table and was impressed to see she'd been served one of Maxwell Vineyards' wines. Any bottle from that well-known winery was reputed to be of fine quality and now she understood the truth of that reputation.

"One of Maxwell's oldest friends is the silent partner in

this restaurant," John said when he noticed the direction of Sabrina's gaze. "We're lucky to have an in with the vineyard. Zak gets all the best vintages."

"It's really good," Sabrina said quietly in return.

She was shy of the Alpha and relieved he hadn't pursued her nascent plans on how to deal with the incoming weather. She wasn't sure what she would have told him other than she'd deal with whatever came when she saw what it was. Not much of a plan, but she didn't know how to make it better. Not now. Not with so little information and so little experience on her part.

"Wait 'til you see what Zak does with the fish," John said in a friendly tone. "He's kind of a genius in the kitchen, as long as you like spicy food. He's a Cajun bear, you know."

John's prediction came true a few minutes later when Zak and the folks who were helping serve everybody brought out the first platters. As promised, a special fillet had been set aside for Sabrina, and Sig brought it over himself, offering it to her with great ceremony and another round of thanks.

They spent more than an hour enjoying the fish and great conversation. The bear shifters were widely traveled and well-rounded men who impressed Sabrina with the wide array of topics and sophistication of their humor. They talked about some of the more elaborate practical jokes they'd played on each other over the years, and Sabrina thought she'd never laughed so much at a dinner party.

Of course, she'd never been to that many parties, and never one like this. The entire community had turned out, it seemed, everyone slapping Sig on the back and saying a few words to him about his adventure that morning. They thanked him and Zak, when he appeared from the kitchen, for the feast. Many stopped by the table to thank Sabrina, as well, having heard through the grapevine about how she'd sent the winds to blow the leviathan and its minions back, so Sig's boat could make it to safety.

Sabrina felt a bit conspicuous and was quite embarrassed by the praise, but Ace was nonchalant, so she tried to take her cues from him. Of course, he wasn't the one everybody insisted on thanking. No, they tended to ask him technical questions about engines and machinery they were having trouble with, and she'd heard him promise to go out to their places to have a look more than once. Seemed like he was building up a list of clients and a pretty full schedule of house calls for the next day or two.

She wondered if there'd be enough work here to keep him in Grizzly Cove for a while—or, perhaps, permanently. Would he want to settle down here? She knew she was thinking more and more about staying, if they'd let her. The town was amazing and the people even more so.

After dinner, Sig and Zak came over and sat with them at the big table as others left. The place was clearing out a bit, but many stayed behind to enjoy coffee or something stronger and the fellowship of their neighbors. Sabrina had talked to Sig a few times, now, but as he started to regale the group with the story of his adventure that morning, she started to learn more about his personality. He wasn't reticent like the other bear shifters she'd met so far. He was very outgoing and not quite as emo as she'd feared, but still, he was a man unafraid to talk about how he'd felt when faced with what looked like certain death by sea monster.

He made it funny, too. Sig was big, like all the other bear shifters, but he was fairer than most of the others, with pale blond hair and weathered skin. He'd mentioned his Norwegian roots a time or two, and when he relaxed, his words took on a slight accent that might very well have been Scandinavian in origin. Sabrina didn't know, for sure. She'd never met anyone from Norway before.

"I regret taking the boat so far out, now, but I have to admit, it was kind of exhilarating. I don't often get to cheat death like that, nowadays. Not like we used to in the unit." Sig smiled fondly as he contemplated his beer, sitting on the table in front of him. He had one hand on the bottle, playing with the torn edge of the paper label.

Sabrina saw nods of agreement from quite a few of the ex-military bears around the large table. The mood of the table changed slightly. Sig heaved a sigh and lifted his gaze to Big John.

"We've got to do something about this, John. It's hell being trapped here in the cove with all this amazing seafood out there that I can't get to." Frustration and amusement warred in his tone, but he said it with a smile that softened the words a bit.

John shook his head. "I agree, but we've done all we can, for the moment. We're waiting on those specialists to come take a look, but they're out in the *real world,* right now, and we have to wait until their mission is complete."

Grumbles of agreement sounded around the table. Ace had clued Sabrina in that, when these guys talked about the real world, they usually meant the battlefield, or some foreign country where they'd been sent to do something for the military. So, she reasoned, whatever experts they were waiting for were active military and on assignment. Hence, the wait.

"It's a hell of a thing," Sig went on. "We all spent a good portion of our lives serving, and now, we have to wait for help because the only folks we know that can do the job are doing the same."

"That's about the size of it," John agreed. "The irony isn't lost on me."

"It doesn't sit well, John," Sig said, shaking his head, "being the ones sitting around, waiting for rescue rather than the ones performing the rescue."

"I hear you, brother." John's tone was solemn. "But, in this case, we have to admit that this particular problem requires special skills. Like Sabrina's. And Urse's and Mellie's. They've all contributed, but it's going to take an even more specialized skill set to finalize the situation."

"You need some kind of water elemental," Sabrina blurted out, unaware until she said it that she'd been thinking about how to solve the problem since the moment she'd heard of it.

It got quiet as all eyes turned to her. Sabrina tried not to squirm, but she felt confident in her words. It made sense, after all. She tried to explain her reasoning.

"Look," she began, her voice softer than she'd expected. She cleared her throat and tried, again. "If I'm some kind of partial air elemental power and I can control the winds, then you need someone that can control the waters. I bet someone like that could lock the monsters in place, at the very least."

Everyone was silent, for a moment, looking at her and thinking about her statement. Slowly, heads began to nod around the large table, but John's regard stayed steady. Finally, he sat back and sighed.

"That's exactly the conclusion we came to," John admitted. "The men we're waiting for have that kind of power. I talked to their commanding officer, who also happens to be their father, and he agreed. The moment they're free to come here, they'll be on their way. The admiral was willing to come up here himself, but he couldn't get away in a way that wouldn't be highly conspicuous to the mortals who work with him and those he works for. He's too high-profile in the human world and its military," he explained to Sabrina and Ace. "He does good work there, protecting shifters like us, who want to serve. He uses our skills and puts us in special units—like the one we were all part of—that allow shifters to use our natural gifts on the battlefield in the service of the Light. He picks and chooses our missions so that we're never fighting on the questionable side of the line. He's a good man, and we all respect the fact that, right now, maintaining his position is more important for all shifters than breaking cover to come help us with our little problem."

Nods all around as the men agreed with Big John's words. Sig sat forward.

"I didn't know the admiral was involved," he said, his tone apologetic. "That changes things, of course."

John chuckled. "Well, if you'd come to more council meetings, you'd have already known this."

Duly chastised, Sig hung his head dramatically, but everyone was smiling. "I hear and obey, mighty Alpha," he joked, then raised his head, smiling broadly. "I promise, I'll show up at the next one. Sorry."

"It's not like we have them that often, anyway," Zak scoffed, throwing his dinner roll at Sig's head.

The fisherman caught it and took a huge bite out of it with an exaggerated nod of thanks while Zak kept eating. He'd cooked for everyone else, so his own dinner had been delayed, but they'd welcomed him to their big table in the center of the room and kept him company while he finally got to enjoy the fruits of his labor.

Sabrina was laughing along with everyone else when a tingle of awareness blew down her spine. The storm was on the move and heading this way. She stood without realizing she'd done so, and everyone at the table looked at her.

"What is it?" Ace asked immediately, standing at her side. She loved the way he was there for her, even when he didn't know what was happening, yet.

"We should get everyone inside," she said, looking through the glass doors that showed a substantial crowd still gathered in the outside areas of the restaurant.

"The storm?" Urse asked in an urgent tone.

"It's coming," Sabrina confirmed, meeting the Alpha female's gaze. "Fast."

CHAPTER 17

"What's going on?" Sig asked as everyone stood from the table.

"You wanted some action," John said. "We're about to get some."

"What?" Sig looked around at everyone else.

Zak was on his way around the table, heading for the glass doors, but he paused by Sig's side to slap his friend on the shoulder. Zak was somewhat smaller than the other guys, but Ace knew that was because Zak was a black bear. They were smaller in relation to the other grizzlies that made up the largest population of the town. But Zak was no less fierce than any of the other bears.

"You gotta come to more briefings, man. Sabrina has *Venifucus* heat on her trail, and while Urse's ward has kept them at bay, they know Sabrina is here, and they've been thinking up crafty ways to get at her. They've cooked up a giant hurricane, or something equally ferocious, that's about to drift over the ward because, you know, weather itself is neither good nor evil, so it can pass right through." Zak's summary was surprisingly accurate. "Come on, Sig," Zak told the fishing bear. "Help me get everyone inside."

Sig jumped into action and went with Zak to warn the others. Ace would have done the same, but his first priority had to be Sabrina. She might need him, and she appeared to be the best defense the town had against what was coming.

"What do you need?" he asked her, ready to do anything she asked.

"I have to go outside. I need to see it. To feel the winds against me," she replied.

Ace understood. He took her hand and led her through the milling crowd. Lots of people were headed inside, but he pushed his way through the incoming stream, making way for Sabrina, who followed right behind him. The others made room for them, apparently, well aware of who they were and what Sabrina could do. There weren't many secrets in this town where outsiders were concerned, which he supposed was only right since this was their town, not Ace and Sabrina's.

Not yet, anyway.

Although he was leaning more and more toward seeing if they'd let him settle down here. If Sabrina was willing. He'd go anywhere in the world she wanted to go, if only she would consent to them being together as mates. It was his dearest wish. And his greatest fear, at this point in his life. He had to pluck up the courage and ask her, but he was waiting for the right time. Whenever that might be.

He knew one thing, for sure. It wasn't this moment. No, right now, they had bigger fish to fry—pun intended. There was a deadly storm rolling in from the east and a sea full of monsters in the west. He hoped Sabrina had figured out a way for the storm to pass by the town without hurting anyone. He didn't know what she had planned, and he wouldn't ask. He had to trust in her, and in the Mother of All who had put Sabrina in this place, at this time.

Ace sent a prayer up to the Goddess as he got his first clear look at the sky. The street lights of the town were reflecting off angry dark clouds, which were roiling with what almost looked like anger—if a cloud could be said to have emotion. Perhaps it was reflecting the emotions of the people who had caused this storm to gather? Ace didn't pretend to know how it worked. He only stood back in awe as Sabrina prepared to do battle with the most hellacious looking storm he had ever seen.

And this was only the leading edge of it.

Wind whipped, quickly stirring all the patio furniture around, but Sabrina held out one hand, and suddenly, there was calm. At least on the patio where the tables and chairs had been only mildly disturbed. Ace sensed the winds were still howling higher up, above the roof of the restaurant.

Sabrina was doing that. He was certain of it.

"I'm holding the winds above the town, for now," she told him, breathing a little faster than normal, but she didn't look strained. Her hands were at shoulder height, palms facing upward, as if holding the wind up somehow.

"It's working," Ace told her.

She nodded quickly. "It is here, but I'm not sure about the rest of the town. Can you get information from the outlying properties? I'd like to be certain I've got everyone covered."

"Can do," he told her, already thinking through who he could ask.

He looked around, somewhat unsurprised to find John and Urse watching them from near the door to the patio. He beckoned John over, unwilling to leave Sabrina's side. Thankfully, the Alpha bear jogged over without hesitation.

"Can you get reports from your outliers?" Ace asked, explaining the situation quietly to John.

The Alpha nodded and moved back toward the building, already on his phone. The roar of the storm above made talking on the phone out here a matter of yelling into the mouthpiece. He'd have better luck inside. Ace trusted him to gather the intel they needed and report back to Sabrina, so she could adjust her magic accordingly.

"You know, it occurs to me that I can protect the town— or most of it, I hope—but there have to be regular folk living in the area that will be affected by this storm." She bit her lip, worrying over those people she didn't even know.

Ace had heard there was an Indian reservation just to the

south of the town. She was right to be concerned. Those people wouldn't have her protection from the whipping winds...or whatever came next.

John came back out at a fast jog. "You've got all of the town and some of the reservation covered, but the storm is pretty massive," he reported with a frown. "There's hail and lightning after the wind and massive amounts of rain."

Sabrina frowned, and Ace wanted so badly to help her, but this was her battle. Her territory. She knew what she could handle and what she couldn't. He wouldn't push her. He wanted her safe, as his first priority.

"I'm going to try something," she said, shouting now to be heard above the wailing winds aloft.

She turned to face the east, the direction from which the storm was coming, and then, she began to lift into the air. Just a few feet, but she was definitely levitating. Ace stood directly below her, to catch her should she fall.

She rotated her arms in the opposite direction of the winds, and they seemed to diminish slightly. Then, she reached out her left hand toward the east and crooked her finger.

All was still, for a moment, and then, lightning lit the sky, followed by a quick burst of small hail, followed by a somewhat longer dousing with rain. She rotated in the air to face the west and made some gestures with her fingers that Ace couldn't really see from his vantage point. Then, the rain was merely a gentle drizzle, and she lowered her arms.

Sabrina sank gently back to the ground, landing on her feet. She was soaked, but her expression was triumphant as she turned to Ace and launched herself into his arms.

"It worked!" They were both soaked through, but her joy was contagious. He held her and squeezed her tight, sensing the danger was past from her exuberant reaction.

Urse and John came over. The Alpha male was only slightly damp, having gone back to his mate before the heavens truly opened up. Urse was grinning.

"What did you do?" she asked in a conspiratorial tone

when Sabrina stepped back from Ace.

"I sent it out to sea. Just over the protective barrier Mellie created. Right down the gullet of the leviathan and its minions." She sounded so proud of her accomplishment. Ace felt true joy for her. She'd come so far, so fast. "I wouldn't be surprised if some of the smaller creatures washed up in pieces tomorrow. That was some storm they cooked up." Sabrina sighed and pushed tendrils of her wet hair back from her face. "We're going to have to come up with a more permanent solution. They can keep throwing that kind of thing at us, and all I can do is steer it somewhere else. That's not really the best thing for the environment. You can't mess with weather like this on a long-term basis without doing harm to the balance of nature."

"They're trying to damage the town and force you out," John said, his expression grim. "But you're under our protection, and we won't let that happen. Don't worry. We all know a showdown has to occur. The sooner, the better."

"How about tomorrow?" Sabrina said, surprising everyone. "They might possibly think I'm weak after what I did tonight. That I have to recover. We could set a trap and spring it while they're still planning their next move."

"I like it," John said decisively. "We've been scouting their movements from covert positions ever since they showed up. We have a good sense of where they are, now, and where they'll be tomorrow morning. I was going to suggest we send out one of the female shifters on your bike—"

"Hold on," Sabrina interrupted him, holding both of her hands up, palms outward. "I don't think they'll fall for that. They're looking for my energy. Or whatever it is that attracted them to me in the first place. I'll have to be the one." She reached for Ace's hand. "Me and Ace. It can look like you're throwing us out of town after the trouble tonight."

John frowned. "I don't like the idea that anyone would think we'd throw you out of our town, or the idea of putting you in that kind of danger."

"I appreciate that, Alpha. I really do," Sabrina said gently.

"But Ace and I have been through a lot in a short amount of time. I trust him to look out for me. I don't think I'll be in that much danger, as long as I'm with him."

She squeezed his hand, and Ace felt emotion well up in his chest. She trusted him with her safety. Would she also trust him with her heart?

They all went back into the restaurant to make plans. Zak and his staff served pots of steaming coffee and snacks to fortify them while a detailed plan was devised. The core group of ex-military bears were gathered around that giant table in the center of the main dining room as the place was turned temporarily into a war room.

Sabrina leaned against Ace. She was weary, but she wanted to hear at least part of the planning before she fell asleep. After all, she would have a central part to play in tomorrow's events, and she needed to know how it was all going to go down.

At least, that's what she thought...right up to the point where she fell asleep.

She woke the next morning in their bed at the hotel. Ace was already up. She saw evidence that he'd been in bed with her. His pillow was dented, and the area where he'd slept was still faintly warm, but he was gone. Hm.

She sat up and looked around, suddenly remembering that they had work to do that morning. A plan to put into action and a trap to spring. She was both apprehensive and oddly excited. She wanted to stop the evil people who would put together a storm of such fury and unleash it on an unsuspecting world, trying to flush out one person. That was just wasteful, disrespectful of the Earth and downright mean.

She got out of bed and took a quick shower. She was dressed and ready by the time Ace returned with take-out bags from the bakery.

"Breakfast for milady," he intoned, like some kind of butler from a British television show.

She giggled and reached for the bag he held out to her.

Opening it, she found it contained one of the delicious egg sandwiches from the bakery she'd come to love, along with a sweet treat. She opted for protein over carbs, knowing the honey bun would still be just as delicious after she'd done her part in the sting operation they had planned for today. The eggs wouldn't keep, so she ate those, enjoying every bite.

Feeling decadent, she ate her egg sandwich while sitting cross-legged on the side of the bed. Ace was checking his phone. It looked like he was reading texts.

"Sorry I conked out on you last night. Did you guys finalize all the details?" she asked facetiously. Of course, they had. These men wouldn't have stopped planning—especially not John—just because she'd fallen asleep.

Ace just looked at her with one raised eyebrow. She giggled. She couldn't help it. Things might be serious, and she might be going into danger in an hour or two, but she felt invigorated. Revitalized. She was finally using her talent for something important. She was helping, which was something she always enjoyed doing. It might be dangerous, but she honestly felt that, with Ace by her side, no harm could come to her. He made her feel invincible—within reason, of course. She wasn't going to be taking silly risks. Not when she'd only just found him. She didn't want to scare him off or lose him to some foolish gamble. Not when she still had a shot at making him want to keep her forever.

And the more she was around him, the more she wanted that. Forever. With him.

She nibbled her egg sandwich while he tapped out messages on his phone. She supposed he'd already eaten. He'd probably gotten up way earlier but had opted to let her sleep, which was nice. He was a very thoughtful partner.

She finished the sandwich and rose to tidy up. "So, when are we doing this?" She tried to sound casual, but she knew there was a bit of nervous energy in her voice.

Ace put down his phone and came over to her. He took her in his arms and kissed her breathless, then moved slightly back to gaze into her eyes.

"Are you certain you want to go through with it?" he asked, his tone low and serious.

"Unless you've come up with something better while I was snoozing, I think this is our best bet."

He shook his head slowly. "Unfortunately, we haven't come up with a better plan, but we all agree we don't want to put you out there if you don't want to do it. So, I'll ask, again. Are you sure?"

Sabrina nodded. "I brought this trouble here. It's only right I should help put a stop to it."

Ace chuckled. "Something tells me the bears in this town attract trouble, so don't feel bad about bringing them a bit more. You didn't see them at the planning meeting last night. They actually enjoy this stuff. Going into battle seems like fun to them."

"I can't believe that," she told him, giving him a sidelong glance.

"Okay, maybe not fun, exactly, but they definitely seem to enjoy the challenge. If you'd been awake to see them, you would agree. Trust me."

She smiled and gave him a considering look. "Something tells me you enjoy a good brawl, now and again, too. I mean, you're a bear, after all, right?"

Ace seemed to consider her words. "Well, if it was just me and my brothers, you're probably right. Mixing it up, once in a while, helps us let off steam. But having you involved in this…" His words trailed off as he shook his head and his expression got serious. "I have to tell you. I just don't like it. You're too important to me to risk lightly. I hate that you're in danger, and the only reason I'm going along with any of this is that I'll be by your side the entire time, and at the end of this operation, what little is left of our enemies should back off if they have any sense whatsoever."

"You mean a lot to me, too," she admitted, waiting for him to say more.

But they were interrupted by a ringing phone. Ace shook his head and stepped back, reaching for the device that never left his side when he was in human form.

"They're ready for us," he said quietly after he ended the short call.

Just fifteen short minutes later, Ace and Sabrina were mounted on their bikes, heading out of town. The plan called for them to ride out, seemingly fleeing the town before breakfast. Careful reconnaissance had told them where the *Venifucus* had dug in, just beyond the boundary of the permanent ward, alongside the main road, in the forest.

What the *Venifucus* didn't know—at least, they all hoped the *Venifucus* didn't know—was that before dawn, the ex-military bear shifters of Grizzly Cove had come out from behind the ward and positioned themselves in the most advantageous spots possible. They would come down hard on the *Venifucus* forces the moment they tried to make a move on Sabrina.

Ace privately thought it might turn into a blood bath. He'd seen some of the equipment the men of Grizzly Cove had at their disposal as they suited up in the wee hours of the morning. Highly illegal military hardware seemed to be the norm among this group, and Ace was just glad they had his and Sabrina's backs in this mess.

Unless they had some kind of magical defenses that could block conventional weapons, the *Venifucus* were going to bleed. And, if the weapons did turn out to be useless, the shifters would stash them and go furry. Bears could withstand a lot of magic, and they all had natural weapons—claws and teeth—that could be used to great effect. Either way, it didn't look good for the enemy.

Ace felt it the moment they left the safety of the permanent ward. They were moving fast. Running like they would be if this was for real. With any luck, that would help them avoid some of what the *Venifucus* had lying in wait. The bear shifters had done as much reconnaissance as they could without being discovered. They'd found a number of both magical and mundane forces arrayed on either side of the road, but there was no way they could sniff out everything without tipping off the enemy.

That was the sketchiest part of the plan. If the *Venifucus* hit them with something big that nobody expected, this situation could get a whole lot more interesting. And, by *interesting*, he meant *terrifying* for a man who had a mate to protect.

As if he'd conjured trouble just by thinking about it, something slammed into him and his bike, sending both careening off the road and into the shrubbery along the side of it. He saw Sabrina do the same. She landed in a bush not too far from him and immediately sprang up, lifting herself into the air with the wind power she could call. Good girl.

With the winds whipping around her, she would be safe from most magical attacks. As for Ace, it was time to go bear and kick some ass. He'd hoped they'd be able to get past the trouble and let the other guys handle it, but if they couldn't do that, he sure as hell was going to do his best to protect Sabrina. Right now, he would be most effective in bear form, so he stripped and shifted in record time.

He roared out a bear call and was gratified to hear it answered from all around as volleys of magical fireballs streamed out of the forest on both sides, aimed directly at Sabrina. Ace positioned himself directly below her as he saw her twirl one finger, causing the fireballs to swirl around her without touching her at all.

Then, she flicked a finger in each direction, and the fireballs returned to their senders at triple speed, moving so fast the mages who had fired them had no chance to get out of the way. Ace heard one man shout as his coat caught fire and he dropped out of the tree he'd been perched in, rolling on the ground. On the other side of the road, a woman screamed then disappeared in a puff of evil-looking smoke. Whether she was dead or had dematerialized, or something equally bizarre, was anybody's guess, but Ace thought she probably had gotten fried by her own foul magic. Either way, she was out of the action.

Ace saw Zak expertly applying zip ties to the man's hands,

now that the fire was all but out. A judicious tap to the temple sent the mage into unconsciousness where he couldn't hurt anybody. Zak winked and melted back into the forest.

All around, Ace heard screams cut short as the Grizzly Cove guys took care of business, taking out those that had been waiting to ambush them. But they didn't get them all.

Ace felt a bullet graze his shoulder, and he roared, spinning to assess the new threat. Three men had come out of the forest, holding military assault rifles. They smelled of blood magic to his sensitive bear nose, which put them on the wrong side of this battle. Ace charged, and they leveled their guns at him. This might hurt a bit, but bullets wouldn't bring him down easily, and he could get to them before they did too much damage to him.

He expected the sting of gunfire, but as he watched, their firearms were ripped from their grasp by localized winds. A mini tornado engulfed them, whipping their clothing and gear all over the place before lifting them off their feet and dumping them from about fifteen feet in the air, a few feet away.

When they landed, Ace was there, roaring at them. One fool raised a knife. Ace bit his arm, breaking it with a satisfying crunch. The knife dropped to the pavement while the other two men limped away—right into the waiting arms of the Alpha bear and his friends, who were ready to accept their surrender.

More magic made the air feel electric, but whatever it was the remaining mages were throwing at Sabrina, it never touched her. The barrier of wind that circled around her like an orb seemed to redirect every last mage-bolt. Ace watched with satisfaction, even as he scanned the area for more mundane attackers, as she sent the bolts back, with interest.

Ace felt a bit of magic aimed at him, where he stood guard under Sabrina's levitating form, but either she was deflecting most of the charge or it was simply sliding off his fur because the mages weren't of that high caliber. Chances were good that the two fireball-wielding folks were their first string, and they'd been taken out early. What was left was strictly second-string. Not that they couldn't do some damage of their own, but they were clearly no match for Ace's natural protections—or for Sabrina.

The growling and roaring in the woods went on for a while. Apparently, there'd been quite a large number of conventional fighters drafted into this confrontation. But they, too, had met their match in the elite fighting men of Grizzly Cove. Hardly a shot was fired, but within a few minutes, the enemy had been captured or otherwise neutralized.

Ace stood guard as Sabrina continued to stand in the whirling, protective bubble of winds that kept her safe. Right now, that was the best place for her, even though no further attacks against them had been made for several minutes. He'd wait for Big John to sound the all-clear before he stood down from his alert pose, and even then, he wouldn't take anything for granted. Sabrina was his to protect.

CHAPTER 18

About ten minutes after the noises ceased in the woods, Big John came out from the trees flanked by Brody and Zak, appearing like ghosts out of the mist. Not there one minute, walking toward Ace and Sabrina the next. Spooky. Even for shifters, these guys were impressive.

"It's safe to come down, now, ma'am," John said quietly, addressing the air above Ace's head where Sabrina still floated. Then, he looked at Ace. "We'll form a protective ring around her while you get yourself together and check the bikes. I hope they're not too damaged." John frowned. "I'm sorry you two got hit. That definitely wasn't part of our plan."

Ace grunted agreement and watched while John, Brody and Zak took up guard positions around him and Sabrina. They were turning their backs on him while he was in bear form and they were in their more vulnerable two-footed shape. It was a mark of trust that wasn't lost on Ace.

Still, Ace waited to shift until Sabrina was on the ground. They would be most vulnerable while he was shifting, though he'd pass through the battle form which was half-man, half-bear and all-badass, but he'd have to give that up to resume his human form. Naked. Exposed. Not totally without skills, but not quite as resistant to magical attack as when he wore his fur.

With Sabrina on the ground, he let the change come. He paused in the battle form to take a look around. In this shape, he was taller than the other guys and could see out over their heads into the forest. His bear side sensed nothing hunting them. His human side saw that the threats had been dealt with. He allowed himself to slide into his fully human form and took Sabrina in his arms for a quick squeeze.

"You okay?" he asked, unable to stop himself from checking on her welfare.

"I'm fine. What about you? Is this blood?" Her voice rose in alarm, making John turn his head to look over his shoulder as Sabrina drew back and started examining Ace's shoulder.

"Just a graze," John observed, then turned back to his guard position.

"John's right," Ace confirmed. "It just passed through my fur and grazed the top layer of skin. You won't even know it was there by lunchtime."

Wanting to get back into the safety of the town, Ace walked a few paces away, reaching between Brody and Zak to grab his clothes from where they'd fallen on the pavement. He dressed quickly while Zak fetched Ace's boots and brought them back to him. Ace nodded and put them on.

"Thanks, guys. How did we come out?" Ace asked cautiously. He wasn't sure if John wanted to share that intel, but Ace was really curious.

"Everyone we were aware of, and quite a few we weren't too sure about, have been neutralized. We have a lot of prisoners to send to the Lords and other friends of ours who might have an interest in interrogation. We also have quite a few mortal fighters that seem like they're under compulsion to me. Gus will check them out before we figure out where to send them. It might be as simple as freeing them from whatever blood magic spell that was used on them. I suspect the grannies will have something to say about what we do with those people. If they're innocent, of course, we have no reason to hold them further—except for the fact that they've now seen us in action. It poses a bit of a problem," John paused, grimacing as he looked around, "but we'll sort it out. Want some help with your bikes?"

"Sure. Thanks," Ace agreed, taking it as a positive sign that John had been so free with the information. Having John's confidence would be a bit step toward being accepted among the rest of his Clan.

"Just wait here a minute. I'll get your bike, okay?" Ace said gently to Sabrina.

She looked shaken, now that the confrontation was over, and he didn't want to stress her any further. He watched to make sure Brody and Zak stayed with Sabrina while he and John tracked the bikes into the brush. They'd flown a good few yards away from where they got hit by that magical pow.

John went for Ace's bike while Ace made for Sabrina's. He wanted to take a good look at her bike, especially, before he'd let her ride it back to town. If they had to, they could hitch a ride on one of the trucks that were just starting to pull up to pick up the other guys and their prisoners. Ace could always come back for the bikes later. Ezra had access to a truck with a trailer he could probably arrange to borrow.

"I'm no expert, but everything seems to be okay with this one. Just cosmetic damage from what I can see," John reported from a few yards away as he lifted Ace's Harley up to a standing position and began to roll it toward the road.

Ace fell in beside John, rolling Sabrina's bike, which looked surprisingly good for having been blown off the road by a massive puff of magical energy. He suspected the bushes had cushioned the fall. Either that, or Sabrina had done something in the split seconds of the attack to help the bikes land softly. He'd have to ask her later.

"You know, your lady is something special," John said as they rolled the bikes slowly toward the road over the rough terrain of the forest floor. "Urse is hoping your Sabrina will decide to stay in town, for a while, and as far as we're concerned, she's already proven her mettle."

What was the Alpha bear saying? Ace stilled inwardly, even as he kept moving.

"I think Sabrina will be relieved to hear that. I know she's come to love it here, and she's found friendship with your mate and the other members of the magic circle, as she calls it. They've been good to her."

John stopped moving, pausing with the bike just as they were about to break out onto the road. He turned his head to regard Ace, catching his gaze even while he held the bike's handlebars.

"What about you? Have you given any thought to settling down here?"

Damn. John was asking rather than telling. Ace hoped the Alpha wasn't about to crush his hopes, but he had to take a chance.

"Lately, I've thought of little else," Ace admitted. "Settling down, I mean. But it all depends on her." He broke eye contact with John to turn his gaze to Sabrina. She looked so small between the two bear shifters who were guarding her at the moment, but she was mighty in all the ways that counted.

"I thought so," John said with satisfaction, drawing Ace's gaze back to meet the Alpha's. "She's your mate." John's smile held a sort of benevolent joy that lifted Ace's hope for the future. No wonder so many followed this Alpha. He truly cared about people. That much was clear.

"I believe she is, but she's got to feel it, too." Ace frowned. "How do you manage being mated to a mage? How do you know she feels the same bond? It's not like it is for shifters, right?"

"We shifters just know, of course," John allowed. "Each species has their own ways of knowing, and each individual may be more attuned to their fate than others, but mages have their ways, too. They're mysterious to us, but I feel my mate in my heart. In my soul. I know she feels as much as I do, and once you both admit it to each other, you'll know whether your bond is fully reciprocated. Trust me."

Ace sighed. "I hope you're right."

John chuckled and started rolling the bike onto the asphalt. "You'll be fine. Just find your balls, pluck up your courage, and tell the woman how you feel." Thankfully, he kept his tone low enough that their conversation was private. "Trust in Sabrina if you don't trust me. It's pretty obvious she's crazy about you. And, in case you're wondering, Brody already ran our standard background checks on you and your brothers. You passed."

There was no opportunity to speak further as they rolled the bikes closer to where Sabrina and her two bodyguards waited. Ace didn't have time to puzzle over the Alpha's revelations. He was too busy watching the alignment of each wheel, trying to judge whether they were safe to ride back into town or not.

He gave the bikes as thorough a check as he could under the circumstances and deemed them safe enough if they kept the speed down. Sabrina looked relieved to be able to reclaim her bike and head it back toward town. Ace was right there with her, and they took off with a convoy of trucks filled with John's men. The vans full of prisoners would be dealt with separately. Frankly, Ace was fine to let John and his team handle that stuff. All Ace was concerned with, right now, was Sabrina.

They drove back a lot slower than they'd ridden out, but they weren't all that far from the ward, and once they were within the safety of it, Ace felt himself breathing a bit easier. Some of their escort turned back at that point, leaving them with only one truck following them into town.

Sabrina was trembling a bit from what they'd just been through, but riding her bike—albeit slowly—through town, and right into the hotel parking lot, helped settle her nerves. The truck that had escorted them back to town had left them as they drove down Main Street. The truck went into the town hall parking area, and the bikes continued on their own down the street to the hotel. It was safe enough. They were in the heart of Grizzly Cove, after all. Sabrina suspected Big John had taken the opportunity to come back and start placing sensitive phone calls to their allies. But that wasn't her problem. Right now, she just had to stop shaking.

When she shut off the engine, she sat there for a moment, getting her bearings and trying to still the fine tremors coursing through her limbs. She was very much afraid that, if she tried to stand up, her knees would buckle.

"Okay?" Ace's low voice came to her from just a couple of feet away.

He'd parked his Harley and come over to her, all without making a sound. She met his gaze and saw the gentle concern in his eyes. Suddenly, she wanted nothing more than to be in his arms. She got off her bike and stood on wobbly legs, reaching for him. Ace got the message, closing the distance between them and taking her into his arms.

"I feel like such a wimp, falling apart like this, now," she whispered, her cheek pressed to the reassuring beat of his heart. She could just hear it faintly under the layer of thin fabric covering his chest.

"Hey, now is the best time to fall apart. After the action is over, and everyone is safe. You did good, sweetheart. Real good," he crooned, swaying just the tiniest bit from side to side in a rocking motion that seemed to help calm her.

"I was scared," she admitted. "I was so scared I was going to let you down, and you'd get hurt." She rubbed her cheek against his chest, clinging to him as her nerves steadied. It felt like she could tell him her deepest secrets after what they'd been through together. "You were so brave and so amazing. I love your bear form, Ace." She took a deep breath. "Just as much as I love your human form." She lifted her head and sought his gaze. "I…just…love *you*, Ace."

"You do?"

His eyes swirled with shifter energy, and she knew she was talking to both the bear and the man. She nodded, feeling hopeful, though they'd never made such open declarations to each other. She nodded and held her breath. Waiting.

"That's good to know, darlin'," he told her, grinning as her heart soared in anticipation. "Because I love you, too. I've been agonizing for days to figure out how to tell you." He leaned closer and whispered low so that the words were just between them and the wind. "You're my mate."

Joy flooded her, and the winds around her rejoiced. Or, maybe, they were just dancing to her own happy feelings as her spirit floated on the air around them.

"I am?" She had to be one hundred percent certain. "I mean... I know shifters mate for life. Is that what you want? To be my mate...forever?"

Ace nodded slowly, his grin lighting her world. "Forever, Sabrina. You are my mate, my life and my hope for a happy future. Will you consent to share your life with me?" He dropped to one knee and smiled up at her. "I think this is the way humans do it, right?" She laughed, happy tears gathering in her eyes as he went the extra mile for her. "Will you marry me, Sabrina?"

"Yes! Oh, yes!" She reached for him, and he sprang back to his feet, taking her in his arms and lifting her off her feet. He swung her around in exuberant joy as she laughed and tried to hold onto this moment to remember forever. The moment she found true love. Forever.

She felt like she was floating on air, and then, she realized...she was. Or, rather, *they* were. She'd been so caught up in the moment, she must have allowed her power to wrap around them both and lift them into the air. Sabrina giggled a little self-consciously. She looked around and saw a few people in the lobby of the hotel, staring at them out the big front window.

"Sorry," she told Ace. "I'll fix this."

"No worries, babe. I like flying with you." His sexy smile might've caused her to lift them higher if it hadn't been for the audience watching them.

"I'd like to get better at the whole flying thing before I take you up with me. I'd die if anything happened to you." And, just like that, they landed gently back on the ground.

"Same goes for me, Sabrina," Ace told her. "From now on, we have each other to consider whenever we think about doing potentially risky things. Promise me you'll remember that."

He looked so serious. She reached up to rub his deliciously muscular shoulders. "I will if you will, but to be honest, I never intended to do anything dangerous. It all just sort of happened."

He gave her a quick kiss that felt like approval. "And you handled everything that came at you with style and aplomb, but now that you've had a taste of danger, I hope you won't seek it out."

"Are you kidding me?" She shook her head. "I thought you knew me better than that by now."

Ace gave her an appraising look. "I do. And…I don't. We haven't been together all that long as humans count time, but that's what happens, sometimes, when you find your perfect mate. We get to spend the rest of our lives learning every nuance of each other's personalities." He started walking, his arm around her waist as he guided them both into the hotel. "For my part, I can't wait to get started."

She giggled, again, as he lifted her in his arms and carried her across the threshold. For a shifter, he certainly had covered all the human traditions. She loved that he was making such an effort to meet her halfway. She'd do the same for him, she vowed.

But, first, she was going to make love to her mate. These moments were the start of the rest of their lives together and she wanted to mark it with a tender, wild, delicious mating.

Ace carried her all the way to the big bed and lay her down upon it. He then spent the next ten minute alternately teasing her, kissing her, undressing her, and then tasting the skin he uncovered, bit by bit. Her body ached with need by the time he stood next to the bed and removed all his clothing. She'd tried to push it away, but her efforts had been thwarted by his focus on her. She didn't mind, of course, but she wanted to feel his skin against hers.

She didn't want to wait any longer. She'd gone from shaky with fear and delayed reaction to being shaky with need for her one true love. Her mate. She still couldn't quite believe it.

He'd been feeling the same undeniable attraction. It all started to make sense to her, knowing what she now knew. The instant liking. The magnetism. She understood why she'd been powerless to stop herself falling in love with him. She couldn't stop Fate. It was destiny that they be together.

When he slid his pants down his powerful legs after kicking off his shoes, she caught her breath. He really was the most handsome man she'd ever seen in the flesh. Everything about him appealed to her. Everything about him turned her on.

She reached out for him and he didn't make her wait. He put one knee on the bed and lowered himself over her.

"Slow and steady or hard and fast?" he asked when he was positioned above her. His gaze met hers and she could see the humor and love in his eyes. It made her want him all that much more. It made her want to show him how much she loved and wanted him.

"How about somewhere in the middle?" she replied, her tone teasing.

"Your wish, is my command," Ace said, nodding his head to the side. He finished the movement with a kiss to her neck, in the sensitive spot that made her squirm. Yummy.

He kissed his way down her body, pausing here and there at interesting parts. Ultimately, she had to reach down and drag him upward again, tugging lightly on his hair, his ears, whatever she could reach. He gave her a silly grin and raised eyebrows when he met her gaze.

"Yes?" he asked in a dryly amused tone.

"I changed my mind," she said between panting breaths. "Hard and fast. Now!"

His grin turned devilish and he wasted no time sliding within her. "Hard and fast, indeed. My favorite."

There was no more time for talking as he applied himself to her pleasure. His strokes started out slow, despite their earlier banter, but moved rapidly from languid to urgent. Just as she wanted. He was so powerful, so masterful, so athletic, and yet so loving. She could feel the care he took with her in every movement, every touch.

For the first time in her life, she knew what it was to make love with a man who loved her heart and soul, completely. For the first time, she understood what it meant to love and be loved in return. She was complete. And completely ready for whatever he had planned for their future, including right this minute, when she felt like the top of her head was going to come off when she hit orgasm.

Son of a...

She screamed his name as she came, gratified to hear him shout hers as well a moment later. They strained together, reaching for the stars and finding each other there, waiting, willing, wondering how they had each been so blessed as to find each other.

"I love you, Ace," she whispered into her ear as he dropped his weight momentarily onto her, his arms giving out at last. She loved that she could affect him so deeply. Just like he affected her.

He rolled after just a moment, taking her with him, keeping her close. He growled low, near her ear. "I love you, too, mate."

She wasn't sure if it was the man or the beast talking, but she figured, in the end, it didn't matter. She loved both sides of his nature. The growly protector and the tall, lean, biker who owned her heart.

*

They might've spent the rest of the day in bed, making love, but the phone rang. Ace sighed heavily and answered it, sitting up against the headboard of the bed. Sabrina snuggled against him, unwilling to let him go too far.

She knew she was being a bit needy, at the moment, but they'd both been through a lot that morning, and she was still coming to terms with everything. She'd give him space if he gave her the least indication that he didn't like her clinginess, but so far, he'd returned every caress and seemed to enjoy the way she'd wrapped herself around him.

She knew she'd have to give him some space eventually, but for right now, all was well with her world and her man was close enough to touch. She was damned well going to touch him. Where the sudden feistiness came from, she wasn't exactly sure, but she liked it. Being with Ace gave her confidence she'd never really had. Especially after the disastrous events up north with the wolf Pack. That had shaken her right down to her foundations, but Ace had helped her rebuild and then some.

Sabrina felt stronger than ever before, with his presence in her life. He made her better. More stable. Happy.

She knew she probably had a sappy smile on her face, but she didn't really care. She was drunk on newfound love and happy just to be alive.

Ace ended the call and put the phone back on the bedside table. He was grinning.

"Apparently, news really does travel fast around this town," he said in a musing tone. "We've been invited to our own mating party. It's being held tonight in the town square. They've arranged for a band, and all the refreshments are being paid for by Ezra's employer—a guy I know pretty well—whose mate is a freaking heiress. You haven't met Trevor and his mate, Beth, but you'll like them both. They're good people."

"But why would they pay for our mating party?" Sabrina was astounded by the generosity of these bear shifters. They were truly exceptional.

"I'm guessing it's because my brothers and I helped Ezra get Beth's businesses back under her control. Her stepfather had turned her late father's business empire into something truly sleazy and downright evil. Ezra has been helping Trev and Beth systematically go through the holdings—and there are a lot of them—to figure out what's legit and clean up those things that are not. My brothers and I lent them a hand not too long ago, and this feels a bit like a belated thank you, though we were all well paid for the job." He shrugged. "It could also be that age-old bear shifter thing—any excuse for a party, you know. You're going to have to get used to that if we're going to live here."

Sabrina sat up a little higher, meeting his gaze. Did he mean...? "You want to live here?" She caught her breath. "Will they let us?"

"Yes, and yes. If you do, and they've already cleared us if we want to stay." He put his arm around her shoulders and hugged her close to his side. "Come to think of it, the party might also be a way for them to show us that we're welcome. Bears are clever like that. They suck you in, and before you know it, you're family."

"I haven't had a family in a long time," she whispered, awestruck at the open-hearted kindness of these shifters. They were so different from Tobias's wolves...except for Marilee.

"You've got me, now. And don't forget my younger brothers. They're going to love you." He kissed her, and she forgot to worry about meeting the brothers until he let her up for air, again, sometime later. Then, another thought occurred to her.

"What am I going to wear?" She had only the clothes they'd traveled in, and nothing was really suitable for a celebration where she and Ace were the center of attention.

Ace chuckled. "Urse thought of that. She wants you to meet her at the bakery in an hour. She's taking you shopping, apparently."

That afternoon was filled with shopping with the girls. Urse had brought along her sister and Nonna to help Sabrina find the perfect dress. There was only the one boutique in town, and it was run by a mermaid. She had all kinds of pretty frocks, and the *strega* witches insisted Sabrina try on a dozen different options before they all settled on the perfect one.

It was sky blue and had subtle sparkles, a simple cut and a feminine silhouette. The *strega* women conspired to hide the price tag from Sabrina, insisting that they were paying for the dress as a mating gift. Sabrina teared up at the way they had welcomed her into their circle. She almost felt like one of the family, though she had known them only a short time. They were just already so special to her. So caring and accepting.

She hugged each one of them, thanking them for the incredible gift of the dress and the fun hour spent shopping. She hadn't done that kind of thing in far, far too long.

Then, they took her to another new mermaid-run business in town—the one and only salon—to get glammed up. They told her they would release her only at the party. They wanted her to make an entrance and wow her mate with how beautiful she looked and how much thought and effort she'd put into dressing up for him. They seemed to imply that Ace was doing the same, but Sabrina couldn't picture it. He was already so handsome, there was little he could do to improve the way he looked, and she might not recognize him if he put on fancy clothing…but she began to wonder what he'd look like dressed up a bit.

Too hot to handle was her private conclusion. She thought about him wearing different outfits from a spy tux to a sport jacket while the blow dryer whirred. Damn. She couldn't wait to see if he'd actually made an effort. Excitement buzzed through her as the time drew closer to go to the party.

Ace was impressed by the way the party had come together on such short notice. It sure looked as if the entire town had come out—probably to hear the band and make merry. He waited somewhat impatiently for Sabrina to arrive with the Ricolettis. John had assured him that his wife and sister-in-law, as well as their Nonna, had basically kidnapped Sabrina—in a good way—for the few hours leading up to the party. Ace trusted them, but he was getting anxious at the separation. The mating was so new, he wanted to be with her all the time.

And, then, she was there. A vision in sky blue, she walked toward him, the light fabric of her dress wafting in the wind and sparkling an invitation at him, to come hither and claim his mate. The crowd parted, making an open lane between them, and Ace found himself walking forward to meet her. Closer…and closer…until she was right in front of him. She smiled, and he lifted her in his arms, spinning them around in the joy of just being together.

A cheer went up around them, but Ace hardly heard it. Music started playing, and folks started dancing, but he was caught up in the magic of being with his mate, looking into her eyes and knowing she was the only woman in the world made just for him.

"You look stunning, sweetheart," he told her. "Sky blue to match your eyes…and your talent. It's definitely your color." Sabrina blushed a bit as he kissed her cheeks gently.

"You're the most handsome man in the world," she said, her words ringing with truth to his sensitive ears. Now it was his turn to blush a bit. "Thank you for fulfilling a fantasy." Her smile was devilish, this time, and made him wonder what she meant.

"What sort of fantasy?" he asked, playing along.

"Well, when they hinted that you might be getting some new clothes for the party, too, I started dreaming up what you would look like in different things. I like the button-down shirt and khaki look on you. Rugged and urbane, all at the same time."

He decided retreat was the better part of valor in this situation, since he didn't quite know what to say to that observation. Nobody had ever called him urbane before. He figured his mate would keep surprising him for a good long time to come. He looked forward to that with every fiber of his being. Speaking of which…

"There's a piece of land up the mountain a ways. I had a talk with John about it while you were shopping, and it's available if you want to go take a look with me tomorrow." He wanted her input on where they would live. "The advantage of this particular lot is that it has the highest vantage point on the cove. I figured you could see all the weather from there, if that's something you want. John said you'd be most welcome to do your weather thing for the town, and if you decide to take that job, it would come with compensation, since you're using your talents on behalf of the entire town. You'd be a town employee, though they're still thinking about what title to give you. *Weather witch*, while appropriate, isn't quite covert enough."

She laughed with him, her expression filled with joy. "I can hardly believe how welcoming they're being. The wolves were nothing like this." She put one hand on his chest before he could say it and repeated it for him. "I know. Bears rule, wolves drool."

"Damn right!" came a voice from nearby. Zak was grinning at them as he danced past with Tina in his arms. "Bears rule!"

A few others took up the chant, and soon, the entire area was filled with raucous bear shifters and their indulgent mates, chanting and laughing up a storm. It was the best party Ace had ever been to.

"I love this town," was Sabrina's comment as she watched the happy crowd, just shaking her head.

"Me, too," Ace agreed, then added, "but I love you more."

They kissed, and the people around them started wolf-whistling. Sabrina was smiling and blushing when Ace let her go. The night went on like that for hours. Dancing under the stars with new friends and old, his mate in his arms and good music, flowing refreshments and the welcome he had never really expected. At least, not like this. Things were definitely looking up.

The only things missing were King and Jack. Ace sent a prayer up to the Mother of All for their safety and a reunion with them sometime soon. He knew they had to travel their own paths, but he hoped, and prayed, that their paths would lead them to the same kind of amazing happiness Ace had found. He wanted them to be as happy as he was right now.

EPILOGUE

White Oaks Wolf Pack Territory, Iowa

King ended the call from his brother Ace and shook his head. He'd gone and done it. Ace, the eldest, had gone and found his mate. King was just a bit worried about what the mating would mean for the brothers. Things were going to change, now.

Of course, they'd always known they couldn't go on as they had forever. They didn't want to go on as bachelors for their entire existences. The whole point of going off and having adventures was to meet new people and hopefully find mates.

King was happy for Ace. In fact, he was intrigued by the little Ace had told him about Grizzly Cove and the bear town John Marshall's unit of crazies had founded for themselves. He'd had a good time hanging out in Iowa, but there were no mates in sight for him here.

He knew that, for sure. He'd taken every single female in the territory on at least one date, and none of them had made his bear wake up and take notice. They were nice girls, but he figured his mate just wasn't to be found among werewolves.

Maybe there'd be a cute lady bear shifter—or even a

mermaid—in Washington state that would make his inner grizzly growl in appreciation. He figured he was just about done with roaming, for now. It hadn't panned out for him at all, though he'd solidified his contact with the Alpha werewolf here in Iowa. It was always handy to have friends in far off places that you could count on.

King decided there and then to make his farewells as soon as possible and head west. He wanted to see Ace and meet his new sister-in-law. And he most definitely wanted to check out the town known as Grizzly Cove.

Meanwhile, in Canada...

Marilee was fed up with Tobias and his edicts. His indifference and shoddy leadership had cost her Sabrina. The only true friend she had in this crappy town. Marilee wasn't a dominant wolf. She would never stand up to Tobias in an overt way, but Sabrina had given her the perfect excuse to leave town, and she was going to take it.

Tobias didn't have to know she had no intention of returning. He'd figure it out soon enough when she didn't come back. And, by then, hopefully, Marilee would have found herself a better place to live among people who were more accepting and friendly.

That thought firmly in mind, Marilee put her efforts into packing up Sabrina's stuff. She didn't have much. Her apartment had come furnished, so the only things Marilee had to pack were personal items and clothing. It all fit in just part of the trunk of her car—leaving quite a bit of room for Marilee's possessions.

She packed quietly. Methodically. Taking only a few things a day out of her apartment—conveniently in the same house as Sabrina's had been—and packing them away in her car. They were safe enough there until she made her great escape. One thing Tobias wouldn't tolerate in his town was petty crime.

When Sabrina called to let Marilee know she had landed on her feet in Grizzly Cove of all places, Marilee knew it was time to go. She packed up her last few things and left town one morning as the sun rose over the mountains. It was a beautiful day, and she hoped for a much brighter future ahead.

She'd left a note for her landlord, along with the keys and a little money she owed him. He'd find it that night when he got home from work and saw the envelope she'd left in his mailbox. By then, she'd be well on her way.

She had one thought as she left the remote mountain town behind…

"Grizzly Cove, here I come!"

# # #

ABOUT THE AUTHOR

Bianca D'Arc has run a laboratory, climbed the corporate ladder in the shark-infested streets of lower Manhattan, studied and taught martial arts, and earned the right to put a whole bunch of letters after her name, but she's always enjoyed writing more than any of her other pursuits. She grew up and still lives on Long Island, where she keeps busy with an extensive garden, several aquariums full of very demanding fish, and writing her favorite genres of paranormal, fantasy and sci-fi romance.

Bianca loves to hear from readers and can be reached through Twitter (@BiancaDArc), Facebook (BiancaDArcAuthor) or through the various links on her website.

WELCOME TO THE D'ARC SIDE…
WWW.BIANCADARC.COM

OTHER BOOKS BY BIANCA D'ARC

Welcome to Grizzly Cove, where bear shifters can be who they are - if the creatures of the deep will just leave them be. Wild magic, unexpected allies, a conflagration of sorcery and shifter magic the likes of which has not been seen in centuries... That's what awaits the peaceful town of Grizzly Cove. That, and love. Lots and lots of love.

This series begins with…

All About the Bear

Welcome to Grizzly Cove, where the sheriff has more than the peace to protect. The proprietor of the new bakery in town is clueless about the dual nature of her nearest neighbors, but not for long. It'll be up to Sheriff Brody to clue her in and convince her to stay calm—and in his bed—for the next fifty years or so.

Mating Dance

Tom, Grizzly Cove's only lawyer, is also a badass grizzly bear, but he's met his match in Ashley, the woman he just can't get out of his mind. She's got a dark secret, that only he knows. When ugliness from her past tracks her to her new home, can Tom protect the woman he is fast coming to believe is his mate?

Night Shift

Sheriff's Deputy Zak is one of the few black bear shifters in a colony of grizzlies. When his job takes him into closer proximity to the lovely Tina, though, he finds he can't resist her. Could it be he's finally found his mate? And when adversity strikes, will she turn to him, or run into the night? Zak will do all he can to make sure she chooses him.

Phoenix Rising

Lance is inexplicably drawn to the sun and doesn't understand why. Tina is a witch who remembers him from their high school days. She'd had a crush on the quiet boy who had an air of magic about him. Reunited by Fate, she wonders if she could be the one to ground him and make him want to stay even after the fire within him claims his soul...if only their love can be strong enough.

Phoenix and the Wolf

Diana is drawn to the sun and dreams of flying, but her elderly grandmother needs her feet firmly on the ground. When Diana's old clunker breaks down in front of a high-end car lot, she seeks help and finds herself ensnared by the sexy werewolf mechanic who runs the repair shop. Stone makes her want to forget all her responsibilities and take a walk on the wild side...with him.

Phoenix and the Dragon

He's a dragon shapeshifter in search of others like himself. She's a newly transformed phoenix shifter with a lot to learn and bad guys on her trail. Together, they will go on a dazzling adventure into the unknown, and fight against evil folk intent on subduing her immense power and using it for their own ends. They will face untold danger and find love that will last a lifetime.

Lone Wolf

Josh is a werewolf who suddenly has extra, unexpected and totally untrained powers. He's not happy about it - or about the evil jackasses who keep attacking him, trying to steal his magic. Forced to seek help, Josh is sent to an unexpected ally for training.

Deena is a priestess with more than her share of magical power and a unique ability that has made her a target. She welcomes Josh, seeing a kindred soul in the lone werewolf. She knows she can help him... if they can survive their enemies long enough.

Snow Magic

Evie has been a lone wolf since the disappearance of her mate, Sir Rayburne, a fey knight from another realm. Left all alone with a young son to raise, Evie has become stronger than she ever was. But now her son is grown and suddenly Ray is back.

Ray never meant to leave Evie all those years ago but he's been caught in a magical trap, slowly being drained of magic all this time. Freed at last, he whisks Evie to the only place he knows in the mortal realm where they were happy and safe—the rustic cabin in the midst of a North Dakota winter where they had been newlyweds. He's used the last of his magic to get there and until he recovers a bit, they're stuck in the middle of nowhere with a blizzard coming and bad guys on their trail.

Can they pick up where they left off and rekindle the magic between them, or has it been extinguished forever?

Midnight Kiss

Margo is a werewolf on a mission...with a disruptively handsome mage named Gabe. She can't figure out where Gabe fits in the pecking order, but it doesn't seem to matter to the attraction driving her wild. Gabe knows he's going to have to prove himself in order to win Margo's heart. He wants her for his mate, but can she give her heart to a mage? And will their dangerous quest get in the way?

The Jaguar Tycoon

Mark may be the larger-than-life billionaire Alpha of the secretive Jaguar Clan, but he's a pussycat when it comes to the one women destined to be his mate. Shelly is an up-and-coming architect trying to drum up business at an elite dinner party at which Mark is the guest of honor. When shots ring out, the hunt for the gunman brings Mark into Shelly's path and their lives will never be the same.

The Jaguar Bodyguard

Sworn to protect his Clan, Nick heads to Hollywood to keep an eye on a rising star who has seen a little too much for her own good. Unexpectedly fame has made a circus of Sal's life, but when decapitated squirrels show up on her doorstep, she knows she needs professional help. Nick embeds himself in her security squad to keep an eye on her as sparks fly and passions rise between them. Can he keep her safe and prevent her from revealing what she knows?

The Jaguar's Secret Baby

Hank has never forgotten the wild woman with whom he spent one memorable night. He's dreamed of her for years now, but has never been back to the small airport in Texas owned and run by her werewolf Pack. Tracy was left with a delicious memory of her night in Hank's arms, and a beautiful baby girl who is the light of her life. She chose not to tell Hank about his daughter, but when he finally returns and he discovers the daughter he's never known, he'll do all he can to set things right.

Dragon Knights

Two dragons, two knights, and one woman to complete their circle. That's the recipe for happiness in the land of fighting dragons. But there are a few special dragons that are more. They are the ruling family and they are half-dragon and half-human, able to change at will from one form to another.

Books in this series have won the EPPIE Award for Best Erotic Romance in the Fantasy/Paranormal category, and have been nominated for RT Reviewers Choice Awards among other honors.

WWW.BIANCADARC.COM

Made in the USA
Columbia, SC
27 May 2019